NO FAIR MAIDENS FROM EARTH TO MARS

ROWAN HILL

TREPIDATIO PUBLISHING

Copyright 2024 © Rowan Hill

All rights reserved. No part of this book may be used or reproduced by any means, graphic, electronic, or mechanical, including photocopying, recording, taping or by any information storage retrieval system without the written permission of the publisher except in the case of brief quotations embodied in critical articles and reviews.

This is a work of fiction. All of the characters, names, incidents, organizations, and dialogue in this novel are either the products of the author's imagination or are used fictitiously.

The views expressed in this work are solely those of the authors and do not necessarily reflect the views of the publisher, and the publisher hereby disclaims any responsibility for them.

ISBN: 978-1-68510-129-9 (sc)
ISBN: 978-1-68510-130-5 (ebook)

First printing edition: October 11, 2024
Printed by Trepidatio Publishing in the United States of America.
Cover Artwork: Don Noble
Edited by Sean Leonard
Proofreading, Cover Layout, & Interior Layout by Scarlett R. Algee

Trepidatio Publishing, an imprint of JournalStone Publishing
3205 Sassafras Trail
Carbondale, Illinois 62901

Trepidatio books may be ordered through booksellers or by contacting:
or
JournalStone | www.journalstone.com

For Leila,
Hopefully this future stays in fiction and Mars
is kinder when you arrive.

CONTENTS

FRUIT OF WOMB
9

AURORA AUSTRALIS
first published in Angela's Recurring Nightmares,
May 2022
47

TEEN SPIRIT
first published in Diabolica Americana,
October 2021
59

SWARM
First published in This World Belongs to Us: An Anthology of Horror Stories About Bugs, *May 2023*
77

A BETTER CHIMERA FOR THE TOXIC WORKPLACE
83

COME IN, CAMP ZUMA
110

VOID
123

SPACEPORT MARTE
132

GODS OF MARS
158

ACKNOWLEDGMENTS

ABOUT THE AUTHOR

No Fair Maidens from Earth to Mars

FRUIT OF WOMB

ALL AT ONCE, the lane ended in a vine-covered gate. Ripe and green. Henry exhaled frustration like a popped balloon and began turning his cumbersome car. Verdant land smothered the slopes of this private valley. Glutted, lush trees right up to the fence, the greenest he'd ever seen. The kinda green to make your mouth salivate. After endless miles of dry soil, burning tarmac, and relentless heat, he naturally thought this road was a small lane leading to the river and the fabled ocean somewhere west.

As usual, Henry was wrong.

In the back, young June coughed dusty air. Now that her medicine was all spent, she had developed a dry, scratchy utterance deep within her lungs that both irritated and worried him, reminiscent of sandpaper on wood. His three daughters slept in his little rectangle of mirror, heads lolling on each other's shoulders as if they hung from nooses. Sweat thick on their blanched brows, the heat from a burning noonday sun was inescapable with windows that stuck.

He reversed for the three-pointer and the car stalled.

Mae in the front seat chuckled without moving her chest, but hushed when the engine didn't turn over. "Aw, hell," she muttered.

The car, choked on years of dust, died, and Henry pressed his head against the steering wheel, his own thirsty throat clenching tight, an effete desire to bawl trying to escape his body through his eyes. Mae's hand massaged his clammy neck.

"Hun. That gate."

Strangled with tendril vines, the gate held a wooden sign only visible from a closer angle.

Land's End Farm

"Maybe they could help? Bet they'd even invite us for supper. Country folk like helping each other. Nice like that."

"Beggin'," he said, hungrily.

"Asking for help ain't the same as beggin', and hell, they'll have to if they wanna get us outta their driveway."

Henry nodded, his rusty door squeaking open, and a cool wind rustled his hair. The last town they visited, the very concrete had been unbearable, temperatures baking the street as if trying to reach their innards and cook them alive. But here? Henry closed his eyes and smiled at the memory of soft wind, and he left the car.

The gate didn't, couldn't, open. Grape vines with spindly tendrils cinched it closed and it felt sacrilegious to rip such a healthy thing with his dirty, crusty hands. Like a sinner spitting on a church. So Henry mounted it and trudged up the lane, apple orchards tightly hugging either side with their heavy crimson orbs staring at him. His heavy frame lightened with each step in the cool air and the trees rustled. To his tired ears, it sounded like children whispering when suddenly a jaunty, folk whistle broke the facade. Henry realized his faux pas. In times like these, strangers were an unwanted threat. Henry was desperate, but he was an honest kind of desperate, unlike some.

"Hello there in the orchard! Our car broke down in front of your gate, m'fraid!"

"Hold up, son! I'm coming to you. Just stay on the lane there!"

Henry licked his palm, smoothing hoary strands of thinning hair back over his bald spot, and then checked himself up and down as if seeing himself for the first time. His shirt, once white, now yellowed with sweat and ill fortune. His slacks weren't much better, a discolored thinness over his knees and holes around his ankles. Before he could tuck the shirt in, the whistling farmer stepped from behind a blackberry bush as if it spat him out and he stopped short.

"Well, hello there, young'n. Car break down, you say?"

Henry's head bobbed all by itself. "Yessir, guessin' we took a wrong turn down yonder and ended up in your lane. Car just went up and died. This heat ain't helpin' it, I bets."

The farmer grunted and sent him an odd look, his eyes flicking back down the lane. "Wrong turn, huh?" He adjusted his straw hat. An old man. No, that wasn't quite right. Middle age with too much sun maybe. Natural for a chorin' man, a Farmer. The lines around his eyes crinkled like brown tissue paper and he nodded in the direction of the old Packard station-sedan with the family and all their possessions.

"Got anyone with ya?"

"Yessir, my family, trying to make our way to the coast."

"Big family, you say?"

"No, sir, just my three girls and wife."

The Farmer grunted again, his face camouflaged in the shifting shadows of his hat, and waved his hand. "Better get them outta that oven and up to the house then. They'll cook in that thing sure enough. Don't know nothin' about fixin' auto-mo-beals and what not, but the wife could use some company."

He said nothing else and started up the slight incline of the lane, turning his head to talk over his shoulder. "Just keep walking up and you'll hit the house eventually."

The Farmer left and Henry stared at his back. The powerful stride of a young man. Younger than his years. Or older? Henry couldn't decide and went to rouse his women.

Once they abandoned the hot, dead car and forgot their aches, the girls jubilantly skipped up the lane. Lorelai shook her arms and giggled at the pins and needles, while June, his youngest, had a little girl's wonder and fawned over the trees between ragged, diseased inhales.

"Oh, Pa, look at those apples! The color of fancy roses," she smiled. "I can smell strawberries, right in the air!" she exclaimed. "Are those cherries? Dangling earrings! At least, I think they are... I better..."

All four of his charges at one time tried to reach for a vine or a branch or a bush, pregnant and low with ripe fruit, and he had to swat their hands, reminding them they were guests and couldn't arrive at the house with guilty faces, even though his own stomach roared at him to do the same. But the lane was long though the hillock small, and eventually the little band of thieves stopped trying. Their steps grew livelier, as if waking from a dream, recognizing the world full of life and breath and not only burning and stiff. More than thirsty dust and cracked stones.

The orchard abruptly ended, and a house stood alone on the top of the hill. A wholesome cottage, the color of clotted cream against the blue sky, Henry decided it nicer than any painting. In the cleared space, a rusted-red barn stood a ways away, and a confetti-colored speckled garden surrounded the house's wrap-around porch. Henry paused, studying a sole pomegranate tree standing halfway between the orchard and the porch steps. Robust and vibrant and solemn, if such a word could be given to a tree.

"Thought y'all got lost down there!" The old-middle-aged farmer hollered from the porch, and the squeaky screen door burst open behind him, a plump wife wiping her hands on her clean apron, joining him as if they were a pair of salt and pepper shakers. Henry and his women stood at the bottom of the stairs, the Farmer's Wife's arms akimbo, studying them with a good-natured frown but keen and sharp eyes.

"Been a long time since someone took a wrong turn up our lane."

Nervous with new folk, June's hand slid inside Henry's, and Farmer's Wife's gaze drew to the movement, studying the father and daughter's clasped hands. She exhaled, her large bosom heaving.

"Well then, better get you fed. Feels rather dee-vine, must say. Just put biscuits and mutton on the table." The Wife examined June's face a moment longer and then gestured them all inside like they were wasting her time. They drew into the house like gravity pulled them, hunger kneading them forward with its knobbly bones and manners holding them back when they witnessed the table flushed. A cornucopia of delights. Berries staining white porcelain, citrus spritzing the air, steam-ghosts rising from fresh bread.

The girls ate like they'd never tasted fruit before, Mae even forgetting to give polite conversation in the face of abundance, leaving Henry embarrassed and guffing apologies. The Farmer grimaced at the girls worryingly.

"Where y'all headed to before that wrong turn?"

Henry swallowed—the mutton on the table was particularly tough, gray and stringy, and outta place among the ripe fruit and vegetables.

"Was trying for the coast, thought to find work on the trawlers. Always wanted to see the ocean," he mumbled. Henry thought of the ocean often. Water as far as you could see. A pool where you could never touch the bottom. It sounded so fantastical. Something unimaginable, like he was a field mouse trying to envision a warehouse full of cheese.

Farmer grunted. "Hard work on them boats. Not much money for a young man's labor. Even less for an old man."

Henry bit into more tough meat, mostly because he hadn't eaten meat, rotten or otherwise, in a week or so. Down the end of the table, June hacked, turning her neck aside not to contaminate lunch. The old farmer exchanged looks with his wife.

"I'm guessing the recession hit you folks hard."

Henry laughed, yearning for the mood to feel as light as his body now out of the car and away from the cities. Away from drought-sickened fields of the dust bowls.

"Aw, hell, which one?" He laughed, and his eldest, Martha, reached over him, her fingers clawing for more honeyed yams. "But, uh, yessir. Not much work out there for common laborers these days. Not with...everything."

Farmer nodded, wisely, sagely, a man who had seen everything, and there was silence while the transients ate, clinking forks on platters replacing their unpleasantries.

"Anyway, the sea will be good for us." Henry pretended not to notice the farmer and his wife sharing glances. Secret, coded messages not meant for Henry or his brood. He caught whiff of the sweat on his shirt and saw the grime of the last town on his hands staining the white tablecloth. Shame stole through him something awful, and he thought of subtly trying to wipe it away, but then dessert arrived. Sugared fruit cups, sticky granules thick like tiny diamonds. The old farmer inspected the three girls filling the corners of their stomachs before his old-young eyes found Henry's.

"Well, maybe the sea could wait a little while, you think?"

***

"How long will yer be gone?"

Farmer's Wife hefted herself into the front seat, ignoring Henry and arranging her dress.

"Oh, only two weeks. Missus' niece had a new baby. Though I've never spent much time with one, shoulda have enough of the cryin' by then, I s'pose," Farmer said, the final suitcase thunked in the back of his old car, louder than it oughta.

Henry scratched beneath the brim of his hat. Not because his usually dry scalp had ceased itching and he wasn't yet accustomed to the sensation of a full head of hair, but because he didn't quite know what to do with his hands.

"Well, I appreciate you trusting me, us, enough to look after the farm. Never had anyone trust me like that before." His voice cracked, and Farmer erected from arranging their luggage. He arched a brow before his leathery and strong hand clasped Henry's in a firm grip, full of familial kinship.

"Y'all earned that, these last three months. Couldn't have found better help."

He made for the wheel, him and Wife squished together while they watched Henry crank the front end to start the engine. Henry bemusedly listened to the engine catch; such an old car, an original, a relic. With the profit of the various orchards, Farmer could have easily bought a fleet of fancy cars, but perhaps he liked this antique design. Henry often wondered Farmer's age, but wouldn't dare ask. Not that it mattered much. Work wise, Farmer's body was past middle-aged, but it often surpassed Henry's for stamina, damn near shaming him sometimes.

The car grumbled awake and Henry stepped away. Farmer leaned out the window as they passed, seriousness glinting in his old-young eyes.

"You take care of those sweet girls now, and make sure you treat this place like it's your own," he said. Wife looked past them both, somberly studying her house on the hill, her eyes glassy. She remained silent, and after a moment faced the lane ahead. Henry nodded, tongue-tied at the Farmer's kindness, and watched the car disappear into the orchard, the trees swallowing it whole. A cooler breeze traveled up the lane, the *chut-chut-chut* of the aging car lingering on it, and for an undefinable instant, Henry heard a little boy *guff-guff-guff*-ing with laughter, though he knew it was only the car, before his mind turned to work.

Land's End Farm wasn't the biggest property he'd ever heard of, filling a small and gentle valley, only forty hectares, Henry reckoned. But there was always work. Whomever originally seeded the land had chosen a plethora of fruits and vegetables, the variety meaning something always ready for harvesting. And today, the scythe waited, ready for him to stretch new muscles.

Gleaming in a mellow sun, it begged to maim golden wheat.

After months of pleasurable and cathartic toil, Henry understood the Farmer's youthful demeanor and source of energy. Toil kept the body young. Idleness, unemployment, made it weary and stagnant until it turned laden and dead. Henry hadn't enjoyed work as a common laborer before. Not really. Never the kind of toil that made a man proud.

But that had changed. Now when he worked the land with Farmer, learning the ins and outs of fathering, growing, and harvesting, he eagerly awaited each day. Rose before the dawn just as the breeze stirred to caress the trees. Hell, he needed that work. There had once been a day of heavy rain, auguries of changing seasons, where Farmer and Henry had sat on the porch together, rocking on chairs and observing the loam suck that water right up. By the next day, Henry felt as restless as a dog waiting to be let out. Though he was tired and spent at the end of each day, something unfamiliar had possessed him. New muscles in his arms itched with birth and longed for use, a tinkling warmth in the back of his psyche. He *needed* to farm and work the land, gather fruits, real fruits, of his labor. The land called him like a siren. He exhaled, and this time, it was with relief.

The scythe handle was hot and he had only just retrieved his harvesting basket when Mae called him from the shed. They met in the middle, at the pomegranate tree. She wore a new dress, sapphire blue, owing to the harvested grapes sold to wine makers, for those who could afford such luxuries.

"I'm taking that ten dollars for the doctors today."

Henry frowned and hung the scythe over his shoulder. "Doctors? I haven't heard June-bug cough once..." Mae's hand waved away his words like annoying flies.

"Oh, *she's* fine. Just getting the girls checked on, don't worry 'bout it. *Lady* problems. Just wanted to tell you 'bout the ten and we may be late for dinner, that's all," she declared and began walking away, her hips bustling enough to hold his attention. His brow dipped, though, when his two eldest, Martha and Lorelai, exited the house and joined their mother at the car.

Martha, fussing over her dress' hemline, was nearly sixteen, and Lori a year behind. Nearly women. Both with golden-spun hair in ring-curls, their dresses pulled tight over their chests and their momma's hips swayed as they walked.

Lady problems.

Hell, another mouth.

No, no. He and Mae were careful, and his girls weren't like that. Maybe Martha with her looks, but they hadn't even had opportunity, Mae being a fire-breather and lurking close. Picking them up from school instead of allowing them the pleasures of idle youths. Wandering down lanes from the schoolhouse, shortcuts through fields of concealing and conspiring corn. Besides, he wasn't even sure if they had their bleeding yet. He would've heard commotion like that in his own house.

The Packard passed him. Mae and Martha, who coulda been sisters for their same beauty and fiery temperaments, ignored him. But happy Lori with her crooked teeth smiled and gave him a half-wave as they left for the lane. There was no wind this time to relay the car's message. There was, however, a jaunty, familiar folk whistle, and from the backside of the barn, his little June-bug skipped out, examining a bouquet of wildflowers in her grubby hands.

Henry's heart melted into a satisfied, happy puddle. Before, June, twelve years old, couldn't get a big enough breath to speak for more than five seconds. Now she whistled.

She looked up and saw him, then examined the clear yard surrounding them both, the only ones left beside the sturdy pomegranate tree.

"Think we could get some chickens? Seems a big yard like this could use something wandering around it, huh?"

"I think you're right, seems unnatural, huh? A farm without chickens or animals? Not even a barn cat. Never thought to ask Farmer why he don't have none, though he's got enough to do with all the fields and orchards. We'll ask him when he gets home."

June made her way to the house, her braids swinging, not really paying attention to either his words or her flowers while her dreams stole her to other places. "Oh! And cows, like genteel, small ones. Ones for milking, and from milk, cream! And butter! And all the things you can do with your own milk. Oh, no, not just cows and chickens, silly! Ducks! Can you keep ducks? Wouldn't they fly..."

She continued monologuing, or rather discoursing with herself, as she often did. A habit her sisters thought queer but Henry loved. Like a radio program playing from right inside her head. June's conversation with herself kept right on into the house and all Henry could do was smile at his youngest. It was decided. The sea with its vast and never-ending cold water could wait for however long fate said. Until Farmer admitted he didn't need Henry's help anymore and cast them out. Farm life revived his malady-stricken daughter, and that was worth a universe of oceans.

The wheat called to his thoughts, chiding him over his idleness; it needed harvesting then reshaping into other useful things such as bread. He turned for the distant field when a singular pomegranate asked for his attention. It hung low and alone from the branch, and although Farmer said they shouldn't be plucked for a while yet, the fruit metamorphosed into a vibrant, glowing red this last month. Henry held the branch, its master, and the pulse in his hand pushed against the grainy wood, making it alive with the same blood. Such a beautiful fruit, someone should take one of those fancy pictures of it, put it in a book or some such thing that would declare it a perfect specimen.

Farmer was right, of course, it shouldn't be plucked. Not because it wasn't ripe, but because it was far too good a thing to simply pick and eat. It was art, and Henry had the immediate desire to let his girls, especially Martha with her greedy fingers, know it as well. The pome was a bright red, like a massive ruby with light exposing its insides. Far too beautiful for anything as simple or base as eating.

Henry smiled and left it dangling, his scythe comfortable in his grip.

***

The soles of Lori's boots intertwined with the shiny worn ones of a boy who ran too much. Beneath the low and squat mandarin tree, the pair laid outside the radial of firelight. Hidden in fringes of darkness, they were cloistered by dense, glossy leaves above. June subtly watched them, her cheeks warm.

The small fire hit a wet patch in the log and popped, sparks bright enough to show the hump of the boy's back, a moving buffalo covered by the worn hay blanket.

"Sure your pa ain't gonna find us? I've seen the arms of that man, wouldn't want him chasin' me out," the new fella at school, Roy, asked with humor. Trying for conversation, he sat on the log beside her and proved very adept at looking everywhere else but the canoodling couple not ten feet away.

June smiled, drunk on doing something forbidden, and turned around to the grotto of citrus trees. A natural clearing in the orchard on the outskirts of their farm, coming to the drier wheat fields of neighbors and the main road. An oasis for Henry's vagrant progeny. She turned to Roy again; a year older, he had moved to a smaller farm up the road a few months prior, his father and brother raising horses. His hair reminded June of dark sand, and a dimple in his cheek puckered when he spoke to her. She turned away quickly, her face now burning, blood peaking her cheeks, and she watched the clear night sky. There was no moon yet, but the bright orange flicker of a star or planet floated high above them in the late hour, staring at them and glinting like a strange firefly.

"Naw, he thinks we're searching for these cows always trying to escape. I'd say you're safe for another hour." She glanced to him and his dimple beside his mouth deepened. June was transfixed for a moment, her body unconsciously leaning in, and Roy's followed. The trees gossiped in hushed whispers.

Then, only an inch apart and all at once, the spell was broken by the abrasive crunch of leaves underfoot and another three figures broke into the clearing: Martha, guiding two boys through the darkness from the road like the ferryman transporting souls. She responded to June.

"More like two hours I think, he's gotta early start tomorrow if he's gonna drive me back to college later." She sat across on the other log, curling and crossing her legs at the ankles in some kind of finishing-school trick to make her appear like a debutante. "He ain't gonna think about searching for us 'til he's in bed and too comfy."

Her two companions, old school friends, young men on college holidays like Martha, sat either side, comfortably boxing her in. One smiling devil pulled a large flask from the inside of his jacket and Martha giggled, a strange sound June noticed she developed only after leaving home. The newcomers dutifully ignored Lori and her beau, writhing quicker and more desperate beneath the blanket, though a palpable tension settled in June's eyes, often dragging them to the side to observe. The hump of blanket lifted slightly at the end. Lori's feet, wide and pointed to the star-riddled sky, had a mound between them, and in the black gap between ground and blanket, June saw a mouth and tongue. It licked the smooth white skin of an unidentified body part. A long stroke, like a cat drinking milk.

June's stare whipped to the fire at that lick, the flick of pink on white burning her vision. Martha's words, now long past, caught up to her thoughts.

"Wait. You're leaving tomorrow? But you just came home. Can't go back just yet."

Martha raised the flask to her lips with a smooth, experienced motion she must have also picked up in college. She hissed air on her exhale and passed the flask to the man beside her.

"Hell, been home for too long already," she commented casually.

"Huh?"

Martha's gaze reluctantly moved to her kid sister, the baby, whiskey flushing her face rosy pink. Sitting across the small fire made of cast-off boughs, sylphs of rising heat distorted Martha's face. Warping her more than normal. In the years they had lived on the farm, Martha had changed, more than whatever higher learning did to a young woman's mind. Instead of meeting June's eyes, her stare wandered, looking her younger sister up and down. On the precipice of fifteen, June was long and gangly, and often covered in her farm-work clothes to match her long and messy brown hair wrangled into two braids. Martha's glazed eyes settled on her knees, nearly touching Roy's.

"Never mind, Juney, you'll figure it out one day."

Beneath the canopy, Lori made a sound to make a heathen blush and the two men chuckled. Roy, however, nudged her leg, doing his best to steal her attention.

"You really got some cows that escaped? Need any help with 'em? I catch all manner of escaped farm animals, gonna be a roper when I get outta school." His bare forearms flexed, the corded muscles of a man straining to show his truth.

June fiddled with her fingers and searched the clear stars again; his eyes were a weight on her neck. "Naw, they always go for the same place, always to the far end corner, though we never tell our pa that. Always tell him we had to search hours for 'em. I'll swing round and pick this new heifer up on my way back."

He nodded, a frown wrinkling his forehead. "Hard to believe only one family owns all this, bet your pa works you hard, huh?"

"Oh, we don't own it. We just mindin' the place, I guess you could say."

Martha snorted but didn't comment as Lori and her boyfriend had finished whatever they were doing and returned to the group and the firelight. The space around Lori's mouth was scratched red and she patted down the hem of her dress as she sat, smiling congenially like no one knew her transgressions. The boy whose shoes June didn't recognize held his hands up to the fire as if they were too cold.

"What do you mean, 'mindin' the place'?" Roy asked.

June blinked away from the vision of her sister's freshly ruffled hair and stared at Roy for a long moment, her thoughts discombobulated. She half-turned to him, giving them some semblance of a private conversation while her sisters and their boyfriends drank and laughed, firelight illuminating and casting ugly, gaunt shadows on their faces. Roy's, closer to the fire, shone smooth and pure like an angel.

"Oh, uh, well, the Farmer and his Wife left on a vacation about three years ago and just...never came back. Pa tried searching for them after a few months, putting in inquiries with the local police, hospitals, but there was nothing to find. So, I guess Pa just keeps working like they'll eventually show up one day or someone tries to tell us to get."

Across the fire and discreetly listening, talk of the Farmer had turned Martha's face dark, a humorless and dry expression as she ignored her own friends, intent on June's and Roy's quiet conversation. She interrupted in a burst.

"He didn't leave for vacation. He ran away and saddled us with this shithole."

"Mattie," Lori spoke, her tone a warning.

Roy and June, sitting close, whipped their heads to the interruption, confusion stifling any response. June's mouth dropped open, surprised, and then defensive at the label given to Land's End. Something unexplainable and unspoken made her want to defend the farm. Sick before they came, now June stood healthy and alive, grown stout and thriving as if she was a tree in the rich soil. And as for the Farmer, he had always been kind. Though something about his wife had always turned June's stomach, a shrewdness in her gaze, but she wouldn't say a lick of sourness against the Farmer. Roy, however, gathered his thoughts first, a dissatisfied note in his tone that had turned into a man's.

"Helluva 'shithole.' What I can tell, this farm is the most profitable around. Always gets the best rain, least winds. Heard your pa often donates food to the poorer, outta work folks. Heck, everywhere else looks dry and dead compared to your *shithole*." Bitterness laced Roy's words, as if naive Martha, who never did a lick of farm chores, didn't know how good she had it. June wanted to hold his hand right then and there and intertwine their fingers like shoe soles and never let go.

But Martha only had eyes for June, staring right into hers like she was trying to speak with her mind. She ignored Roy's soliloquy and said matter of factly, "This farm is cursed, June. Farmer knew it and his Wife sure as hell did." The orchard around them shivered with the night's dark breeze, and Martha's head tilted to the side, listening intently.

"What are you talking about? How can you say such a thing? Don't you remember before we arrived, Mattie? I do. Farmer saved us. This farm saved us. How you think Pa pays for your fancy college and nice dresses and probably your moonshine?"

Martha opened her mouth, a particularly malicious glint in her eyes, when Lori interrupted, a calm voice among the trio. "Mattie, that's enough now."

Martha glanced at Roy, at their knees wholesomely touching like school sweethearts, and the group was quiet, the men hoping for a good time now confused at the sudden hostility in the atmosphere. The fire had been whipped smaller by the wind, and the cloister of trees dimmed tighter. The two sisters snuck glances, accomplices in a grand secret they wouldn't share with the baby. Finally, Lori, the nice and kind sister who always sided with June during family scuffs, turned her way with a grim smile.

"Don't worry about it, Juney. You'll be fine."

***

The same wind whistled through the hairline crack in June's window. Only a miniscule thing, yet somehow in three years June had never figured how to plug it up. It persistently wriggled through whatever cloth she'd shove against or into the crack and skirled through at all times of the night like faint tinnitus. She looked at her clock, a slice of early moonrise shining on its face. 3am.

A notorious, infamous time, the worst of June's night wakes. Neither tired nor really awake. With her late-night escapades, tomorrow, Sunday, would be hard. Her muscles would be dog-tired, but guilt's oily and stiff fingers would push her to help with the orange harvest.

But it was worth it.

The way Roy's cheeks blushed, his knees and hands always innocently touching hers for some reason or another, the way he defended her farm and her Pa. The way he smiled.

The farm is cursed, June.

Martha's words intruded, rattling around in her head, and the silent message she shared with Lori ground against June's nerves. The two sisters were always babying her yet somehow made her the family mule, the one with the heaviest load, the only one to help out Pa. The only one who felt she had to help on Land's End, a grinding, gnawing notion cornering her every day. Martha had shot off as soon as she had that high school degree in her hand, and Lori, though kind and helpful, looked set to do the same with all her talk of learning. Would probably pick up the same inane giggle.

"She's just sore. Probably failing that fancy college," June whispered aloud, the retort in her own voice already formed in her mind.

You know there's something there.

The gale blew, sharper and higher, perhaps carrying the night train's whistle, and it paused before changing into a broken sparrow's tune outside. Odd for the wind. Or this time of night, she realized. June braced up on her elbow and peered through the pane. Out in the yard, a stone's throw from the house, Roy stood, his head darting side to side like a criminal on the lam. Moonlight blessed his golden hair as a halo.

June smiled and silently slipped into her outside coat. Holding onto her boots and stealing through the house, never had she been so aware of every creak in the old floorboards. Any one of them might wake up her parents down the far end of the hall. She only breathed once the screen door gently closed. Mist sieved low through the orchard, a gossamer waiting to burn in the morning light, and the late-night sparrow near the barn whistled for her again.

Roy hid in its shadow, waiting with a nervous air, and she pulled him by his cold hands through the narrow gap of the open barn door. Blood swooshed like an excited valve in her ears and her voice trembled with nerves.

"What are you doing here?"

Neither had been running, but they were both out of breath. Roy smiled and searched around the dark confines of the barn, mostly grottos of last year's hay sold to others who could keep rein of their livestock. "I don't know! I just... We were walking back home after Martha led us to the road and something...something just *told* me I should try and find you. Like little fingers prodding my brain. Isn't that crazy?" He paced back and forth in a little two-step, running his hands through his hair. "So I told the others to keep goin' and I trotted back, found the lane, and hopped that gate with the sign. Thought I'd gotten lost at first, but then I saw the house and now, well, now I'm here! Isn't that crazy!?" he repeated with a frenetic energy.

June, however, frowned and leaned against the barn door, staring down at the far lane lost to the dark orchard, wondering aloud.

"You found the lane? No one can ever find that thing."

The energy burned itself out in Roy's legs and he leaned on the opposite door, facing June, only a foot away. "I know, I just... Something demanded I march myself right up here, quick smart. Common sense, I guess, chiding me that I shoulda done that thing I've been thinkin' about for weeks."

Roy stepped across the gap of door, only a misty breath away from her, and his trembling hand gently fingered a lock of her unbound hair hanging on her collarbone. "Told me I was a no-good fool to not have done it yet, Juney."

June suddenly couldn't breathe, not the malady of her youth, but a new disease of romance. Enchanted and terrified by the thought of her first kiss, inexperience itching at her legs to run away, but Roy's charm and gentle smile kept her feet planted in the hay-strewn dirt. Her lungs had screwed themselves right up tight and didn't exhale until he kissed her, her muscles relaxing when his hands rested on her shoulders and started kneading them.

Last summer's stiff hay poked her back though her night shirt. But she wouldn't say it hurt. Not as much as when Roy lay on top of her and started moving. A rhythmic and somehow natural motion that pinched at first but then ebbed away. Liquid trickled down her thigh at some point, and a kernel of panic swelled in her chest. Fear of evidence or being caught doing something she shouldn't. Fear of repercussions. Long and permanent and unknown repercussions.

But then Roy's movements began to feel good, a burning kind of good, and all the fearsome thoughts were doused when he breathed hot and fast on her neck. Just when June was starting to move back and in time, gripping and pulling at him, it was all over for some reason and he was off, lying beside her and holding her hand, his thumb rubbing the outside of it.

"Don't have any mice or cats in here waiting to pounce, do ya?" he asked with a stilted humor, still out of breath and trying for normalcy.

June had the disposition of someone retracing her thoughts, securing them in place, trying to understand how she got here or what she might have done wrong. After another long moment of silence, she answered distractedly, "Naw, don't need a cat for no mice. And the sweet little kitten Lori tried to keep as a house cat ran away."

June felt wet down there. Enough to drip down her leg, and lifting her head, she saw white and red smeared together on her bare thigh. Roy also glanced down.

Repercussions. June's heart jumped.

"That's normal for the first time, my brother told me. You got your woman times yet?"

In the half-dark, she blinked at him.

"Woman times, where you bleed every month?"

Her momma nor her sisters had ever spoken of those, and surely she would notice bleeding. "No, I don't have those...yet."

He squeezed her hand a little too tight and nodded, deep in thought. He then sat and pulled on his shirt and helped wriggle her pants back on. "Well, that's good then. That's good." He kissed the top of her messed hair, pulling errant hay from it, and whispered promises of seeing her tomorrow, of coming up to the house and introducing himself proper-like. When they arrived at the porch stairs, his warm hands had intertwined with hers like she envisioned.

June couldn't sleep after that, the wind seeping through her window. Somehow Roy's sing-song tune lingered on the air and in her brain. She lay awake in bed until dawn bloomed the horizon purple, smelling fresh and crowing at her like a rooster. Though it was anxiety at being caught that really tossed her outta bed. Her father was rustling awake, making breakfast in the kitchen with Lori at the table. They caught eyes and Lori smirked but stayed silent while June slipped out the back door.

June and Mae never spoke much. They were different kinds of people, June taking after her Pa. But June had gleamed a few things off her mother, who mostly stuck to the house while she and Pa claimed the fields as theirs. Mae always complained, or rather taught, that it was the woman's burden to clean a man's mess. A man made the mess and a woman cleaned it up, she always muttered. June supposed it was a fancy metaphor that went over her head, but guessed it would count in this situation.

June collected the pitchfork and a bucket of well water, thinking she would turn the mussed hay over where her blood and his seed had run out of her. She stopped short at the little cloister where they had lain. The vivid sunrise shone on the spot through the open door and onto the clean scattered hay laying atop the bare earth. There was nothing like she expected. Maybe a hint of red, quickly fading, on the bare dirt, but nothing else. Mae always said cleaning up messes was the woman's burden, but there was no mess here.

"Guess there wasn't as much as I thought," June said to herself, and instead of her own voice speaking back to her in her head as it usually did, it was Lori's soft tones now.

Don't worry about it, Juney. You'll be fine.

***

Rain and mud warped the outer track into a mess of clotted and raised dirt, the truck bouncing as her daddy carefully winded around the struts. His strong arms grasped the steering wheel as if the two were wrestling in slow motion. June leaned out the window in the warm afternoon air, hazy and bucolic, listening to the distant whistle of a train leaving these parts for other places, and found it strange she didn't want to jump on it like Lori. Like she couldn't hear the whistle of the Pied Piper that lured her favorite sister away and carried her far to the other side of the country. June pursed her lips and mimicked the whistle, her strong lungs keeping it long and low.

The small pear orchard, harvested last August by her and Roy's own rough hands, ended.

"There she is," Pa grumbled, and June searched up the lane. Running along the outer fence line before the Bakers' failing crops, the small body of a calf was lodged in the boundary of barbed wire. Trying to escape.

"Oh, Penny..." June mumbled worriedly.

"Told you not to name this one."

"I like naming them."

"I don't. You cry too much when they go."

He pressed the brake too hard, angry, and the truck lurched to a stop right before the nearest fence post. The black and white calf, six months old and bought last week, had her front leg and head tangled down to her neck through the fence. Barbs stuck her deep, blood trickling over her soft baby fur and down to the soil her hooves churned. Penny bleated when she saw June step out of the truck, her leg and ankle pretzled around the barb wire shook as she wriggled. June winced and patted the white fur between her ears.

"Oh, you dummy... Why'd you go and do this?"

Henry kicked the clumpy loam and rounded the snared animal. "Goddamnit." He studied their latest purchase. Penny's ankle and leg were twisted unnaturally, barbs pricking through skin and into other skin like it a threaded needle. "We're gonna have to cut that open."

"That ankle?"

"Yep."

"But that'll lame her, won't it?"

"Likely. Probably for the best. Won't try to get away if she can't walk far." He frowned at June's frown. "This here's the future of our herd, hopefully. I'm not buying any more if this one ain't good, June-bug. Not spending any more on chickens who don't lay or roosters who suddenly learn to fly." He pulled the knife from his belt and waved it at Penny. "Or rented bulls whose seeds don't take or cows who don't give babies or milk. She's the last."

Henry's knife was too big for her liking. More like a saw made for a child. A machete, really. Used on everything from branches to bovines, it sat on his hip like another limb and he rearranged his grip on it and exhaled. "Alright, hold her head still."

June wrapped her arms through the fence, barbs poking her in the chest, and Penny started to squirm and kick, the cow's hot snorts brushing her arm. June's cheek was wet, though she made comforting sounds for Penny's sake. "Shhhh. Shhhh now, girl, just'll take a quick..."

Penny bleated sharply and the strange sound of serrated knife tearing through thin skin rent the air, her sinew ripping apart like shredded meat. June squeezed her eyes tight, Penny struggling in her cradled arms, until Henry pulled her away and carried her easily to the truck bed like a small child.

June breathed and remained kneeling, the cup of calf's blood soaking the soil near her knee. The ground, shaded dark brown like used coffee grounds, drank Penny's gore. She watched the blood sink into the dirt and blinked once only for it to be already gone.

***

Roy's fingers conspiratorially entwined with hers beneath the table. Not the type of intertwining when they'd sneak away to the barn, but the kind of hold when he comforted her. She squeezed his fingers back and absentmindedly played with his wedding ring.

"Pass the squash, please," Martha asked her husband, Joshua, interrupting his conversation with Henry. Joshua stopped talking, a blank expression on his round face, before smiling and reached for the bowl only a hair outta Martha's reach. June critically examined Martha's swollen belly hidden beneath the expensive canary sundress. Such a thing apparently gave her permission to not even try and reach or strain herself unnecessarily. June looked down to her own linen shirt and pants.

Joshua passed it to her and his eyes met June's as she came up. He took it as a signal to give her attention, as if he thought he should talk to everybody at this first meeting before they quickly left again. His words were crisp and enunciated, as if he thought her hard of hearing, or dumb.

"So, June? You graduated a few months ago, right? Are you going to attend a day college like your sisters?"

Roy squeezed her hand a little tighter. There was a moment, just a brief inhale of silence at the table, that passed, and in her periphery, Mae stiffened slightly and June smiled at the brother-in-law she'd just met.

"No, Roy and I decided to stay on here and help out Henry. I'm doing some business classes by correspondence, though." She chuckled with a good-naturedness, burying small resentments. "Henry ain't getting any younger with all those crops, even need to hire a hand or two from town every now and then. Business is good, so I'm told."

Joshua smiled at her, a limp thing with his weak chin, and he grabbed Martha's hand on the tabletop. "Speaking of business, we appreciate that loan, Henry. This baby..."

But Henry waved his hand, commanding his new son-in-law, the lawyer, to stop talking. "Aw now, just passing it on. Got more than enough here. Gonna do the same for Lori and her brood if she ever comes back to visit from out west..."

Martha yawned loudly, uncaring of any conversation she might interrupt. She *was* pregnant, after all. Her fingers pushed back her golden curls, her clean nails shining glossy in the light. "Oh geez, I'm starting to get tired all the time. Can't believe still got four months of this. Y'all keep it too hot in the house, Momma. I'm gonna get some fresh air."

She rested her fork and abruptly dinner had finished, the rest of the family joining Martha, the favorite, on the porch for respite. June reluctantly also followed, not wanting to seem contrary, and she stepped through the door and greeted by a cool October night. No longer burdened by school, June's days and weeks melted together in a great amalgam of work and chores. Always something to be done—tilling, clipping, harvesting, weeding, sowing—only her recent marriage to Roy broke the staleness she found in her new full-time work.

Together with Henry and Mae, Martha plucked Joshua's hand and showed her husband the surrounds. Touring him around the outer yard, Henry's stubby finger pointed to distant fields Martha had likely never visited or even known about.

Roy and June rocked on the porch, listening to Henry's faint voice explain to a clueless Joshua while Martha's clucked to Mae about the coming baby, another grandchild and Martha's first. June couldn't remember Mae so happy, a new kinda smile on her face that stretched back to her ears. Lori's family had started clear on across the country, too far for a quick visit.

Roy and June, the newly married couple on the porch, eavesdropped, Martha's voice grating on June's nerves with each syllable. Her wide hands splayed across the mound of her bright yellow dress.

"Can you believe that at ten weeks, this little thing already had fingernails? That's what the doctor said. Isn't that something? Probably big, sharp things too, by the feel of it."

The foursome wandered the yard in a gentle amble. In the early evening, twilight near extinguished, Martha's silhouette was already distinguishable by her rotundness, her bright dress a ghost in the gloom.

"You okay?" Roy asked quietly, their hands joined across chairs.

"I guess. Strange having her back. Can't remember last time she was here, and now she's..."

"Pregnant." Roy squeezed her hand, and she felt his gaze staring earnestly at her profile. June didn't reply, wary of betraying anything but indifference, and continued watching Martha and Joshua wander the wide expanse of yard toward the barn.

"It'll be okay, Juney. Doc says sometimes women get 'em real late. Said your sisters were the same, remember? And even if not, I don't mind. We can always adopt, lots of orphans round here who would love to live here with you and me."

June exhaled. Roy's tone was too sincere and sympathetic, loving her even if she failed as a woman. The sting of new tears invaded her nose and she sniffed it away, vexed her new husband had the ability to see past her words and knew her sore points.

"I know. I don't mind though, not really. Lots of work to do round here. Babies take up lots of time, so they say. Always farm chores to do."

Always farm chores to do, silly!

She finally turned to him, his lips pursed to the side of his mouth in a funny little puzzle. Henry and Mae, hand in hand, left their eldest daughter and husband to wander around the outer yard just as the expecting couple dipped into the bordering orchard trees. They climbed the creaky porch stairs and Henry flipped on the porch light, exciting some early moths.

"I wish they were staying longer," Mae lamented, and Henry wrapped an arm around her slender shoulders.

"Now, dear, you know it's for the best." He glanced to the east-facing end of the house. "June-bug, you gonna take Penny over to the barn? Starting to get chilly."

Martha and Joshua had returned to the yard from the dark trees on the far side. Joshua held her by the forearm like she was already nine months and soon to burst.

"Can't Martha do it?" she said casually, hiding her grin, and both her parents looked aside at her, Mae like she tasted something rotten and Pa like he'd gotten a piece of caramel. His smile for her tapered away under Mae's scorning eye and they all looked back to the pregnant couple. Martha appeared so...fragile. The way Joshua held her, the way she waddled, and although a kernel of jealousy stewed in her for having things she couldn't, June inexplicably also pitied her sister for such a malady like pregnancy. To be so vulnerable to her own body.

"Sure, Pa."

She left Roy and the men spoke about the wheat harvest coming soon, Henry tutoring Roy in things June learned years ago. Penny waited in her enclosure beside the house and stepped lively when she spotted June. She lowed at her, recognizing the time of the evening had come for her to be tucked away. The cow still occasionally made a trot for the trees, ignoring her limp, made worse by the soft earth. But those escapes were getting less, and though Henry constantly threatened to put her on the dinner table since she failed with the rented bulls, he didn't because June said she liked the company and Penny, with her sweet disposition, was far and away June's best friend.

She scratched the tuft of soft and fluffy hair between Penny's ears, the full-grown cow leaning into the scratch and pushing for more.

"Alright, friend, time for bed, nothing interesting happening here. You didn't miss anything, I promise." June lovingly slipped her hand around Penny's head harness and started leading her out of the gate but stopped mid-step when Martha cried out, a wrenching sound stealing her breath. June sprinted around the house.

In the middle of the yard beside the pomegranate tree's cleared earth, Martha knelt on the soft grass, Joshua beside her. One protective hand over her stomach, the other holding herself up, her fingers clawing the ground.

She gasped again; shadows on her belly shifted with decisive movements, startling June forward.

"What?! What's going on?!"

Joshua looked at her with wide, confused eyes and a helpless shake of his head.

"Martha? What..."

"No!" Martha suddenly exploded, the hand shielding her belly suddenly clenched into a fist and hit the dirt. "No! No! *NO!*" she shrieked as a banshee. A madwoman belting the dirt over and over again with her weak fist. Joshua snatched her wrist from taking another swing, and in the porch light, tears glinted on Martha's face. Restrained, she found June's eyes, openly sobbing. "I was only here for a day! Less than a day! It's not fair!" She wrenched her arm away from her husband and slammed her knuckles into the earth again, particles of dirt and grass coming away like the aftermath of bare-knuckle boxing.

Stunned at seeing such violence from her older, more sophisticated sister, June stayed stuck, incapacitated for usefulness while pregnant Martha continued fighting and pounding the indifferent earth. Joshua was equally aghast and flummoxed as to what to do until in one inhuman act, Martha roared a cry of frustration and sadness and anger. Roared it to the dawning stars, and it echoed over Land's End. When the last vestiges of the cry were expelled and spent, she slumped right into Joshua's waiting arms and he hugged her like a straitjacket, sharing an impotent glance with June.

Henry's old car reversed fast and harried from the shed, tires crushing gravel, and he drove up to the pair on the ground. June swallowed a lump when the car's headlight struck the crimson creek running down Martha's bare legs. The red of blood contrasting eerily bright and stark against her pale skin and staining her dress. Little specks of viscera among the liquid cast their own minute shadows. June's eyes widened when Martha's belly started squirming like a worm beneath the soil. A raspy stutter escaped, and she was a baby sister again, inexperienced and untried. "Martha?"

A car door swung open and Mae pushed June roughly aside, her town coat already on, her purse in hand. "Outta the way, June! Joshua, get her into the car." The pair dragged Martha into the backseat and the wagon raced ahead, lost to the dense, serried rows of the watching orchard.

June could only stare at the spot where they had left, shellshocked. Sunset had completely extinguished in favor of the night, and the air was stiller than coffin air. After however long, Roy eventually walked before her, towing Penny by a rope. The bovine had tried her luck with the commotion, limping down to the trees for her next escape before Roy caught her. Wrapping his long and muscular arm over her shoulder, he hugged June, tucking her into his warm side.

"She'll be okay. Lots of stuff happens with making babies. She'll be okay."

Though his tone was unsure, June hugged him back anyhow. Holding each other, they swung around to face the house and something shifted at their feet. Like grass springing back after being rudely stepped on. June stared down. In the far porch light, Martha's blood, or her baby's, shone black on grass and soil before seeping away. Releasing Roy, June quickly crouched and pressed her hand into the spot, feeling warmth beneath her hands. She kept them pressed down, ignoring Roy's inquiry, and closed her eyes, gasping when the rich, fertile soil beneath her fingertips throbbed once.

June shot to stand, continuing the disbelief on her face. "Did you...?"

Roy, patting Penny's head, looked at her. "What?"

"Did you see that...there in the dirt? It felt like..."

Waiting for her to finish, his gaze oscillated between her hand, stained with a muddy concoction of blood and dirt, and the ground at their feet. He frowned and offered his hand. "Come on, honey, let's get inside for the night, yeah? Get you cleaned up and in bed."

She stared at the hand like he was insane. Like he didn't understand the unspoken message playing in her head, and she knelt to the dirt again, pressing the flats of her fingers and half her palm into the same patch, now nothing there but warm, sleeping dirt.

***

Moments, minutes, months, and years sloughed smoothly away. June felt time unerringly left the farm alone, wreaking havoc on all others outside its confines. She blinked and she wasn't young anymore, not that her body felt much different. Still strong and healthy, at least healthy in the way that meant you weren't dying, not necessarily that you were functioning properly. She and Roy, Henry and Mae kept to the farm and chores with unwavering steadfastness, rarely inquiring or bothering with the outside world. Uncaring until quite abruptly one day, her parents expressed interest in a vacation.

She now watched her Pa lug Mae's suitcase. In that moment, that very moment of hefting something gargantuan, her father appeared younger than he should, younger than nature allowed. Henry should have been old and decrepit, though he couldn't pinpoint what year he was born. Shedding his work coveralls like a snakeskin, he now wore nice town clothes, the big knife replaced with a wallet in his pocket. From behind, he and Roy could have been brothers. Strong, defiant shoulders time never assaulted. He pushed the large brown suitcase into the back seat and June's throat tightened.

"How long you thinkin' of being gone for?"

Henry paused in the car door, his old-youthful figure filling the frame. "You know? Not quite sure. Month, likely two? Can't remember last time we went on a vacation. Can't even remember when I wanted to, to be honest."

June's eyes glistened, recognition shining in his own, and his weathered hand gripped her shoulder, concern pressing into her muscles. "Hey now, after we go and visit Martha and the kids for a week or two, the drive 'cross country oughta take another week. Gotta see Lori and see how many great grandkids they've made out there.

Finally get to take my trip to the ocean." He watched Roy heft the last suitcase from the house.

"Be back before you can spit, June-bug."

June's throat finally cinched. Like an unkind hand squeezed, desiring her to choke on something and nothing and everything.

"It just..." She gasped and her father stopped, the frown on his face turning his smooth skin, tanned boot-leather-brown by years of sun and work, into unnatural lines. She continued, the hand relinquishing to let her talk. "It just feels like you ain't coming back. Like the Farmer didn't."

Henry's face adopted a queer expression, puzzled at her somberness, while his hands squeezed her strong arms. "Now, June, you're just talking nonsense, I swear." He frowned. "You're thirty years old. Thought you and Roy could use the time alone, thought you'd be grateful to have this big ol' place to yourself for a while before I get old and dodderin', before you gonna have to feed me with a spoon."

Henry's blue eyes, deep as wells and endless as the sky, held her gaze, a slight tilt to the corner of his mouth. No, he wasn't lying. He didn't wanna escape her and the farm. Didn't feel trapped by their family, though they were the last and there wouldn't be any grandbabies from her. A tear rolled onto June's cheek and she shook her head. "There you go again. We both know you're gonna live forever, the way you work."

He smiled and rubbed her shoulders with finality. "Before you can spit, promise."

Roy sidled along her, replacing her father's hand. "Not enough time to miss 'em, Juney. Got those oranges need pickin' soon, then the olives shortly after. Won't even have the time to spit, I reckon." The two men smiled at her, coercing her in a way to smile back even though she didn't feel it in her heart.

Leaning into the car, June kissed her distracted mother one last time, her firm apple cheek happy and plump, and June was surprised to see her eyes glassy as she stared up at the cream cottage on the green hill. As if she knew a terrible secret and it hurt.

"Momma?"

Mae blinked, the glazed sheen evaporating to study June with a more serious air. She gingerly kissed June's cheek in return, though not enough to wear off her lipstick. Another light, little thing June didn't feel in her heart, like it wasn't strong enough to reach that far.

"Now, June, you take care of the house and grounds now. And of you and Roy, won't you? Gotta stay healthy, no liquor after five and no late nights, hear?" She said it with a note of worry, and June was oddly touched for the instruction. Even with them gone and only writing letters, Mae had always favored Lori and Martha, June often saddled with Henry. But now her mother worried for her.

"Course, Momma, we'll see you sooner than you can spit, apparently."

Mae smiled in a way that was more a frown, no doubt happy for the vacation, but not for the inconveniences that came with leaving your home. June stepped away from the car and Henry beeped the horn.

When the old family sedan rolled down the hill and was swallowed whole by the orchard, June remained in place, listening to the wind chittering up through the trees, carrying the sound of the old car. Was there something she had forgotten? She listened to the wind for a moment longer, likening it to crowds of old men and women guffing away. Though they'd all had a full breakfast, June's belly felt empty and hollow, concentrating on the ghostly discourse. Like her parents were adding to it. She gasped, realizing all at once she had forgotten to say, "I love you."

Now, June, stop moping for no reason. Too busy for moping! That hay needs tending after all. Lots of things to do!

"Yeah, yeah," she retorted against the voice of reason persisting in her head. Roy leaving to close up the shed, she crossed the center of the yard with its pomegranate tree, pausing to study the ripe fruit Pa commanded to never touch. Downright forbade anyone from laying a hand on the fruit or tree because he thought it looked perfect, something about when you searched for the definition of a pomegranate, this would be the picture the publisher would choose, he often said. A perfect specimen. Her hand itched to snatch one. The biggest one. The fattest, fullest pomegranate that hung right in front of her, taunting June with its ripeness and Henry's protection like a challenge.

But the wind whistled through the trees, and somewhere in a far-off field the hay called, wondering why she wasn't already there with her scythe. She stalked away from the center tree, Penny limping after her.

***

Three weeks had passed when Roy, coming straight from his daily delivery to town, searched out his wife and found her pruning the lemon trees. The small cluster of trees had been Henry's charge, having an affinity for the clotted citrus fragrance in the air. He once said the crisp scent was how he imagined the smell of the ocean. So thick you could swallow and taste it. June secretly enjoyed it because she imagined it a similar smell to holding a baby, fresh and clean and new and bright and happy and all the things her imagination sometimes ran away with.

"Juney," Roy said, and she looked down the rungs of the ladder at him. He should have taken twice as long from delivering the latest orange pickings. But he held a piece of paper in his hand and woe on his face. June's knuckles tightened around the clippers and her mouth was abruptly swollen, the word viscid and thick in her mouth.

"Pa?"

Roy shook his head slowly, like he was stuck in time or in a dream, and June's fingers unclenched. "Honey, I'm... Your Momma took a turn when they got to Martha's. She...died a few days after they arrived." He swallowed, his voice high and strained, his words disbelieving. "About two weeks ago, I guess. Josh says she was just...tired and died in her sleep one night."

He grabbed the bottom of the ladder, maybe to hold it for her, but also to hold himself up. A whisper of déjà vu suddenly caught June's mind, something someone mentioned long ago. Only a susurration of memory she couldn't quite grasp, and June's throat and the upper part of her nose stung, swelling with the sting of salt. She blinked them away, coughed her throat clear, and stayed on the ladder, bathed in lemon blossoms, pink and white, and swathes of thick leaves.

"They bringing her home?"

She already knew the answer. Mail might be slow, or Joshua might've not thought to write 'til a few days afterward, but even so. Martha would never return to Land's End, the place of her first and only miscarriage, and if Henry was bringing her back to the farm for a burial, he would have arrived by now.

Roy shook his head again on slow repeat. "Didn't say, says Henry is outta it, you know, understandably. Lying in bed and what not... Oh God... Henry." Roy's voice broke, and June blinked out of her daze and down at him. Sweet, loving Roy. Her husband leaned against the ladder, his hand massaging his temples, sweaty in the midday sun. She descended and he wrapped his arms around her waist, his head cradled against her stomach. She held him, the clippers awfully close to his ear, while he sobbed against her rough linen shirt and the reverberation echoed through her own body as a great pulse of sorrow.

June lay in bed two nights later, staring up at her old ceiling, when Henry died.

Roy snored beside her, a gentle stirring she appreciated, knowing he was alive but dead to the world. As usual, around 3am, June had half-woken, murmurs in the far orchard gently caressing her unconsciousness, when a terrible pain shot through her core. At first she thought it a horrid case of heartburn, the way it seized her chest, the way it didn't soothe a minute later like another random pain might. The orchards chittered with a new east wind and the pain creeped lower into her abdomen, to parts without nerves. Deep within her innards. Faint ghostly fingers curling around parts unknown.

June bolted upright in bed, the covers dropping away, and she clenched her lower gut. Henry was dead! He had died! She was as sure of it as knowing when the apples were ready to be picked. Martha spoke of a curse once, and now Henry suffered it. He had died and whatever had held onto him receded across the miles and back to Land's End. June cradled her gut like something lived in there, squirming wild, determined to not wake Roy, though he too now tossed and turned in the bed. After a minute, the pain gradually receded in throbs until only a ghostly memory.

When the spasms in her belly dampened, June's hand covered her mouth and stifled her sobs. Half-listening to the orchard, an unmistakable shiver ran through their leaves, whistling as they were wont to do, as the land had shaped them.

June had been right. Miserably, completely right.

Henry had been just like Farmer.

He would never return.

June laid in bed the entire next day and the day after that. Roy had frowned and fussed over her, but seeing nothing wrong besides June feigning sleepiness and melancholia, he left her be and shouldered his usual chores and some of hers. She hadn't told him Henry had died because she thought it best he find out by himself. Since moving onto Land's End when they married at eighteen, Roy had been Henry's shadow when he wasn't June's. She didn't want to seem crazy, but more importantly, she didn't want to see that look in his eyes until the last minute possible.

By the third day of bed, June's muscles positively twitched with the inactivity, a pervading and insistent guilt telling her she was overdoing it.

What would Henry say? Laying in bed when there is so much to be done?

"Henry's dead, he wouldn't say nothing," she replied, ennui sapping her usual willingness. Henry had worked a lifetime and he still died. Away from her, away from home. What was the point of anything when everything left?

You know he would want you taking care of the place. Not everything leaves.

"That's true. Some things stay. The sun, the moon, the stars, I guess."

Land's End has always been here for you. Gave food for your belly. A place to shelter from the growing heat. A strength for your bones and diseased lungs. Respite. Land's End always stays.

June sat up in bed, confused and staring out the bedroom window. The trees outside swayed. Her voice of reason had a sharp edge to it of late. If it wasn't her own voice inside her own head, she would've called it rather pushy. Demanding. But it wasn't wrong.

June had gotten dressed and filled her stomach with days-old bread when Roy came running in, a ghost chasing him into the house. A new piece of paper was in his hands, but instead of sorrow, aghast disbelief covered his handsome features. His voice, his windpipe had choked, the words lost and crumbling beneath his own pain. June calmly took the paper from his rough hands, the hands of a Farmer.

Henry died earlier this week, peacefully, I think, in his sleep. If you want anything personal of his, please come and take it. I can't go back, Juney.

Love, Martha.

June dropped the paper onto the table and Roy clutched her to him, howling deeply and muffled against her shoulder, turning the cloth wet with tears and snot.

So much to do, June-bug, Henry's voice chided.

She patted Roy's back until the worst had passed and wiped her own eyes of imaginary tears, tears already shed and gone, and left her husband at the table. Henry's knife, the big thing that used to scare her as a girl, hung from its belt by the front door, and she picked it up now, a yearning to use it for work. Land's End called for her, needing her. And she sensed she needed it. Whether she liked it or not.

***

June hugged Adam tight. With freshly washed hair, soap lingered over the skin of his neck. He wore one of the cotton shirts with the collar he and Roy had spent the day picking out for his new fancy college. June examined her adopted son's clothes, thinking them too ostentatious and peacocky for a young man, but styles changed all the time and she couldn't keep up with what the world outside did, let alone wore.

"I'm gonna miss you, Mom," he murmured into her neck, his fingers playing with her long salt and pepper hair, still healthy and thick but no longer in the braids of a young woman.

"I know. Me too," she replied, squeezing him a little harder for the last time. Adam had come to the farm when he was ten. An orphan created by an automobile accident. He was strong and loving, handsome and full of life, a magnet for laughter and people, the most popular boy in his school class.

He also wasn't staying.

Adam sensed her verklemptness and added, "I'll be back for Christmas. Promise."

June released him and forced her mouth into a weak smile. He didn't know it right now, but he was lying. Cupping his cheek that had once been a boy's, she replied, "Have fun, study hard."

Roy, still in his dusty coveralls, leaned out the window of their old farm truck. "Come on, son, train leaves in thirty."

Adam retreated down the porch stairs, his gaze soaking up the house and surrounds, remembering each nook and cranny, each scraped knee on the gravel, each hot summer night drinking bitter lemonade on the porch and studying the night sky and speculating about other worlds, other times. Watching him walk backward to the truck, each moment of the eight years June recalled with beautiful clarity and torment. He was a gift. And he was going. Her heart broke inside her chest.

He entered the truck and Roy cast a knowing, forlorn look at June. Another foster son or daughter who didn't want to stay. Who didn't have the inclination to carry on at the farm, who hadn't even inquired, but just came home from school one day with the notion of higher education or traveling or a girlfriend or boyfriend. No one asked June to stay. The orchard never whispered to them. Even after years of being chauffeured up and down, the entry lane always remained hidden from them.

She couldn't blame them. Who would stay on a farm that didn't want them?

The old truck wheezed to life, rolling forward, and she had forgotten something. June's heart was suddenly in her esophagus. Her thoughts quickly recalling every tactic a mother, a *real* mother, might use to remind a child that she was the only real family they would ever have. Bribery? Veiled promises or threats? Love?

The truck pulled away, Adam leaning across his father to wave to her before it turned and gained speed down the hillock.

She loved him.

Had she said it?

She recalled Henry thirty or forty years ago. Her Pa, leaving, never to return.

She had forgotten then. She forgot every time.

No, she hadn't told Adam, "I love you."

Panic strangled her chest. Tendrils and vines wrapping it tight like a shut gate.

June began jogging, began to run! "Wait! *Wait!*" she cried. But it was too late. The moment, the last opportunity to tell Adam she loved him, fled. The truck was already consumed by the trees, nothing but a cloud of dust to say it was ever there at all. She stopped trying, stopped her run mid-stride, her lungs stifled by distress, her mouth flooding with saliva. She leaned over her knees on the verge of tears.

He knows you love him.

"I should have said it, that was my last chance. The others don't come back. He won't come back."

You don't need them to come back. Too much to be done, June-bug!

June huffed a great exhale, indignant, disbelieving at the alien, errant thought. A tear fell straight onto the earth where it was lost to the grass and greedy soil. She erected. The pomegranate tree stood feet away. Always in bloom, always healthy and alive and sitting right there, in the middle of everything where she couldn't escape it. Its fertility and blossoms pushed right in her face. Even now, a bright red pom sat low before her.

"Too much to be done?" The words escaped June's mouth as if breathed from a furnace. A guttural utterance of resentment and insanity overcame her and she crossed the space and grasped the bright crimson fruit, her fingers clutching its hard-shelled orb. There was a moment of unsurety, all of Pa's warning, lasting some forty years, his words reverberating across time and heavens. Even before he said them, the Farmer before him had, and the Farmer before him. Even June had for some reason carried on the tradition, warning her charges. A never-ending line of Farmers forbidding its progeny to absolutely not take from this tree. Protecting this tree. The farm gave plenty, fruit and otherwise. Leave this.

She yanked abruptly, plucked it, the stem easily releasing the fruit for her. June stared at it in her hand, the fire in her belly dimming in realization of what she had done, what she betrayed. Her heart beat fast, belying fear. The same beat that thrummed her veins and pressed against the fruit. It pulsed. The fruit pulsed.

June plucked Henry's knife from her belt and too hastily cut into the pom's tough hide. Just a slit. Replacing the knife, June used her two thumbs and dug in farther to rip the fruit into two ragged pieces, pulp flying away.

Its depths were beautiful, glorious, and deep. A catacomb of plump pulp, vibrant crimson with pink jewels in each center, white tendrils of pith wove around bountiful clusters that sat innocently and watched her like little glinting eyes.

June stared back, mesmerized by its beauty, and then horrified something so beautiful could exist and be hoarded for no reason. Without another thought, she mashed her face into the parcels of sweet and tang, her teeth indiscriminately gnashing and piercing the fruit with sharp canines, chewing the thick skin of each pulp and savoring the juice. Gnawing the seeds within and sometimes swallowing them whole. Juice ran a bloody river from her chin. Ambrosia. Elixir. She bit a large chunk and ripped it from the cavern. Penny lowed across the yard, a warning sound, and cautiously approached, her limp now old and worn in, a natural restriction.

June breathed in and out of her nose while frantically chewing as if the Farmer would suddenly emerge from the trees and stop her. With each breath, each swallow, the adrenaline and fire subdued. Extinguished and satiated by the sacrilegious act. Penny ambled forward, and something stuck in June's soft gum. Something not fruit. Not seed.

She plucked it from her gum, her hands dripping in gore, and peered at the small thing between her thumb and forefinger. A little thin thing with a curve to it. A tiny, translucent thing, so small it could have easily been invisible. Perhaps a small, hardened part of the stem? She wiped the crimson juice away, the translucence of the object revealed, the small crescent shape unmistakable.

Can you believe that at ten weeks, this little thing already had fingernails? Martha's voice echoed over the yard, across time, her howl following when viscera ran out of her body and into the earth.

June's fingers pinched the calcified fetus nail, its sharpness piercing her fingerpads, the juice thick and gummy running down her hand and flowing over her forearms. Her heart squeezed and throat gagged. She retched onto the emerald-green grass, crimson and brown vomit splattering her boots, tears and snot, a waterfall issuing from her face. The holy pomegranate given back to the farm. Penny stepped back and forth, anxiety tensing the cow's muscles.

When her stomach had emptied, the acidity of juice and bile lacing her tongue, June stared at the tree with hatred, new and deep and unreserved. Swelling and strong, a strange kind of hurt twisted her heart. One that made her want to cry and scream and rage and sob and reign destruction on the pieces of wood.

She unhooked Henry's knife from her belt, an extension of her arm. A flaming sword. Penny stepped away, always wary of Henry's knife that maimed her fifty years ago, the memory always fresh.

June howled into the air when she took the first swing, the branch with the offending fruit swiped away as if it never was. Left and right, June hacked with the strength of a young woman, with the fire of a woman wronged. Exterminating what Land's End provided. Over and over, indiscriminately all the delicate branches with shiny leaves fell to the ground under her knife. June crying, wailing, a tear for each leaf. How many babies had the Farm stolen? Left and right, branches hewn in half. How many babies hewed in half? How many chances? Anger and sorrow fueled her muscles, her will.

How much blood and sweat had the Farm, this leech, sucked for its own fertility? How much stolen from June? Her blade swung insanely.

Left and right, over and over. Since time immemorial? Leaves like confetti, fruit dropping as blood bombs, bursting and exploding on the ground. Everything given, everything taken. Futures stolen.

Finally, June hewed away the last inconsequential branch, fruit broken and hacked as a battlefield full of debris. The detritus of *her* vengeance. Her chest heaved, sucked air tinged with far-off lemon, assessing the trunk. The blade's handle was sticky, juice making it tacky.

June swung widely for the body of the sturdy tree. The first tree of Land's End Farm. The one to see families come and go, the one who chose which desperate families were privy to its gift. The tree that would be there when there were no families left and humanity gone, leaving for other places, other worlds. June swung hard, her metal singing as it ended in the wood with a *thunk*.

Something inside June's body broke. Gored.

A powerful twang, a ripped muscle, buried somewhere she never knew. She released the knife, stuck in the tree, and leaned on her knees. Her tears hadn't stopped, but the piercing sensation had taken her breath away. Startled her. The connection all at once evident and surreal.

She breathed through the words. "That's it, huh? A hurt for a hurt?"

A long life for a long life, June-bug.

She yanked the knife out and swung again with a grunt, a cut of triangle shorn from the tree, and another, harsher pain rent her insides in retaliation. Eyes squeezed shut, her arm swung again, and again, and again, speckles of red showed and sap thick as clotted ichor began snailing down the bark and warmth trickled inside June's pants until it freely flowed. Crying with pain she had never known, been shielded from by Land's End Farm, now wracked her body, her gut, her shriveled womb. She screamed at the pomegranate tree, painful and raw, bleeding and breaking beneath Henry's machete, and she swung down on a thick, core branch, the wood screaming, a stolen baby squealing.

June's insides were falling away from her, forsaking their shell, her husk, the pain intolerable, but her anger kept her from falling to her knees in submission. The land grumbled unhappily, rippled beneath her unsteady feet, a waking earthquake, a giant near bedrock. And raising her arms high, June, a woman lost, denied so much and no longer thinking about any future, swung at the hemorrhaging, dangling branch and the slender string of wood it hung from. The knife cut right through it and Penny bleated a terrible, coarse sound.

June spun, dizzy, disorientated, and wounded. Her pants, holding viscera in like a bulging bag, were soaked in gore from her groin down, and her boots slipped as if they were in mud. Halfway cross the yard, Penny, her beloved friend, forever trapped on the land but gifted a healthy life if not barren, was knelt on her front two knees, an odd way for a cow to be. Behind her, the branch dropped to the ground and Penny lowed again, sharp and distressed, and a gush of blood cascaded from her still-raised behind, splattering to the earth.

"No, nonononono." June mumbled, her own hurt roaring everywhere and in everything, and she stumbled to Penny just as the cow collapsed. June cradled her head and looked down her long, mottled, black and white body, the blood rushing out of her and onto her back legs. Her big eyes were surrounded by long, full, clean lashes and they blinked at June, and in the pink, puffy flesh of her maw, more red.

"Penny... I'm sorry. I didn't think."

Never do, June-bug! So much to do! Why you wasting it on useless to-dos!

Penny bleated again, a pathetic sound, a cry asking June to stop.

"Okay, girl, okay, I know, I know. That was silly of me," she said with lips drenched with tears and copper tang spread across her tongue. The pain in her lower abdomen juddered every nerve down to her toes, but with each breath, with each remorseful thought, it receded slightly, slowly. As if it never wanted to go, as if it reprimanded her and wanted the last word.

Her hands covered in juice and blood, June frantically petted down Penny's soft face, her eyes now closed, and examined the chaos of the pomegranate tree, asking its forgiveness. She would clean it up. Tend to its wounds. She would make it pretty and healthy again. She would make it right.

***

A warm breeze brushed June's hair from her face. Standing atop the ladder and nearly through the lemon tree's canopy, she searched eastward where it hailed from.

"Awfully unusual feeling something like that, it's almost November! Shouldn't be that warm."

Seasons change back and forth all the time.

June harrumphed at the thought and reached farther for the last scraggly branch needing pruning. Her back oddly twinged with the reach, her old-young bones straining after so long up the ladder, reaching and pulling. Adam's last letter, detailing his latest baby, had begged her to stop her daily work routine and hire some help. *Hell, sell the farm!* he wrote. This week was the first week she had ever seriously considered it.

Clipping the branch, she descended slowly, an uneasiness in her feet for each rung. June picked up the wicker basket, only half full of the season's last lemons. It creaked as she hugged it into her hip like a laundry basket, and her thoughts turned to the last time she had a new gathering basket. Roy had bought this one back when Adam lived on the farm as a little boy. Over thirty years?

June began whistling as she weaved her way to the house, through the cluster of lemon trees that melded into the apple orchard. The tall and elegant trees cast a labyrinth of shadows on the ground that shifted and swayed.

She was in the middle of the orchard when she paused, a curious sensation stilling her legs. June's voice of reason kept curiously quiet, as if sleeping. Then all at once, as if they were subjected to an earthquake June couldn't feel, every apple tree before June shook and juddered. Like the hand of God smacked them all. Their shadows moved hurriedly and queer, as if the sun fast-forwarded an hour. June watched them, careful not to move in case something else should happen. When the shadows stilled and every tree was silent again, June exhaled and the breeze resumed.

"Hello in the orchard! I'm afraid we need some help if you're there?" a distant man asked.

June frowned at the unfamiliar voice hollering a request she'd never heard before.

"Hello?" the deeper voice asked again.

"Uh... Yes! Hang on, just stay there on the lane!" June replied to the trees and distant driveway. Gripping the lemon basket tighter, she wove through the orchard, the break for the lane becoming clearer, until eventually June made out two adult figures. She made for them, a puzzled, bemused expression on her face at the strange event. Penny, lying in the shade where June had entered the orchard, now stood, her weary legs starting to shake when she walked for too long. She trotted until she caught up to June, and they made for the strangers together.

The two crossed the last apple tree and were on the driveway, staring at a man and woman. The pair were younger and smiled with genuine relief when June emerged from the trees, smirking further at the cow acting like a personal companion. June frowned at them, not because they were awfully young, not because their clothes were disheveled and worn, patched tens of times over with odd threads, not because a toddler clung to each of their backs like possums. But because they were here, on her lane.

The man seemed to understand her critical assessment and dipped his head, a hungry gauntness in his cheeks. "I'm sorry to bug you, ma'am. Our old Jeep broke down on the main road a few hundred yards up from your lane. Hot as hell out here today and no cars were passing. Was hoping we could use your phone for a tow?"

June's mouth parted like a stunned fish and then sharply closed. She thought for a long moment before remembering to reply. "Sorry, don't have one of those."

The woman's eyebrows now arched in surprise. "A phone? You don't have a phone?"

June nodded, her thoughts running away. "No, sorry."

From the other side of the orchard, footsteps and a whistle approached, and Roy popped out the other side, a bemused expression on his face, and both parents turned to him, the children on their backs now facing June. The little girl, no more than five years old, met her eyes and curled into her daddy's back like it would protect her. A daddy's girl.

Roy tipped his wide-brimmed straw hat to the lady and the man spoke for both of them. "Sorry, sir. Our car broke down a ways down the road, guess we drove it too hard these last couple weeks, trying to get to the mountains, you know? Trying to get away from people, you know? Secondhand hunk a' junk wasn't meant to go that far, I guess," he said in a string of fast words, as if he could expel his embarrassment all at once and be done with it.

Roy's eyebrow arched. "Y'all just...came up the lane all by yourselves now, did ya?" He glanced at June. Her breath grew fast, her heart starting a silent and unexpected race. The man nodded, unaware of Roy and June's secret language.

"Yes, sir. Beautiful place you have here. Living off the grid and the land, huh? That's the dream, for sure. And no neighbors? Heaven on Earth, for sure." He laughed at his own joke. The little girl holding around his neck smiled likewise at his laugh and June studied them surreptitiously, unaware a silence had grown, the young family, weary and anxious, now thinking they had made a mistake coming up and crossing the fence.

On the woman's back, a little boy, maybe four, reared his head, a whine pairing with his little voice. "I'm hungry, Mommy."

The woman twisted her head and bounced him. "Shhhh, have patience, we'll eat at the next town." The little boy groaned but laid his head on her shoulder. June stared with glazed eyes, though her body's organs were racing with prospects, and she recalled the cold calculation Farmer's Wife studied her with decades ago. June's breath hung in her lungs.

She wondered about the ocean.

She wondered if she could make it.

She wondered how far Farmer had gotten with the three young girls replacing them.

How long he had lasted.

Henry hadn't lasted long at all with just June and Roy.

She glanced at Roy again, seemingly waiting for her to make up her mind. She nodded, only the smallest of motions, and there was recognition and surprise in Roy's eyes. But then his easy smile returned, the skin around his eyes crinkling, and he addressed the little boy.

"Well then, can't have the little ones hungry now, can we? Seems serendipitous, really. We were 'bout to have lunch. Why don't you folk come up to the house and stay a while? Rest your feet and fill your belly."

AURORA AUSTRALIS

ANGELA HACKED ICY water lodged deep in her esophagus as she crawled from the ocean's brackish embrace. Her forehead fell onto the shore's cold pebbles and the light-headed feeling of drowning morphed into freezing misery and despair. She stumbled onto stony, wet ground and faced the luminous sky. Dawn rose from the northwest, and the Southern Lights, broad, ethereal ribbons of gold laced with crimsons she had never seen, quickly faded with the sunlight.

Angela propped onto her elbows in time for a blistering wind to sweep the shore, cutting through the thick and wet fur coat clinging to her slim frame. In the pre-dawn light and unearthly glow of Aurora Australis, the tip of the meteorological research vessel *Fairwinds*, was visible a mile offshore. Mostly obscured by the destructive iceberg, after a few minutes, the wreckage was subsumed into the rough sea and Angela sucked breath in anticipation. Her eyes, stinging with salt, searched for splashing in the water, evidence of another team member who hadn't been asleep below deck, hoping, praying, she wasn't alone. Alone and castaway on an obscure, frozen rock in the Antarctic Ocean. Surrounded by hundreds of identical micro-islands and approximately fifty miles away from their intended route because the unusual magnetic activity justified a detour.

But there was no one.
No splashes.
No survivors.
Utterly alone.

Angela sat curled on the rocky, unforgiving shore, shivering while floes of ice sailed past and her sodden boots kissed the waterline. The sun lazily breached the horizon and the aurora dissipated like melting ice. She watched, knowing the orb would never rise high enough at this time of the year to be of any warmth. A useless sun.

After five minutes of self-pity and mourning her fifteen colleagues, Angela stood on shaky legs. The water-logged and heavy clothes had long begun to steal the heat of exercise from her bones. Shucking the coat off, the great weight sagged to the ground and Angela began examining the island. Boulders taller than men littered the shore in between coves brimming with baseball-sized gray stones, cold water and flecks of ice licking them. Rubbing her arms for imagined warmth, she walked away from the shore and up the hillock, every laden step the effort of three.

Cresting the small hill, Angela fell to her knees with the view and cried, sobbing relief. The small island, maybe the size of a football field and surrounded by broad channels of choppy, icy water, blessedly housed a whaler's hut, stuck right in the middle. Tears burning cold on her cheeks, she thanked whatever higher power helped her escape a sea burial and then provided shelter.

The whaler's hut, discernible for the decrepit skeleton of an orca loitering outside, was shut tight. A beige tarpaulin covered a tall stack of cut wood at the end, the door had been braced shut by a solid plank snug across it, and the one window was boarded haphazardly. The whaler who built it was likely warm in his home north, maybe as far as Chile, for these autumnal months when the sun only presented itself for a few hours each day. He would not likely return until after October, eight months from now.

Lifting the door's bar away, Angela's eyes shut in prayer as she reached for the rudimentary handle, a simple piece of metal against a wood notch. The latch lifted easily and another fresh round of relief clinched her chest through the spreading frigidity.

The interior was simple and cold, but dry. The whaler had definitely left for the winter, the few wooden shelves empty and barren except for one old can of beans with a faded Spanish label. A new calendar displaying a white sandy beach hung over a pile of rags and showed the months of 1970, successive red crosses explaining the whaler had indeed left only two weeks prior. The one thing of permanence or worth in the hut was a small cast iron stove in the corner, a full thatch of wood waiting patiently beside it with a sharp flint and jar of possibly sperm oil.

"Bless you, sir," Angela mumbled through chittering, blanched lips and began making a fire. Twenty minutes later, she sat half-naked before the stove, showing as much skin to the fire as possible in an offering, a trade for warmth. Sitting naked and somberly, it wasn't long before her mind turned to food, her stomach voicing similar concern. An empty, hollow feeling consumed her insides, like she would soon desiccate from the cold sapping whatever energy and heat remained. She hadn't eaten since early last night, eons ago it seemed. A simple meal with laughter and cards and bourbon and company. Her stomach growled.

A faint rust circled the top of the bean can, and only when she touched the pull tab did she think twice, the gravitas of her predicament now plain. Angela had been on the bridge with the captain, discussing her insomnia and examining the sky full of aurora, when they had hit the submerged iceberg. He sent out the emergency SOS with their location. There had been no reply before he pushed her out onto deck with a life-preserver. They were far southwest, past the South Shetland Islands, and the rough Antarctic Ocean churned with the latest storm system, an unforgiving and hostile part of the seven seas. No one would cast off immediately just to face that. At best, it would be fifteen days before the wreckage was located and Angela found.

Two weeks and one can of beans.

She could try fishing if she found any leftover equipment. But Angela's previous attempts with her father, even in good weather, yielded little results. Leaving the can of beans alone, she was scouring the small hut when there was a strange sound outside the door. A high-pitched chirp. It rang again and again like an insistent salesman at a doorbell, and Angela tensed her weary and tired body to withstand the outside chill, opening the door.

The rough wood scraped against the frame and Angela's eyes widened at the fledgling emperor penguin standing erect on the doorstep. Its head tilted sideways to inspect her like a puppy might, and it chirped again before shuffling unexpectedly forward. Angela frowned but moved aside for the penguin as it waddled into the shack with familiarity, right across to the little bundle of rags beside the fire.

Stuck at the open door in near-bewilderment at the confident penguin, a gust of Antarctica air bit Angela's bare skin and she closed it, returning to the cot and staring at the wild animal making itself at home. No longer a chick, but not an adult, a pluck of old fluffy gray feathers enveloped its rump. Maybe the equivalent of a teenager? After circling the rags, it plopped onto its belly, its beady-dull eyes hooded like it neared sleep, and Angela spotted its deformed wing.

An obvious plight to Darwinism or a parent.

The bed of rags, the comfortableness with humans, the familiarity when it sauntered into the hut. Darwin had been circumnavigated and cheated. The shack's owner had clearly adopted this chick. Abandoned by its mother for the malformed wing, a natural selection criteria only to be cruelly left by the whaler when he returned north.

Angela considered herself a pet lover with a kind heart, a soft touch. A heavy, remorseful sigh escaped her chest and she knelt beside the penguin, offering her hand to him. It eyed the hand, but wasn't scared of it as a wild animal might be, and a moment later, it leaned its head forward into her palm, curling into it like a house cat might. Angela grinned at it and obliged by rubbing its head, suddenly thankful she would not go through this alone.

***

Angela was hungry.

A hunger she had never known, could never imagine, coiled her stomach in on itself. It had only been four days since the crash, and she fervently hoped to be wrong about the supposed two weeks for a rescue.

Since the crash, Angela had created "SOS" with the white rocks littering the shore closest to the sunken ship, hoping any rescue crews visited in the sparse daylight hours. As yet, no flotsam or jetsam had washed along the shore. All she could do now was wait.

And not starve.

The can of beans had been opened on the second day and finished on the third. The penguin Angela named Buddy stayed by her side near the low burning fire, a constant, faithful companion. When Angela refused to use more than the daily wood ration and curled up on the bed, her muscles revolting in uncontrollable shivers, Buddy would snuggle beside her. His slick oily feathers over his plump, fatty body were a strange comfort, and Angela held him like a childhood snuggly.

But Buddy would also leave the cabin daily, ambling to the door, tapping it until Angela, tired and lethargic, let him out. He would return an hour or so later, incessantly chirping to be let in. One day, she observed him waddling across the barren island in his lopsided manner only to plunge into an ice hole. Ten minutes later, he surged up through the same icy ingress, landing on his belly with a slide.

Returning up the well-trodden path to the cabin, Angela smelled fish on his breath and noted his swollen stomach. The little bugger had just eaten.

***

Angela lifted her head from the thin pillow, weary and lacking strength to make it off the bed. The fire had burned down over the long, cold night. The stack of wood beside it dwindled since she last ventured outside to restock from the large stack. It was day seven, and kernels of regret niggled inside Angela's tired mind, wishing she had died in the wreckage. Gone down with her colleagues in their watery tomb under the hypnotic sky.

Even in the two daylight hours, Angela still felt Aurora Australis in the sky above the shack. Its magnetism stroked the Earth like the finger of God caressed the stratosphere. In the first few days when she had reserves of energy, she would open the door and stare at the intense colors against the night and the occasional overcast clouds glowing like bright nebulae. Unlike anything she ever experienced in her five years of meteorological research, beautiful blondes and crimsons flowed through the air, unexplainable by thought or logic or science. Red meant intense solar activity, but crimson and gold? It was unnatural and hadn't dissipated since her arrival on the island.

If Angela had the energy and equipment, she might be able to understand the phenomenon. How such beauty stayed in one place. As it was, however, she could barely remain standing for more than a minute. It wouldn't be much longer until she would fall asleep and stay asleep. Maybe she could last two weeks without food in a warm climate, where melting water wasn't an issue and a deep ache didn't ring in her bones. But here?

No, not much longer.

Erratic tapping of beak on wood echoed, and Angela lifted her head to Buddy at the door, demanding to be released, wanting to feed himself. Fill his fat little belly. Even with his gimp fin, the adolescent penguin still survived in this cold, desolate section of the world.

Groaning, Angela pushed herself up and opened the door. Holding its frame to support her shaky legs, Buddy exited and waddled down his path to his ice hole. A biting gale tore Angela from her stupor and a new thought entered her mind as she watched the penguin disappear beneath the ice. A thought that clutched the shriveled remains of her stomach and squeezed it with hunger, her mouth flooding with saliva.

A deep exhale whooshed from her lungs and she returned to the fire, stacking it with more wood than needed for simple warmth. Flames spread to the new tinder, eating it quickly, the fire growing hotter, enough for warmth to return to her near frozen flesh. The metallic poker lay forgotten beside the iron stove and she picked it up. The weight was unusual in her weak hands, holding something unmalleable and sturdy against shaky muscles. She willed herself to be just as tough as the metal. Just as strong. Unaffected.

A chirp erupted outside the door not long after, and tears rolled effortlessly onto Angela's cheek. She opened it without watching Bud... the penguin return to comfort and warmth and his friend. Only when the door was closed in its ill-fitted frame and there was no escape did she turn to the penguin, continuing to his little bed, stopping momentarily to watch the new, raging fire.

Angela's grip on the iron tightened and through the tears blurring her vision, she swung the poker right at Buddy's soft head.

Plucking Buddy's strange mix of adolescent and adult feathers was more difficult than she hoped but easier than she imagined. A spoiled penguin, loved and cared for by the whaler, his thick fur hadn't fully developed against the polar climate. In the end, it didn't matter; the fire singed the feathers away from his pink flesh, and really, Angela didn't mind feeling the tuft against the roof of her mouth as long as his meat greased her tongue.

An oily, fishy flesh with a beef-like texture, she needed her canines to bite through it, as if the penguin wanted to make her work, suffer for her ill-gained energy. Angela couldn't actually taste it well because the tears continued down her face along with snot and mucus. A byproduct of guilt and revulsion at killing an innocent animal solely so she could survive a few more days. She wasn't vegetarian, but killing what you ate was a hardship for a less effete person.

When the tears finally subsided and her stomach rejoiced as she laid on the cot, the week until her anticipated rescue didn't seem so long, the burden of time not so great or troublesome.

***

Angela lifted her head from the icy stones, hacking abrasive salt water from her lungs; it burned her throat on the way out. She pushed herself off her belly, bewildered. Soaked in her furs and boots, the wind numbing every place it touched, Angela sat on the shoreline again, waking as if she had just emerged from the water.

With disbelieving eyes, Angela saw the tip of the *Fairwinds* meteorological research vessel sink slowly into the ocean once more. Reliving its own death. Angela gulped air, the beginnings of hyperventilation, and she gripped her icy scalp, staring at her sodden boots and wondering whether she had actually died.

A fever dream? A hallucination? A premonition?

Tendrils of aurora curled overhead in bright snaps, their spectacular, unearthly colors sending a shiver down Angela's freezing spine.

Through mumbling lips, whispering delirium, she stood and made her way over the island's rough-hewn rocks, decimated from previous enormity through years, decades, eons by the harsh carvers of Earth's ancient ice. Traveling into the center of the island as if in a dream, she cried when she saw the whaler's hut, standing exactly as remembered.

On approach, she saw it was, in fact, *exactly* like she remembered after her first shipwreck. Boarded up and dark, all evidence Angela had spent a week inside had been eradicated, like she was never there. The wood outside replenished, the can of beans stood full on the shelf, the sperm oil jar restocked. Sloughing her wet clothes, Angela proceeded with a fire, making herself warm just as she did the first time. Only when she was half-dressed, her open palms begging the fire for warmth, did the chirping start, and her forehead creased with worry.

Timidly opening the door, Angela gasped when Buddy stood before it, just as healthy and alive and uneaten as a week ago when they first met.

He looked her up and down as he did once before. No mistrust or timidness in his gaze.

No idea that she was his murderer and he was her ghost. He waddled in and moved to his little bed. Angela followed him cautiously and sat on the cot across. His sharp little beak shone in the flickering light and his slate irises with their dull black in the middle examined her.

Angela started to cry.

***

It was day eight by Angela's last count. Or...day fifteen. Sixteen? She didn't know exactly what she should count, because she still didn't understand what had happened to her. Days loped away, the night sky riddled with alien colors, the weather, the penguin's schedule, they all happened the same as before.

But Angela had learned from her premonition, or déjà vu, or prognostication. An unwilling oracle. Only a spoonful of beans every day. A heaping spoonful, but still only a spoonful. Instead of finishing on day three, she stretched the one can until day six. She had also attempted to fish, but with the icy gales and snow drifting on the wind as tiny bullets, the activity sapped more energy than a fish would have ever given, and she returned to the cabin hungrier and weaker for trying.

Buddy continued to enjoy her warm hand petting his soft fur, and Angela wondered how long the whaler took care of the penguin. From birth? When his family migrated and left him behind? Each day, he walked to his ice hole, filled his belly, and returned to the warmth of the cabin and his blankets.

And each day there were no ships on the horizon.

On day nine, Angela's stomach began to remind her it was there.

On day eleven, Angela's weak hands ensnared Buddy's small neck while he was asleep and stole the breath from his plump body. She tried to break the neck bones to make it quicker, but was too weak and sobbed as his feet scratched the blankets and the malformed wing flapped fruitlessly against her hand. His meat wasn't as moist or dense as she remembered the first time. Imagined? Imagined the first time?

When misery and tears were spent, Angela gnawed on his stripped, cooked wing, sucking the marrow absentmindedly, and stared at the crimson and gold flashing in the sky like long, alien serpents. Alive and sentient.

They watched her eat the island's only other inhabitant. Angela let Buddy's innards and skeleton burn to char in the fire as fuel and counted the three days until the imagined rescue ship arrived.

***

The shore's pebbles were sharper against her face this time when she woke, coughing, soaked, and half-drowned. Pushing herself to sit, she watched the last of the *Fairwinds* sink into the dark, rough water, and Angela pressed her wet palms against her eyes and wept. She sat for much longer than the first two times she washed ashore, physically numb and emotionally exhausted.

The weak autumnal sun had risen well above the horizon and a thick layer of frost had formed on Angela's wet coat before she wiped her face, and without preamble, she trudged the well-known path to the whaler's hut. As before, everything had been replaced and another round of bawling, howling, cursing racked Angela before Buddy chirped his arrival.

The door scraped open and they met for the third time. He chirped and tilted his head to the side, and in the twilight sky behind him, the aurora flashed. A strange sight in the weak daylight, like a rainbow trying to break the laws of science and appear without rain or sun.

Trying to tell her something. Something important.

Buddy, again, took the open door as an invitation and waddled in, moving to the new-old fire. Angela, however, stayed by the open door, stuck, nearly literally frozen to it. But a harder frost clawed into her bones as she ignored Buddy and stared at the iridescent colors in the sky, her mind turning over the last two weeks of existential torture and why it was happening. How it was happening. She landed, survived, and ate the penguin. Both times. Her stomach growled, breaking the hypnotic spell of the aurora, and she closed the door against the wind and phenomena. She sat on the cot across from Buddy and stared at the sleepy bird.

Both times she... Buddy had left, the day of the shipwreck reset, and her two weeks until salvation restarted. A torturous cycle that finished or started with death.

Angela was a scientist, and a good one. The first in her family to attend university in the new age where women helped men land on the moon. But even she recognized when something beyond science was at work. A miracle. Or a curse.

She exhaled and examined the penguin with new, philosophical eyes, wondering at the nature of spirituality, time, self, and where Buddy fit into it all. He had died, and was then reborn. Save the penguin, save yourself.

He chirped at her and, as if he could read her thoughts, waddled over and rubbed himself against her cold, limp hand. As if he knew the motion. As if they had done this before. Did he also remember? No, he wouldn't be friendly if he did. Angela had been ashamedly savage in his final moments, a vicious, hungry animal. He would be frightened and avoid the shack. Whatever this was, it wasn't Buddy's doing. Angela obliged and scratched the head she once smashed, the neck she once strangled. The skull she took his little brains from and watched his ocular gel bubble in the fire.

"Okay, let's try it the other way."

***

Angela had nearly destroyed her willpower until it was nothing but a decimated reminder that she used to be human. Nearly as shriveled as her stomach and intestines. She had survived, if that is what one could call it, for nearly ten days. No, this wasn't surviving, this was hanging onto a ledge with stiff, dead fingers, too cold and frigid to unhook. But that was all she needed.

Lying prostrate in the narrow cot, all her energy was gone. She had been smarter this time. Learned from the past. She didn't need to thrive, Angela just literally needed to continue her pulse until the rescue ship arrived. Rationing the beans to only a few a day, she had melted enough water for two weeks and stocked enough of the outside firewood inside so she wouldn't need to move in the last, final days when rescuers would see the smoke from her weak fire.

But even agonizingly rationed, the can of beans wasn't enough for ten days, and she tried not to cry for fear of expending energy. Buddy, however, thrived. She had let him in and out every day, and even resorted to begging him to bring her back a fish. He, of course, didn't understand, and returned with nothing but his own full belly and satiated appetite.

Angela had been so frustrated at the futility of the cycle, she had taken one plank of wood off the sole window in near hysteria. The splinters sank thick and deep in her pale fingers. She rationalized that if she wasn't allowed to eat the one animal on the island for her own survival, she would at least watch the mesmerizing display of auroras from the cot where she lay and would die.

In the deep of night and a thousand miles away from any lights, behind the veil of aurora, stood the bright prick of stars. Stagnant fireflies in patterns. The Southern Cross, the Centaur, alien and unfamiliar constellations, beautiful and eternal. She recognized Mars, or was it Jupiter? Bright and proud, holding unimaginable terrors and wonders in its red illuminance. Angela blinked lazily and adoringly at them. Endless stars equaled endless space equaled endless time. Space and time were one and nothing. There was so much and too much out there. What else was out there? In the stars, other planets, other systems? If she ate Buddy, Angela would have endless time. Was she immortal? Immortal and doomed to live the same frostbitten days over and over in guilt and shame.

By day thirteen, Angela couldn't move. Torpor consumed her, and she was no longer mad or frustrated or upset or panicked by the thought of death and the recurrent loop of survival from the shipwreck and death of a fucking penguin. There was no more energy for those feelings.

Buddy seemed to sense Angela neared her end, her death, because he had somehow hopped up onto the low cot and lay beside her, nuzzling his head beneath her slack hand and arm. So she could experience a connection one last time, even if she had killed him many times before, and now, he would be the death of her through his survival. If time was a river, Angela would now float down its current and leave this island.

With drowsy eyes, she searched through the gap in the boarded window, the sky on fire with the aurora. A gossamer of chromatic display covering this isolated section of the world, beyond and away from human eyes. As radiant as it was foreign and terrifying, Angela now knew it had somehow kept her here, here until death.

Tiredness swept over her entire body, like God covered her with a heavy, weighted death shroud, and she stroked Buddy with the last movement she would ever make. Relief flooded her mind as she sensed it was finally the end. She would die, Buddy would live. Something heavenly, angelic, ethereal wanted this damn penguin to live and there was comfort knowing something higher looked out for the little guys. Buddy would continue this time, while she died and forever slept. Her eyes closed on the Aurora Australis. A particularly bright flash seared across the sky as Angela breathed her last and welcomed death's river.

***

Angela's slender frame, heavy with soaked clothes, washed onto the icy shore, and she sputtered as a baby fresh from the womb. Her lungs retracted as if they had just experienced trauma and she swiveled on her hip just in time to watch the *Fairwinds* research vessel sink into the desolate waters, Aurora Australis painting the sky above.

TEEN SPIRIT

NIRVANA'S "COME AS You Are" blasted from the Mustang's speakers, cruising a slick thirty miles per hour down a dusty service road, and Janey watched the grand estate pass in the dark. A black tennis court, an empty pagoda by a Stygian pond, a covered Olympic-sized pool, and a distant mansion hosting some kind of party in full swing. Through ceiling-to-floor doors, she glimpsed flashes of bright crimson silks twirling, waiters holding trays, drinkers on the open patio mingling and laughing.

Janey wanted to ask her date about it, this festive party they obviously weren't attending, but was arrested by the silhouetted forest drawing ever closer, signaling the end of the Kennedy's affluent lands and the start of the wilds. Without slowing, the car plunged into the pine forest, old trees towering as the road sliced between them. Through the densely packed trees, a blazing light flickered, closer and clearer, until the car slid to a stop in an informal parking lot with several others.

Partially concealed through layers of pines, a large bonfire flared, a teepee of tree corpses stacked as high as a man. Flames licked the air, casting shadows onto the soaring foliage, and several teenage figures were outlined against the roaring inferno.

Janey glanced to her date in the driver's seat and inspected Mark's letterman jacket. A bright red chest with black sleeves and a black S on his pectoral, the other side held the football team's patch of an attacking tiger. The punk tune, loud and abrasive, continued even though he turned the engine off, and she frowned. Weren't people supposed to talk on first dates?

Mark had waited down the end of her driveway, his muscle car purring far from the house, but the music blared enough that Janey's anxiety blossomed, thinking it might wake her sleeping parents and the night would be over before it began.

Finally turning to her, Mark flashed her a smile no amount of orthodontics could buy. White teeth against the dark, and she blinked twice to clear her thoughts. That smile with his strong jaw and Grecian nose? Maybe it didn't matter if he talked to her tonight. She was new to public school, but even a recluse could recognize a miracle when wealthy Mark Kennedy, rising-star high school quarterback, approached the new girl and invited her to a private party.

He didn't bother to touch the music and instead nodded his head, gesturing they leave the car. Without waiting, he then exited, leaving his door open, and Janey scrambled to follow. The Mustang's music, an album on repeat, drifted through the trees, ricocheting between them in an eerie, hollow echo.

"So, are your parents also having a party tonight?" Janey asked as they walked. He strode too fast, Janey always a step behind. But he stopped at her question and his smile dropped for a moment. Instead of answering, he reached for her hand, interlacing their fingers and pulling her closer to him while they walked. His rough hand was warm in her cold one, and his thumb rubbed against the outside of it. Janey's heart climbed up her throat for the intimate action, and he grinned noticing the blush spread across her cheeks.

They circled the last of the wide, ancient trees and into a barren circle. Maybe a hundred feet across, the bonfire sat in the direct center. Ten or twelve teens, all dressed in the black and red of footballers and cheerleaders oddly dressed in uniform, milled in the space and looked to the newcomers. Janey eyed the girls' pleated miniskirts and white sneakers with spotless socks and resisted glancing at her capri jeans and plain white button-up tee hiding her slim frame.

A ring of logs circled the fire, half the distance to the trees, and Mark and Janey stepped through a gap. Janey's flat ballet shoes immediately sank and she looked down. The ground inside the ring of trees had a nearly sandy quality. As if hundreds of bonfires had burned here before and the ashy-gray detritus slowly replaced the soil.

An esky inside the ring of logs held the attention of two particularly burly teens, and one of them narrowed his eyes at them.

"Yo! QB! Light or dark?" he called across the fire and above Mark's sonorous music.

Mark replied boisterously, too loud for the space. "What? Did I lose my dick somehow, Coop?"

The teen laughed and hurled a beer can like a football. Janey flinched, but Mark gracefully snatched it from the air and immediately snapped the tab, froth exploding while tilting his head back to drink, and his teammates *whooped* in feral tones like a pack of wolves. Janey watched him crush the can in his fist and shake his head violently, wisps of his golden hair flying with specks of beer from his wet face. An easy laugh escaped his throat and he hung a lazy arm over Janey's slim shoulders.

"Coop! What about the guest of honor here!? She seems like a 'light' kinda girl, huh?"

Janey frowned, tucking her mousey brown hair behind her ears and adjusting the glasses sliding down her nose. "I'm the guest of honor?"

This time, Coop tossed the beer underarm and Mark caught it for her. His mouth gaped but then snapped close. "Yeah...of course, new to town, new to school, my date. 'Guest of honor' worthy, right?" He finished with another million dollar smile and popped the can open, handing it to her.

Janey sipped and winced at the bitterness, but still smiled and nodded agreeably. Mark laughed again and released her from his passive hug, leading them to a log. Across the ring, a boy called out something above the drifting music, holding up a football, and Mark's attention left Janey to enthusiastically nod.

"Hey, I'm gonna go throw the ball for a few. Be back soon," he said before shucking off his jacket to reveal a tight black t-shirt. Janey watched the thin cotton strain against his biceps as he placed the jacket around her slim shoulders, drowning her body in its folds. "Stay warm," he commented before joining his friends.

Left alone, Janey glanced at the other teens spread across the circle, their shadows stretching thin and lanky into the woods, melding with darker silhouettes. All beautiful, young, healthy, and likely affluent if they were friends with Mark. But from the quick glimpse of his house and lands, Mark was probably the richest kid here, and Janey subtly scanned the other teens. Confidence and privilege rolled off them in enviable waves and she ignored the cheerleaders' glances in her direction. At the girl in plain clothes, limp hair, and Coke-bottle glasses.

A new song reverberated through the forest from Mark's car, the angst thick and hostile in the chorus, and Janey sipped her beer while sitting alone on a log. This was awkward. She knew it, felt it. Why hadn't Mark introduced her to anyone? Four teammates now passed the football outside of the log ring. In the weaker radial of firelight, their agile bodies turned to amber ghosts against the gray sand and dark forest. Janey watched them, lulled into a sleepy haze with the late hour, warm fire, and the soft leather of Mark's jacket. Their bodies, taut and firm with youth, leaped and tossed each other into the sand-dirt and she wondered what it would feel like to be able to make your body do those incredible feats of strength. To do anything incredible with your body.

Janey was abruptly jostled on both sides and her stupor broke when two cheerleaders sat beside her. Their manicures tapped against Diet Coke cans and they sat far too close for strangers, nearly knee to knee. They aimed perfect smiles at her, and Janey was reminded of Mark's. The fair-haired girl on her left leaned over, smoothing out her black pleated skirt with red inlays.

"New girl, right? What was your name again?"

"Uhh, yeah, right. It's Janey."

The girl on her right snickered, but quickly stifled it with a scathing look from the blonde.

"Right, right, right... Janey, I remember. I'm Carla, this is Bianca." The cheerleader's smile was genuine and Janey's shoulders relaxed. She tucked a lock of hair behind her ear.

"Yes, we have trig together. You sit up the back."

Carla's smile widened. "Yeah, you're right. Ugh, I hate that class. Mr. Turner is a straight-up perv. Always *innocently* touching a shoulder here or there. Don't worry, you'll see."

"He's not the worst at Sherman High," Bianca mumbled, sipping her Coke before adding, "Fuck, Sherman teachers aren't so bad. Not when you compare them to Oakdale."

Carla snorted in agreement, "Ugh, that fucking Assistant Coach Tucker, the way he slides up to Oakdale's cheer squad. Even I feel sorry for those bitches."

Janey, flicking her head between the two speaking across her, stuttered, "Oakdale?"

"Oakdale High, rival school down the valley. Lots of perverts and sick fucks."

A deep voice interrupted from behind, as if waiting for the perfect time to deliver his line. "Lots of sick fucks, mediocre offensive line, and officially no mascot AFTER TOOONIGHHHHT!" The voice ended in a victorious boom, and the three girls turned to another brawny teen dressed in a practice jersey. He held a rope trailing a small, gray donkey.

The other teens heard the cry and joined, raucous laughter lost to the music and pines. Janey watched the timid donkey flinch at the roar and then tremble as it was led around the fire. With jerky movements, its wide, darting eyes glinted in the firelight, and she felt sorry for the creature with a royal-blue *Oakdale* cape hiding a swollen belly.

Mark and the other players joined inside the ring, more cans of beer flew into waiting hands. A matching blue football helmet emerged from someone's gym bag and beer was slopped into it before set in front of the donkey for it to drink. "One for the guest of honor!" someone howled.

Janey's brow furrowed at the phrase and she pointed at the donkey. "Is...that..."

Carla answered, "Oakdale's mascot. Team's lucky charm."

"And...it's a guest of honor?"

Carla's spine erected, her high ponytail jerked. "Oh, well, I mean, it's a special donkey, right? It's *really* special to the team."

"Let's see how well they do on Saturday without it, huh?" Bianca chimed in with mischief.

"There's a game on Saturday?"

Carla huffed dramatically. "Oh yeah. Big one too. I don't know if you noticed, but football is kinda life round here. Like, the whole town comes to the games."

Janey nodded; she had noticed. Every shop window in town housed a red and black Tigers flag. Even the real estate agent, befriending her while showing them around, had sported a Tigers tie. They'd driven into their new, upscale town, and at first, Janey thought red and black were the *town* colors.

"So, big game, lots of people."

"Lots of people, *lots* of money. Gonna be a few scouts there too, huh, Kennedy?" Bianca hollered.

Across the circle, scratching the donkey's tuft of hair, Mark pursed his full lips, vibrant red in firelight. "I'm not worried. Big D ain't gonna let us down."

He continued talking to his friend and petting the donkey, calming it, and Janey whispered to Carla, "Which one is Big D?" She looked expectantly at several of the bigger, muscular teens.

Carla smiled shyly, unnatural on her handsome face, and she twirled her long ponytail between her fingers. "Yeah, Big D, he's not here...yet, but he's...like an honorary coach. Always has something special to pull us over the finish line. Gives us gusto, etcetera."

The current song finished and there was a pause in Mark's music. The echo died and Janey realized other music also played in the forest. An old, unearthly tune, where voices carried the melody instead of instruments and time meant nothing. A song where there was no beginning and no end. Distant and faint, maybe not even in the forest. Janey's head swiveled behind where she thought it came from and remembered the mansion's party. But then the Mustang's new song began and the other music was drowned out.

Carla followed Janey's gaze behind them and stole her attention.

"Anyway, enough stupid football. Let's hear more about you, Janey. What school did you transfer from?"

Startled from concentration, Janey turned back to the fire and unconsciously pushed her glasses up her nose and clenched her empty can. Condensation ran over her fingers and her throat tightened. "I...uh... Nowhere, I was homeschooled...before we moved to town."

Bianca and Carla's eyebrows rose and she had their full attention. "Wow. You're sooooo...normal," Carla mumbled, amazed.

Janey laughed in relief. Entering high school as a junior after years of homeschool had been weighing on her like the new feeling of hauling a fully loaded backpack. "Thanks...I think."

Carla affectionately brushed a lock of Janey's hair from her shoulder, fingertips touching her neck as she inspected her like an interesting creature at a zoo.

"Probably have overprotective parents, huh?"

Janey snorted, an unconscious noise. "Oh yeah. I mean, I needed school if I was going to get into any good colleges. But yeah, definitely frown on things like...this." Her hand waved in an arc to the party, full of loud, anti-establishment grunge music and teenage drinking.

Bianca frowned. "Parties?"

"Sheesh yeah, parties, drinking, dating, you name it. Frowns all-round." Janey giggled with a high pitch, a sound she never heard herself make before, and she proudly added, "It's actually my first kegger."

Both cheerleaders showed surprise but a shout drew their attention to the group of rowdy boys now wrestling in the ashy-sand. A strip of

Mark's toned and tight stomach flashed. Muscles flexed and strained over his ribs and Carla whistled. "And with Mark Kennedy."

Janey's cheeks, rosy with beer, blushed deeper, while Bianca continued the thought and leaned over her knees to prop her fist beneath her chin. "Just look at him."

And Janey did.

His backside flexed in tight jeans as his legs dug in the soft sand. She quickly turned away to stymie the swell of tension curling below her waist.

"Can you imagine all the things you can do with a body like that? I mean, things you could do *to* a body like that?" Carla whispered salaciously. Janey hoped her curtain of hair between them hid her red cheeks, or she could claim she was too close to the fire. It made her warm. It made her whole body warm.

But it didn't matter. Bianca saw and leaned over to pointedly speak to her friend. "You know, I *don't* think she knows what she could do to a body like that. I don't think she's gotta clue."

"Shut up, B!" Carla whispered furiously and her hand whipped around Janey to slap the back of the other girl's head. Bianca huffed in pain and her lips pursed, about to retort, when Carla cut her off. "Don't be a bitch. How about you get the others ready, okay? Can you do *that*, Bianca?"

Bianca's cherry-red lips, glossy in the firelight, pursed tighter, but she stood and walked over to the three other cheerleaders on the other side of the fire.

"Sorry... She's kind of like...the bitch in our squad who's too good to drop, you know?"

"No, it's okay. I mean...she's kind of right..." Janey's voice trailed off. She didn't know why she just confessed that. She should keep her mouth shut about herself. Give compliments, laugh at jokes, agree with gossip. Be as small as possible until she was actually friends with these people. Isn't that how socializing worked? Don't let all your private secrets out on the first night? But secrets built bonds, didn't they? Secrets were the currency of friendships.

Carla, however, latched onto the information, a rapt expression over her features. "Oh... So...you're a...virgin?" She whispered the last word as if it was a disability and wanted to help Janey.

Janey glanced at the groups of teens in their little gossip mills, and instead of answering with her small voice, she nodded just once. Carla leaned away with a large exhale, a smile growing wider on her face, her voice rising at an alarming tone.

"Well, that's news… It's news that WE HAVE A VIRGIN HEEEEERRE!"

She ended the declaration in a triumphant howl and Janey's stomach furled into a knot, her shoulders bunching up to her ears, terror flooding her as the beautiful cheerleader declared to all the popular kids the new, freak homeschooled transfer student was a bona fide virgin.

Janey couldn't breathe.

Instead of the laughter, humiliation, and expected insults, the teens cheered and raised their beers. A good-natured cry, as if they were really happy Janey had been locked up for sixteen years and remained unwanted by the other sex until Mark Kennedy noticed her.

Janey frowned at the response, her shoulders unbunching, and she looked at her date walking to her with two beers in his hands. A wide smile, full of those perfect fucking teeth, stared at her. Not one of bridled disappointment or derision. A happy, wide smile. He sat in Bianca's empty seat. "My jacket looks good on you," he commented, handing her another full can, already opened.

Carla stood and said, "Well, I'm gonna get my squad ready, you guys have a nice *talk*." Janey was mortified, unsure of what to say to someone who just screamed her virginal status. They watched her leave and she glanced aside at Mark, staring at her with such happiness, the curled knot of muscle in her gut loosened slightly.

"That was awful. Why would she do that?" Janey asked, shaking her head.

Mark's heavy arm hung over her shoulders again and he squeezed her into his body. "Doesn't matter. I already knew, honey."

Janey stiffened under his arm, unsure of what to say with the endearment, and he laughed with such a happy laugh, like it was the best thing in the world, and he whispered, "I'm glad. I'm glad you're here with me tonight. Everyone's glad."

Neither spoke, silence between them as he studied her petite features with such intensity, her blush deepened and Janey had to look away, the moment too intimate for her inexperienced emotions. She changed the subject.

"So, big game this weekend? Shouldn't you be laying low? Getting good sleeps? Staying healthy?"

"Psssh, naw. We good, it's gonna be easy. And a few beers never hurt. Speaking of, drink up, slow poke, I think I've lapped you." His arm squeezed hers and Janey felt the dopamine of his touch shoot through her veins like a hard drug. She tentatively sipped the new beer, wincing at the bitterness mixed with something like herbs. Studying the can's label, it was new to her and definitely not a "light."

Mark shrugged. "Sorry, the light ran out and all we had left was this hippy shit," he apologized before drinking his own. Janey nodded and tried it again, still terrible, and she didn't drink as much.

"Someone mentioned there's a lot of money riding on your games? What's that about?"

The rare frown marred Mark's face and his free hand threaded his honey-blond hair. He shifted in his seat, fidgeting, and stretched his neck. "Yeah, I mean... Sort of. The two towns kind of use it as an excuse for betting."

Janey smiled at his unexpected awkwardness, endearing that someone so handsome should look any other way. "Betting what?"

"You know, rich people stuff. Land, cars, portfolios, fuck if I know," he admitted, maybe frustrated. His legs bounced on the balls of his feet for an unsure moment and it suddenly felt like he would make an excuse to get up and leave, but instead, a determined expression crossed his lips and he brought their interwoven hands up to kiss her knuckle. Any thoughts Janey had about making conversation were lost when his tongue touched her skin and her lips parted. He smiled at her reaction.

"How's that beer?"

Her mind drew a blank on words and instead sipped, though she was too discombobulated to even drink, liquid sitting in the can's rim. Watching her mouth, his smile widened and his hand squeezed hers again. They then stared at the fire in comfortable silence, hands pretzeled, listening to its crackle and others talking in soft, hushed tones. The moment of perfection, everything a sixteen-year-old wanted, needed. Her eyes closed all by themselves, wanting to remember this time, this place.

Janey smelled the deep pines and needles drift on the breeze and her body felt comfortably mellowed in the warmth. A new song came on, echoing through the pines, and even though it repeated the same album, Janey sensed she never really heard it before. Curiously distant and altered, it wailed through the forest to the bonfire. Playing slower.

Distorted. She opened her eyes and saw the flames were blurred around the edges. Janey squinted, raising her hand to adjust her glasses, but found an unbearable weight consuming her body, like lethargy from a deep sleep.

The cheerleaders outside the logs held pom-poms, and Janey could tell their limbs waved in a mesmerizing choreographed dance. Bodies flipped into the black air, fans of sand flew up and spread open only to dissipate. Red and black streamers oscillated in the firelight like eels. Bodies moved to the slow, uncanny tune, and Janey smacked her lips like peanut butter coated her mouth.

Mark's heavy hand slid down her arm, clenching and kneading, until he pinched her elbow through his own jacket. It didn't hurt, more like she had hit her funny bone five minutes ago.

"Owww," she mumbled through sleepy lips.

"Oh geez, I'm sorry, baby," he replied, grinning before rubbing it. She frowned and tried to push her glasses up her nose but found her hand wasn't really inclined to move at all now.

The cheerleaders' bodies stopped moving with their bright flares of crimson and black and a collective cheer ricocheted through the teens that Janey didn't understand. A hand came in front of her face, the glasses pushed back up her nose with Mark's thick finger, and Carla was suddenly visible, walking toward them with a strut almost indecent. A big smile consumed her face and she wiggled her forefinger in a small circle at Janey, the fire behind lighting her blonde hair into a halo.

"Well hey, you two!" She grinned and sat on Mark's waiting knee, his hand clasped around her waist.

Janey lips mumbled a question and Mark's finger came to her lips, pressing down to silence her.

"Shhhhh, I know, but the guy told me this roofie was super mellow. Like, not really a roofie. Apparently it's just like smoking half a joint, but for your body. And the other stuff in there...is like a pre-game."

Carla giggled and Mark kissed her with a lewd carnality Janey watched through hooded eyes. Their bodies pressed tight, one of his hands disappeared beneath a fold of her skirt, and Janey wanted to tell him something vulgar, but found she no longer had energy. The pair's jaws, nearly unhinged to swallow each other, mashed with spit and bruised lips that only broke apart suddenly when a strange *whizzzzz* sizzled through the air.

Above the circle of trees, hanging low in the clear night sky, a firework detonated. A singular explosion of red sparks drifting down to the earth as fragments of a dying star.

Janey's nerves shook with the sound, so loud, so close, and a little more control returned to her body. All the faces of the teenagers collectively turned to the sky, and beside her, Mark said confidently, "Ready to go, team?" He called across to a group of bulky teens who collectively nodded in eerie unison, and three of them left the circle. Janey's pulse quickened, her chemical lethargy lessening with the new fear and fast blood coursing through her body as she lost sight of them walking toward the faint outline of Mark's car. After a moment, the Mustang's music suddenly stopped and the trees were silent. Palpable tension covered the party like a heavy gossamer without the pretense of music.

Janey breathed deep, willing her muscles to regain their will as Mark and Carla ignored her and moved to the donkey, speaking quietly. Her foot tapped, just once and slowly, but enough to give her hope. Hope that quivered when the new silence suddenly ended with another sound. Muffled screaming and dull thumps growing closer.

Janey's eyes flicked to watch the three large teens reenter the space, and she realized why Mark had kept the music loud on the drive: so she couldn't hear the hostage in his trunk. They hauled the hooded, heavy form of a half-naked man, his feet dragging over the soft ground.

The teens stood around the logs, watching their friends carelessly drag the man only to throw him beside the fire. With the captive's entry, the jovial atmosphere had changed to one with purpose. Beer cans tossed away and into the fire, the pigskin stowed, the laughter gone. The carefree party had changed to something with purpose. A meeting.

Janey watched Bianca stand in front of the hooded captive and clutch his scalp through the bag with her long nails, painfully pulling it up so he kneeled. With her chest at his eyeline, she ripped the sack away and a portly man appeared, sweat glistening on a brow below sparse black hair and a gag in his mouth. Bianca adopted a tone of an overly sweet teen girl too mature for her years as her nail scraped his double chin, leaving a painful red line.

"Hey, Coach. Or should I just call you Tuck now? I mean...we did...you know."

Janey assumed it was Assistant Coach Tucker whimpering through the dirty rag filling his mouth, tears coursing a stream through the grit on his face and over his plump apple cheeks. He shook his head at Bianca, thin, errant strands on his mostly bald head highlighted in the firelight.

Janey's eyes welled as she watched others join Bianca, poking and lightly assaulting the adult. "*Tuck likes to fuck*" wafted through the fire on children's voices and the scene began to feel more foreign, more life-threatening.

Janey wasn't leaving this circle.

It was past the time to run, a fearful ending coming up that she refused to acknowledge. Janey needed to flee and lose them in the dark. Plunge into the forest and risk finding her way out. Let the trees hide her. But Janey's legs wouldn't move yet and she raised her hand, happy to see she could, and thumped it on her thigh like it simply slept.

Between the fire and the logs, Mark assumed an air of natural authority and began to draw in the sand. He drew a wide circle between the log seats and flames with interior designs she couldn't see. His finger was a paintbrush, moving fast but practiced. The small pictures within the larger circle were complex but also somehow primitive.

Janey's foot suddenly wiggled and began to bounce on its ball with nervous energy. Exhaling relief, she subtly glanced around to see a wide-open gap of darkness between the trees. A pathway.

"How ya doin, huh?" an effete but warm voice asked, and Carla sat down, her gentle hand dropping the pom-pom to brush away Janey's hair, and Janey sniffled.

"What's happening? What are you going to do?"

Carla's face held some kind of pity, and her thumb wiped a broad stroke beneath Janey's eyes, her glasses finally falling off her nose and left on the ground. "Jannneey, we *really* need to win this game, you know? You would not believe how much pressure Mark's dad puts on him. I mean, between the university scouts, the cashed-up alumni, the blood oaths, and the fundraiser for the new football stadium, we really cannot fuck this up, right? Lots of people, the town, count on us. We need a little...guarantee, you understand."

Janey could do nothing but sniffle when Bianca called out from the fire, "Carla, you got that paintbrush? I cannot fuck up my nails again."

Carla looked between them and smiled into the corner of her mouth, raising her forefinger to point conspiratorially at Janey. "Don't you go anywhere now, I'll be right back."

She gleefully skipped away, and Janey watched as the several teens were all focused and engaged in other activities, their care-free natures evaporating. Janey tensed her muscles, and instead of following Carla's orders, she willed her body to finally shake off the last of the drug in her system. She swung on the log and with shaky steps, began to run for the tree line.

A moment later, Mark swore behind her. "FUCK!" Janey risked a glance back. He had started to chase her, vaulting the log, strong legs pumping for her, and Janey put extra push into her step to leap into the darkness when she turned her head forward and bounced into a hard wall of muscle. About to fall backward, a strong hand snatched her wrist and pulled her up, and Janey came face to face with a tall man dressed in a tuxedo. An unadorned black mask covered the upper half of his face, but his stern blue eyes caught hers and froze her.

A vacuum of noise covered the clearing, and Janey sucked in breath as the strict man studied her with a frown. Mark's footsteps came beside her, calmer and reserved. The adult, this tall man with a grim face, gripped her wrist so tight Janey thought it might break, but he then looked to Mark and lifted the mask to sit on his hair. Janey gasped, a striking resemblance between the two.

"Sorry, Dad...sir. We're ready if you are."

Instead of answering his son, something black dribbled from the corner of his lips, and he leaned toward Janey and spat a viscous liquid violently in her face.

Shocked, her mouth gaped and she wished it hadn't. The vile, inky sludge dripped down her face and a little entered her mouth as her free hand wiped it from her eyes.

She sobbed in distress, squinting through the paste in time to witness the glint of old metal in Kennedy Senior's hand, and felt the rip and pull of her shirt being cut away. Mark's strong grip held her still, but she whipped her head side to side, the black paste of his spit strangely numbing her face and growing thicker. Janey wailed when the dagger came to her fragile skin this time, cutting away the plain bra. Then her jeans. Then her underwear.

Her scream continued as the men stripped her, exposing her slim body to the quiet circle even as she tried hiding herself with her free hand. Kennedy Senior offered Janey's wrist to Mark in a bored manner, as if delivering a pizza, before replacing his mask and nodding. Without comment, Mark began to drag her with ease back into the center.

Janey struggled, fought him, slapped his hand, frantic with what her nakedness might mean, when the strange, melodic tune she'd heard through the trees reappeared. Through her gluey eyes, she searched around the circle of trees. Between the strong pines standing as sentries, bodies of men and women now emerged, filling the black spaces. Elegant women dressed in couture ball gowns, brushing the forest's needle carpet. All in differing shades of red, from Valentino Crimson to Dior Blood. Men in tuxedos alternated between them and the trees, all wearing the same black masks. They watched Janey's naked body dragged by the stronger teen. They all chanted in a foreign, melodic tongue.

Mark hugged her by the waist, easily lifting her over the log, and Janey's shaky legs crumpled beneath when placed on the ground, unwilling to move further. He exhaled frustration as she sprawled forward, gritty sand sticking to her numb, ichor-plastered face. His hand ran through his messy blond locks.

"Look, Janey. I really appreciate this. This is huge for me, I won't forget it. Promise."

The other teens, cheerleaders and footballers alike, had left, subsumed by the forest. Only the adults in their masks and opulent dress remained. Deep voices spoke archaic words in chorus. Janey eyed Coach Tucker on the right side of Mark's crude sand drawing. Hog-tied into kneeling, his chest had been cut with a large bleeding X and a strange circle, painted with his own blood, sat above his groin. His raw flesh pulsed and blood streamed to the ground with the designs. Janey spluttered incoherently, eyes wandering over the gray sand and adults observing them. Mark kept talking, adjusting her hair, and something stuck into her scalp. A crown. "The Notre Dame guy is going to be there, I've already set a meeting," he continued happily, sharing good news.

Her date knelt beside her and adjusted her crown, though she couldn't feel it. The black paste completely numbed her face and encroached on her neck. "You're the most beautiful sacrifice ever." He paused and his face turned puzzled. "I mean...the most beautiful I've ever sacrificed, you know?"

Janey's features set with wild fear at her new title, and her mouth gaped, a stutter on her lips. The drugs had worn away. She was awake, totally awake, but panic froze her bones so all she could do was stutter as she kneeled in the hot, liquid sand.

Sobbing through breaths, Janey gestured to Tucker. "Wh–why do you need both of us?"

The tall team captain frowned, and from his back pocket came a switchblade. The chanting grew louder all at once, more insistent, words Janey didn't understand but recognized their malicious tone. Mark pointed with his knife between the three sacrifices.

"It's like when you get married, right? Something old." He gestured to Tucker. "Something new." He pointed at Janey's groin. "Something borrowed..." The knife swiveled to the stolen donkey, its leash nailed into the ground while its gut bled and dripped to the ground. Mark's empty hand whipped out and clasped her wrist, the thumb caressing the tender flesh of the inside, her pulse below. "And something...red."

The switchblade cut a long, thin line down the center of her forearm, below her palm leading up, and a wild shriek erupted from her throat. Another sound she had never heard herself make, one she didn't know she could.

Blood fell onto Mark's drawing in the sand and it *rippled* like a water surface. More drops fell and the sand transformed, glistening in the flames, as if the entire clearing was now a pond of gray liquid, smooth and calm. Janey's heartbeat filled her ears, incessant thumping, and Tucker's gagged mouth screamed when something alien swam beneath the clearing's surface.

Mark's broad, confident hand grasped the back of Janey's hair lovingly and tilted it to the sky. Stars stood bright overhead in the circle of black, the treetops reflecting the fire, and Mark's handsome face filled her view.

He leaned down and sweetly whispered, "Janey..." before kissing her.

Not a peck or a polite kiss. Not a short or a congenial one. A deep, plunging kiss involving lips and teeth and tongue and the whole of his mouth covering her numb one in a smothering embrace. Her first kiss.

He opened wider and regurgitated into her mouth.

Mark's black mucus smothered her orifices, and he pinched her nose, forcing it down her esophagus, pulling her into nausea.

Mark broke away and Janey fell forward, hacking, spluttering, crying, the same numbness enveloping her body as the chanting overwhelmed everything everywhere. The donkey *brayed* and Janey erected in time to see what alarmed it.

The sand purled violently and a leviathan serpent, obsidian as the void, reared from the gray lake in an arched coil. Sand fell in rivulets from the great dragon. A beast of antiquity, swollen long ago from gluttony of man flesh until its wings were useless and it was confined to crawl the earth until it learned to swim in its depths.

It raised, high and thick as the trees. The corners of its mouth below a long nose writhed with a legion of tentacles, sentient worms by themselves, sensing the air, vibrations of the summoning chants, the rapid breaths of its offerings. It leaned over, smelling, inhaling the donkey's musk briefly before striking in a flash, biting the head in a messy bite, innards and blood plopping into the sand. Janey screamed and the donkey's body was consumed in another two bites. The monster's throat gurgled loudly, its rumblings thrumming her ears.

Janey no longer felt tears or the sobs racking her naked breasts, but could sense the terror deep in her sternum. Swelling until she couldn't breathe, crippling her insides when the great worm of ancient earth and older space, from somewhere unknowable, beyond human thought or time, turned its hunger to the kneeling pedophile. Smelling his stink, it snatched him from the ground as a coiled viper with a pest.

Assistant Coach Tucker's bones crunched between large molars, and Janey shook her head wildly in despair, whimpering to the indifferent, chanting adults through numbed lips. "Please... I don't wanna die, please!"

Standing behind her, her escort Mark's gentle voice lowered to her, trying to comfort.

"Shhhh, shhh, Janey, Janey, Janey. No, no, no, I'm sorry, I didn't explain it well. You're special, sacrifice was the wrong word, I'm sorry..."

The serpent tilted its head back to that same eternal sky, and the lower half of Coach Tucker slid into its gullet, limp legs flopping upside down, and the bulge of his body coursed down beneath the slick, reptilian skin. Once swallowed, its black doll eyes the size of baseballs found her. Mark whispered frantically in her ear, his excitement rising, with each breath stinking of beer and mucus.

"You're not a sacrifice. You're the bride."

Janey's entire body, beyond numb with the pitch ichor coursing over her skin and inside her veins, sat immobile as the fat worm-snake towered. Looking to her head, scenting the vile paste dripping down her naked chest, recognition gleamed over its void-eyes.

It leered from its great height and Janey whimpered as the black irises twitched. It came so close, its breath whipping her hair before rearing over her and opening its jaws, revealing old, blackened teeth. Janey's lungs wouldn't, couldn't expand or catch air as the mouth slowly lowered and that thick gurgling bloomed louder from the empty void inside his maw.

Darkness poured, retched, a plague, spewing over her in a solid wave, blanketing her human flesh until no white, untainted skin remained. The paste wriggled over her, alive, filling everywhere, foulness reeking, and Janey still couldn't breathe once the wave passed. Her mouth gasped like a dying fish, sucking in whatever available, whether inky vomit or air. Janey no longer felt her body and was unsure if she still had one. Had it melted? Her thoughts were a nebula, unbound and floating, her eyes heavy, often closing by themselves in the sticky goo.

But they were open enough to see the great deity now lay placidly along the sandy pond, calmly, expectantly flicking its eyes between her and the chanting adults. It spoke with no words, the command clear. *Janey.* Strong arms lifted her limp figure and walked to the benevolent serpent whom she somehow now knew would take care of her. Needed her. They were together and one now, she knew.

Janey's body, dripping, solvated into a primordial disposition, was gently, tenderly, reverently laid on top of the thick snake with soft, pliable skin. A collective exhalation trembled the forest, and every atom in Janey's body shivered as she sighed through bubbling, decomposing lips.

Relief swelled through the family's ranks as the black blood of their lineage worked on Janey's DNA. Stifling and blending it, they continued chanting, sensing the new bride merge with their benefactor, their ancestor. Divining her youth, her purity, her untainted organs, her new, fresh eggs were sinking into its receptive flesh. Janey's body melted like snow on water, subsumed into a greater being, adding to it.

Adding a fresh course of life, of blood, of spirit. She added new scientific connection to the Earth, to the trees, to the roots pulsing with their life, with their rotting death. A connection renewed for another year. The next bride. Their next mother.

Her body dissolved into the one beneath. Until they were together.

Then Janey was no more.

They were greater, rearing above the forest as equals, a rival among giants of ancient flora, a survivor of ancient fauna, and they surveyed their progeny. Once landed on this third planet, separated from its main body and host, this great worm altered its own evolution, diverting their cycle of procreation and regeneration. Stemmed from many and then only one, it adapted. Now generations removed, iterations altered and diverged, they merged with humans. Humans still revering their creator, hungering for their trivialities, still needing their inherited fortune. They felt them all, all their desires, lusts, sins. An amalgam of emotions and commands of what their ancestor could provide.

The offspring really needed this win on Saturday.

The cozy, cavernous Earth beckoned—it always liked caverns and grottos—and they longed to find a warm burrow deep near the core to coil into and begin the annual process of life. To use those eggs it couldn't make itself and create anew.

But they felt the heirs whisper prayers. The progeny of progeny innumerable and their upcoming need. They would help where they could. Bequeath favor and good fortune and help as long as they still honored them with their yearly tribute.

Their jaws opened again, and their voice, full of chaos and deep cadence, echoed over the forest and hurt young, mortal ears. The humans winced, but understood the simple phrase to let them know the sacrifice had been accepted, the bride and her eggs pure. Everything would work in their favor.

"GOOOO TIGERS!"

SWARM

"PEOPLE GO MISSIN'" in West Virginia all the time, ya know?"

"That right?"

"No rhyme or reason to it." Marni grinned. "Second most caves in the whole US of A. Just go walkin' and *pfffffff*... Gone." She leaned in the porch's rocking chair and it creaked. Her elfin face matched her short hair, and in the twilight, her pale skin glowed.

"Ol' Appalachia burial. Swear it," she added, the grin turning mischievous.

My lips pursed and she abruptly exploded with laughter, sharp cackles swallowed by the hovering forest. "You city boys are so easy..."

Todd groaned inside the cabin, a deep, vulgar sound, and Marni laughed harder in concerto. Strange guffs a woman shouldn't make, her lips baring back and exposing a chipped left canine. Something I missed in the dim bar where we met.

"Well, at least *easy* city boys know how to have fun."

A bug tickled my nape, tangled in the short hair. I slapped it only to really sting myself. "Yeahhh, Tinder is fun, huh?"

Planting her whole foot, Marni began rocking aggressively, the chair squawking, and she picked at something between her teeth with a thoughtfulness on her features.

"That how y'all save money? Tindering across America? Swipin' right through these great states?"

Blood rushed to my cheeks, warming them too much against cool night air, and I turned to the forest. Looming high and dense, it was now a shadowy pitch.

"Hey, no shame, lotsa men whoring these days. Equality and all that shit."

I cleared my throat, thinking of how we "saved" money this road trip, tensing and readying for Todd to come out and give me the signal. My whole body too tight.

"So whose shack is this anyway?"

The space between the house and forest, littered with clunky metallic detritus, might have been a junkyard. In the near-night sky, the rusted skeletons of several cars, old and new, plates from everywhere in the U.S., lay hidden in the dark eaves of the yard, vines strangling their corpses. Our '99 Corolla fit in perfectly, camouflaged in the decay. Marni didn't reply and I glanced at her. Gone was the smirk, her lips set into a sharp, thin line.

"This *home* is our old pa's."

I shifted, the knife in my boot scraped against my ankle, and I regretted bringing it. These girls had less than shit in their *shack* to steal unless Marni suddenly dropped a gold tooth outta... Suddenly, behind Marni's head, a pinprick flare of warm light illuminated her greasy hair. "What the hell..."

She followed my eyes. "Y'all don't have fireflies in LA?"

She lifted her hand and a black bug suddenly sat on her white knuckle, as if it materialized from gloom. Long and ovalish, little antennas waved frenetically as it crawled over Marni's knuckles like a pony trick. It flashed again, mesmerizing lime on her cream skin, and then it was gone, dissolved back into the black air.

"That's dope."

Marni's finger, a slender thing too rangy for her wide hand, pointed to the forest.

"Naw, *that's* dope."

A firefly flashed ten feet from the porch, then twenty, then beneath the dark canopy, more lighting one after another like the guiding beacons of an airport runway. A hypnotic stream leading from the house on an invisible path.

Todd moaned and began huffing exertion, wood knocking wood in a carnal drumbeat. Marni suddenly grabbed my hand with her cold and clammy one, leveraging her petite frame to pull me from the stoop. "Come on, LA, let's leave the Tinderers to their mating ritual. Arlene can shake that whole house sometimes. Goddamn nine point ohhhhh on the Rick-ter, ya know?"

She didn't wait, nearly yanking my arm from the socket, chuckling at her own joke. I was about to reclaim my hand when the wholesome string of lights flickered, delving into the forest, and stunned any thoughts. Their cozy light cascaded hypnotically, rhythmically, dominoes falling away, and Marni led us into the darkness like she saw perfectly. Like the luminance of the ephemeral trail was enough for her bucolic eyes, used to shadows and night air.

The fireflies grew in number as we followed, accompanying like they were the Ferryman and this was the River Styx. Their off-green light illumining dirt mounds and woodland castoff, passing old trees with bark molting as slough. Leaves, felt more than seen, crunched beneath my boot, and the soil beneath them was soft like sand.

"Come on, Las Vegas, I gotta good feelin'..."

The rhythm faltered and I blinked from stupor. "Wait, what did you say?"

"I said I gotta good feelin' 'bout tonight..."

She tugged harder, a mysterious, infectious excitement edging her voice as the trees broke for a clearing. "Oh shit, looky here. They're swarmin'. I've only seen this a few times. You're in for a treat."

Beyond Marni in untouched wilds, a cloud of heavenly light, a beacon, pulsed at the base of a gargantuan gnarled oak. Dozens, no, hundreds of fireflies illuminated its knots and rough edges in sharp shadows, deep crevices hid a grotto in its base. She yanked again and we stumbled into a plateaued depression with knee-high grass and soft, sodden dirt. "Hey!" I protested, before being cut off by another insistent jerk, her grip a vise on my wrist. The forest canopy was thick, the gloaming nearly completely night, the only illumination from the swarm's hypnotic display.

The ball hovered, growing brighter, radiating that spectral green, and parcels within the swarm began harmonizing. A strange, asynchronous union. Mesmerizing, hypnotic, swelling, throbbing light. Flashing of warning lights.

"Is this...safe?"

Marni finally stopped, mere feet away from the nimbus. Her arm encircled my shoulders, her body heat thick and cloying, and I smelled the faint scent of meat gone bad. She drew us closer, her urgency exchanged for whispered reverence, our feet on well-trodden ground. "Don't worry, LA. Fireflies don't have any teeth, per se. They just like to gather sometimes, like an orgy, ya know? A wonderful, fiery orgy."

Sensing spectators, the flare pulsed faster, coruscating in this levitating horde, utterly bewitching. Another step, the swarm closer. Where once the fireflies gently flared, they now flashed as if controlled by a wall switch. Pulsed, thrummed, a racing heartbeat of Appalachia. Enthralling, uncanny emanations against the dark grotto and towering pines. I inhaled, forgetting to breathe. Life unexpected in this dreary shithole.

Marni inched us forward and I unconsciously reached for the cloud, as if a magnet controlled my hand, desiring something other than guilt at rolling these girls and turning them into simply bodies. And the bodies before them. And the girls at the start. Would it be warm? Cold light? Electric? My hand breached the ethereal nebula, grime and crime in my thread-worn fingerprints.

"Incredible... I've never..."

The strobe blinded light and dark in flux, a pattern emerging. An odd configuration clearer with each pulse. A shape. My hand hesitated; this wasn't bugs. The shape...

A face, rotten, weathered, and wrinkled, lunged through the cloud of light with an open maw, yellowing, green-lit teeth too wide for the mouth. Blunt and strong teeth swallowed my thumb with warm spit, biting far down onto the palm with a crunch. The fireflies scattered, revealing a deranged old man in their wake. Half-naked and stringy-gaunt, beyond age under dirt and grit, he wore wild eyes above those teeth bared, clamped as a vise on my flesh.

I howled.

Fiery, aching pain, a bomb exploding inside the meat of my hand, and he gritted the teeth harder, ignoring as I pulled. A tug of war. Chaotic embers of light whizzed overhead, frantic, and Marni laughed deliriously to the canopy, her cackle sharp as the teeth gripping my palm. I pulled and shrieked, yanked and the sinews of my palm tore away. Cold air suddenly blistered my hand and I fell backward. Cool and hollow, a subtlety in the way my thumb didn't want to move. Because it was there, but wasn't. My phantom thumb.

Fireflies buzzed, deafening screeches overhead, a cacophonic chandelier of acid green displaying the gaunt man with elfin face scramble from the tree's burrow on all fours like a dog, his jaw cudding wide circles, my stringy meat hanging from his mouth. Fireflies dotted his body, clinging like neon ticks, and his eyes reflected their light. Two little hungry fires burning inside his skull as he slinked forward, his fingers clawing earth.

My ankle pinched in my boot. My knife. The knife in my boot. My free hand pulled it and slashed blindly, wildly, lightning-pain bolting up my arm as I shuffled and turned. My half-hand bled like a river lived inside me, pouring to escape, soaking the loam, and Marni laughed harder, watching me scramble for the camouflaging dark.

"Well, watchu got there, LA? Was that for me? You finally got a pricker for me? Kinda small, ain't it?"

A hand snatched my ankle and I kicked, flailing wild limbs, all my limbs, until something connected and the hand released, leaving me to scurry through the sodden depression to stand straight into a clumsy sprint.

"*Where ya going, LA?*" Marni sing-songed through the wilderness with a child's pitch.

Faint light, straggling swarms of fireflies on mounds arose as I rushed past, eerie lights illuminating their board. A clawed, rigid hand, gray and draped in moss, harbored several points of light above a lump. Bodies. Decomposing, fetid bodies. Long rotten with thick maggots, firefly larvae feasting on the erratic corpses.

A slender moon peeked through the trees, and in the distance, Todd moaned like a distant night train trying to leave for parts unknown. I sprinted, leaping over long, narrow mounds a foot high, some old with soft grass swaying in a breeze, the graves, the leftovers, my hand spraying gore as sacrifice.

"*L-Aayyyyyyyyyy...*"

My panicked sobs drowned Marni out as the edge of the forest and the shack neared. "*TODD,*" I cried.

"*Urghhhhhhh,*" he moaned, and I skidded to a stop in the middle of the junkyard, speckled with points of green light as if the Milky Way had descended to Earth. Todd moaned louder.

"*AURRRGHH!*"

Not a moan, a wail.

The shack door flung open. Todd, blond and athletic, naked and dirty, fell to his knees on the rough wood porch. Hands covering his groin, a creek of black ichor ran down his thighs. Blood dribbled from his mouth, and when he spoke, all I heard was garbled and distorted. Half his bottom lip was bitten away, torn and flapping on his chin. Hovering fireflies approached his wounded body.

"*Toddy... Hot Toddy, wher'dya go, bay-bee?*"

He stumbled from the porch just as the door opened again, naked Arlene ambling idly out, her white breasts iridescent in moonlight. She held something long and floppy and drenched black in her hand, her chin bloody. A crack sounded inside my skull, an unbearable pain buckling my knees, and the dry August grass ruffled against my face.

Groggy with pain, I rolled, and the stars in the sky doubled, points of lights moving and blinking awake. So many stars, so many hungry little mouths waiting for their turn, until only Marni's face hovered over. Her eyes gleamed, familiarly emerald and wholly strange; her jaw also moved in a circular motion, a wet clacking sound at each apex. Chewing.

A bug landed on my hand, the same tangling of hairs. Little exploring legs, first one, then many, then hundreds. A legion of tickling antennae. Marni licked her fingers, those slender, strange fingers, in a long broad stroke, sopping up blackness like it was caramel. "Sorry, LA. Tinder is like...our UberEats."

Knobbly, old phalanges began crawling up my legs, bright light emanating from somewhere below my chest, and Marni's chipped canine ripped into a chunk of unidentified meat, and she spoke, her mouth full to burst.

"And we always hungry."

A BETTER CHIMERA FOR THE TOXIC WORKPLACE

GUSTS OF SAND, caustic, red, and burning, rattled the closest window in its track. Desert winds picked up in the early hour, whistling sharp everywhere, and the sun slowly baked the tops of the surface buildings of Marianna Mining Camp.

"My scales are itching crazy bad."

CeCe gnawed her jerky. Kangaroo meat. 'Sun-dried.' Fancy label for roadkill scooped up after several blistering hours on hot blacktop. She kept her attention on the diner's far corner and the small hologram of the news reporter raised in the top corner. In the vastness of the hostile desert between Marianna and Perth, Category Two winds undoubtedly erupted with the dawn, because the transparent woman flickered in and out of existence as if someone played with a light switch.

There was never any audio, but news of the race to colonize Mars always peaked CeCe's interest, and scrolling subtitles made easy guess work. Another record-breaking global heat index disrupted the latest launch on the American coast. Boiling water spouts, hundreds of meters tall, played havoc with the astronauts catching a ride off-world. Tossing launching equipment and space shuttles as if they were paper airplanes.

Jodi persisted, the lisp from her recent transmogrification scraped against CeCe's nerves. "I said my—"

"I heard you," CeCe calmly cut her off, matter-of-factly. "I just don't care."

CeCe chewed slowly, careful not to smack her lips open, and avoided Jodi's hurt-puppy-dog stare by focusing on her e-reader and the job application. Grit had settled into the machine's lens, and she blew sharply into it, wiping with her soft gloves until the holographic keyboard flickered awake. Across the booth, Jodi's eyes tried burning a mark at the top of CeCe's beanie.

"No need to be a bitch..."

CeCe dropped her company ration to the plate and replied with the tone of a frustrated mother. "I'm not being a bitch. You always do this. This is the third time. You're not shopping for fuckin' shoes. You gotta wait til they work out the kinks with new DNA genomes. The input code is never perfect on the release date and even the first iteration. Adaptation will always take longer. Hell, I have *never* bought below a gen four-point-oh, and it still takes me three weeks to assimilate."

CeCe ended her rant, the longest she had spoken since returning from "vacation." The most words so far she had given her only girlfriend, or whatever word was appropriate for less than a friend but more than an acquaintance. Jodi slumped, her pout an unnatural, angular shape on her altered and pointed chin bone. Marianna Mine's only diner was near empty in the morning, the coolest part of the day, the time others not on-shift would be able to enjoy fresh air not recycled or stale. Still, CeCe searched for eavesdroppers. Three old timers sat at the counter. Grandfatherly figures and early-birders, slowly spooning their coffee jellies and watching the news because it was in front of their eyes.

Jodi reached over to the side wall, waved her wrist ID over the table's scanner, and pushed its call button for her water ration. She muttered low, intending a curse, but her lisp made it her sound closer to a cranky toddler. "You've been so testy since you came back. And you don't need to be mean about it, not all of us get first pick of which mine..."

CeCe's partially forked tongue flicked unconsciously, sharp and fast, and Jodi stopped talking, her sulking replaced with mortification.

"Sorry. I don't know why I said that."

CeCe grunted, tugging the protective dust scarf on her neck, suddenly too tight, and muted activity filled the diner. The tinkle of spoon on ceramic, the faint hum of the news projector, the balls of tapping feet reverberating over the tiles.

The new waitress, 100% human with the water ration tips to prove it, broke the silence with her light tread, her skirt swishing above unblemished and long tanned legs. She was so out of place in the remote mining town, packed with gruff, dirty men layered with reptilian skin mods, she could have been an alien. CeCe's eyes lingered across the legs for a moment before traveling up to the young woman's kind face. Heart-shaped. Symmetrical. She stopped at their table holding a gelatinous water cube on a plate aloft.

"Water order?"

"That's me," Jodi said, sliding over to collect. CeCe turned away from the waitress and continued typing her credentials into the form. The waitress, still nameless until the gold name tag adorned her chest, continued standing at their table. Her shoes, a sensible, clean white-neon sneaker, remained visible in CeCe's lowered peripheral. After another moment of the waitress' still feet, CeCe looked up.

The waitress raised her eyebrows, as if they had accidentally bumped into one another. "You girls been working here long? I haven't seen many women, though I guess I've only been here for a few days." She chuckled and CeCe couldn't recall such a sweet sound in the diner before. This woman was still a girl. "Still... I thought there would be more..." The sweetness turned worried at the thought of so many men. CeCe grimaced.

But Jodi laughed, good naturedly, though gruff and swinish in comparison. "No, not many women. I mean, not many women want those DNA sequences, do they? Can't come out here to the desert and work the mines with a simple mammal genome. Gotta get the whole kit n' caboodle, you know?" She removed her lightweight beanie unashamedly; her domed skull of mottled and pebbled scales, beige and gray, was in the process of shedding. Transparent flakes drifted to the tabletop. The reptilian skin, covering 90% of Jodi's body, began where her hairline would have started, rounding around the eyes, nose, and lips, and continued down to her neck, lost beneath her work uniform.

"Not exactly gonna be on a *Vogue* cover like those cat ladies, huh?"

The waitress' eyebrows arched, but not with disgust. In fact, her hand, svelte and the frailest thing CeCe recalled seeing out here at camp, unconsciously raised as if she would touch Jodi's head. Jodi also raised her hairless brows, surprised. "That's so cool," the waitress mumbled distractedly, her hand raising until abruptly stopping, aware of the collective gaze. It retracted, and suddenly CeCe understood this new waitress a whole lot better. A mod-chaser. Someone who liked the look and thought of body modifications but couldn't bring themselves to forever harm their frail human body. Well, she would have her pick of anyone of the three hundred men likely dying for a bit of her attention. If she was like that.

"Sorry, don't get many with the reptile mods in the city. It's all cats and useless stuff, huh? Maybe an avian sometimes. It's so interesting though... What do you have?"

Jodi straightened, generally considered unattractive with her masculine features, especially now her hair had shed, delighted in the interested audience. "I got some Horny Devil sequences and the latest Gila Monster, the one from Mexico they just decoded." She wriggled her brow, though it didn't have the same effect without eyebrows, and finally turned her attention to the water cube, sticking it with a straw. "Can sustain a thirty-five Celsius internal temp." She scratched her neck and it sounded like sandpaper on more sandpaper.

"Wow," the waitress mumbled. Her eyes traveled across to CeCe, now typing. "What about you?"

"What about me?"

"Whatcha got?"

"What I got?"

Her eyes roamed CeCe's gloved hands, hungry to see some of her genetically altered skin, and moved to her coveralls, then her neck liner and beanie covering her skull and sensitive ears. "Yeah, I mean, you look... I mean I can't see anything." Like most, CeCe's mods were comfortably and well hidden, but more importantly, her body was out of sight. To inquiring eyes, CeCe was now genderless.

CeCe stopped typing and stared at the waitress, bubbly with straight blonde hair and that heart-shaped face ending in a fucking pert chin. She'd likely only be here for another week, at best. There was a reason Mike at the diner hadn't given this girl a nametag. CeCe made her face as impassive and deadpan and unfriendly as possible. "I got stuff," she replied stiffly.

The waitress frowned until the entry chimed and she turned to the outer door opening. Sylphs of hot winds roiled sand inside the entry chamber, a two-door system into the cooler diner. The women watched three men pass through. The first lowered his dusty balaclava, his handsome, totally human-flesh face was rimmed by a devilish serpentine pattern only in the space where his hair would have been. Harrison. CeCe turned away, disgusted, a small part somewhere in her brain convinced she should scamper and hide, make herself invisible and camouflage among the scenery. Another more disgusting part of her noted his virility and the way the muscles of his hand flexed.

The men, three sets of heavy feet and the sporadic drag of a tail oscillating back and forth, strode across the floor, and CeCe felt *his* presence as if a literal weight straddled her back. The waitress left for the new customers and CeCe listened to her footsteps, heavy on the outside heel. Swaying her hips. Maybe unconsciously, but probably not. Harrison's grin did that.

"You seem different today," Jodi said abruptly, earnestly studying her. "You didn't get any new mods—" she began when CeCe punched in the last few pieces of information, pressing send before returning the reader into her chest pocket, and quickly replied.

"I'm off, my shift starts in thirty."

Jodi forgot her question and quickly sucked her cube through her straw, careful for every last molecule. "Wait up, we'll walk over to the terminal together."

CeCe didn't reply and stood from the booth. Her eyes, sharp and exacting, immediately met Harrison's smug face. She kept her stare neutral and he winked, his second membrane slower than the first eyelid. He smiled, and even though he hadn't any facial mods besides the protective eyelids, his exposed teeth were somehow sharper than a human's should be. Like he had maxed out his DNA and his body began changing all by itself without any additional resequencing. Evolving into one of the creatures he had stolen a genetic sequence from. Becoming feral to match his personality.

CeCe ignored his wink, her blood flushing and *swooshing* in her ears when she passed him. Jodi's footsteps followed closely and Harrison spoke with a tone.

"Hey there, Jodi."

CeCe flung the entry chamber door and didn't bother to see if Jodi tagged along. The chamber was warm for 8am. Red dust from the Western Australian desert already settled comfortably in the corners. Before she could pull the exit door, Jodi yanked the inner door and the outer door automatically locked so as to not cause a wind tunnel.

"You know, I wouldn't say anything," Jodi said somberly, a marked change from the jovial-colleague persona she projected.

CeCe searched through the chamber's grimy glass. Harrison's profile laughed and smiled with his mates, his head turning ever-so-slightly to the waitress and the hem of her dress and those smooth, long legs. The flash of his fifth, useless limb beneath the table caught her eye, vanity with a hankering for mods. CeCe raised her dusk mask over her face.

"You can tell me, you know? If you ever want to talk about it," Jodi pushed.

But CeCe said nothing and reached for the door handle, leaving for the burning sands.

***

CeCe mounted the stairs two at a time, swiping her ID, and the armed guard opened the unlocked metal grate of the women's quarter for her. He smiled at her, trying to catch her eyes, but she nodded curtly and left the underground, noting he carried two stun guns now.

Safety is also a prison, she thought while crossing the "No Loitering" zone.

As opposed to the crowded dorms for the three hundred men, there were only twenty women's rooms along a lengthy subterranean corridor, excavated and lined with alloy. Unsurprisingly, many women miners quickly decided no amount of crazy money was worth the hardships or other risks, and the corridor remained only half filled.

CeCe didn't mind the solitude. With Jodi working nights, she rarely encountered anyone. Once her door was braced for the night, the quiet hum of sleeping rock and distant machines burrowing deeper and deeper was preferable to neighbors who might observe her too closely.

The sun blared too brightly this morning, even with her sun visor, and her watch beeped an outside temp warning for 51 Celsius. Heat rippled off the open expanse of the mining camp like furious ghosts. Behemoth machines, trucks, diggers, excavators the size of houses lay idly on the fringes of several mine entrances. Too expensive and dangerous to function in the daytime, risking overheating and fire, they slept under the sun and their metal burned at acceptable levels short of melting. They were currently of no use at the fine-tooth digging stage. Using hands, claws, fine teeth. Mining had regressed when men's labor became cheaper than dwindling resources. Men and their bodies were expendable, unlimited bodies. Fine earth metals were dwindling with only one earth in inventory.

The entrance to CeCe's mine shaft, the adit, was located in a small hillock, the opening wide like the start of a mammoth cave. The 9:05 shuttle, an open-air tram on a fixed track, was half-full when she climbed on, miners from other sections sitting patiently. She didn't recognize anyone and no one looked up at her, all men thinking her one of them. But a shorter miner with serpentine eyes, sitting on the back bench, stared at her a little longer than usual. His eyes flickered over her tight-bound chest, likely utilizing some kind of heat vision. Glands in her neck swelled in primordial response, and she swiveled on her seat so her legs hung off the side of the open car. A moment later, the driver called for last passengers and, without waiting, began down the steep ramp burrowing into the Earth. The tram *clunked,* a slowly building rhythm reminiscent of a heartbeat.

CeCe stared at the passing tunnel with glazed eyes as they descended. Radiant sunlight withdrew for shadows, and an occasional fluorescent globe blinded her. Cables and pumps and sewage drains lined the shaft like a great artery of a body. A human body, at least. Pumping air and water inside, sucking the detritus and unwanted waste back to the surface. The shaft tilted to a sharper angle, delving into the Earth's body, and the tram accommodated, the seating remaining level while the base and wheels tilted down. CeCe's legs swung out with gravity, like she was on an elevator now going down. She sniffed the air tentatively, catching the rising fumes. A breath of tepid air, cooler than the burning ones on the surface, caressed her skin, and she finally opened the top button of her coveralls.

The pebbled skin of her body, a hard, coalesced keratin from a lizard in the American desert, flushed blood to the surface, enjoying the subterranean environment, cooling after outside temps.

She closed her eyes, reveling. There was nowhere on Earth with this kind of sensation, this natural dark-cool. Nowhere the common laborer with their mountain of resource debt could escape to besides the extreme depths. Working the ocean trenches was too dangerous; the mods for those jobs were their own kind of jail despite the pay. A "wet" mod meant you always needed to be near water, slowly evaporating and likely gone soon. And getting them scrubbed from your DNA was said to be a bloody nightmare, the genetic tailoring costing an arm and leg, or fin. No, only fools and the beyond-poor population changed into a fucking water mammal on a drying planet.

But desert mods meant one wasn't as bound to one place, and as long as you paid a little extra for genome-tailored design to exclude facial transformation, you could easily hide genetic changes. The tram *clunckclunckclunked* over the tracks, and her inner ear popped with the pressure change. CeCe removed her ear plugs, the tunnel's gentle wind brushing over them, carrying voices from below as whispers.

She wondered about the Mars mission, ruminating over it, thinking about it more than a poor woman would. It had taken seed inside her skull. The next planet, ripe for industry and terraforming. Would they need miners? Probably. Eventually. Knowing her luck, only hundreds of years from now. And even then, probably only fucking men would be given first priority. She didn't know a thing about space travel, but surely desert mods would be useful on a dead planet. Hell, astronauts and future colonists had been training in the desert for the Mars missions for the last two hundred years.

The melodic *clunckclunckclunck* slowed, and a new artificial light shone below her boots on the mine floor. A flood of fluorescents illuminated the excavated dome, and the tram slowed to a stop on ancient bedrock. The other miners exited with lethargy in their steps, mindlessly navigating the routes and branches of the cavernous warren. CeCe let them leave, and making sure no one casually loitered, she forked right.

Passing a large fire door, CeCe's section of the Marianna Mine was slowly drying up, its corpse already carved and sorted. Several tons of holmium had already been harvested from this arm, tendrils of the soft metal scratched and picked clean over the last year, the corpse down to clean bones. With her nose and intuition, CeCe had likely found a third of it with rarely any praise.

Praise used to be nice, but now CeCe only wanted the money. Money was a thing a woman could use. Praise never got a woman anything else but more notice.

Stalking past the backs of miners, her head down, delving deeper and farther from the hub, the tunnel stood mostly empty and string lights in the ceiling flickered every so often. When CeCe left for her forced down-time after the incident, there had been nearly fifty men working this branch. Now she rarely saw more than eight.

Most working this vein realized months ago it neared its end, nature's stolen bounty quickly dwindling, and they applied to more profitable sections or new mines where they would receive higher commissions. CeCe trudged over the misshapen floor, walking close to the wall. Years of labor and machine toil had shaped it into ridges and unyielding stone waves, the sporadic glisten of quartz shimmering sporadically. The supervisor, Terry, a man younger than her and clearly from the cities with his lily-white skin and nocturnal cat eyes, looked up from his clipboard. His face belied his underlying thoughts when he saw her, but quickly schooled them and simply nodded as he logged her in.

She ignored his slight and wound through the tunnel, shadows cutting over the rock like sharp birthmarks between the shafts of light. The tunnel width lessened with each bend; the darkness grew and the cool joined it. CeCe turned on her head and chest lamps.

Tighter and tighter her tunnel narrowed until she could stretch out both hands and touch each wall. The ceiling above her was unsupported, the bare belly of the rock smooth. Removing a glove, her sharp but small nails shaped as claws scratched and trailed stone, her customized metal implants sparking dramatically. Finally reaching the tunnel's end, she palmed the bare rock wall.

Unlike the rest of her body, CeCe had paid the lab tech an extra twenty credits to re-sequence and keep her palms and feet soles bare. The pebble of her reptile exterior protected from the fatal heat and abrasive sand, but it sacrificed the feel of smooth rock and deeper reverberations. Useless for finding big payloads that hid between crevices. The big money. She just needed one more to prove a point.

Rubbing the stone face like a woman wishing for luck, she stopped at yesterday's groove, confident something lived beneath. Something left. Her sixth sense told her a deposit lay sleeping. Hiding. Something the techs and surveyors with their fancy radar had missed. With the mining regression, the art of prospecting had resurged. Of whispering into rock and hearing its secrets. Machines weren't infallible, only pinging the widest and most obvious pockets.

The *clatter* of a rock fell in the distance, far along the tunnel or perhaps even in another vein, and CeCe stopped, eyes closed and listening. Removing her lightweight cap, the padded low flaps covering down to her neck came off and exposed her ears, radial and widened for her sensitive inner ear. Silence.

No footsteps. No tail drag. A memory of hot breath brushing her face wanted to resurface, stained with artificial rye liquor, and she squeezed her eyes tighter, pushing him away. CeCe's own breath held her lungs tight for a long minute until sure she was alone.

Finally, taking her tools from her leg pouch, she extracted a tiny hammer whose handle fit snug in her palm. Platinum but without the chrome finish. Hard, sturdy, a good conductor. Placing the side of her head with its widened cochlea and implanted shell flush against the wall, CeCe tapped along the rock face. Sound traveled deep into the rock, little reverberations cascading away, a minutiae of echoes tingling along the face and inside.

Pressure resonated through normal silica rock, the density familiar to her canine ear. *Tap tap tap.* She hammered, a step across each time its resonance signaled nothing distinguishable, maybe the odd pocket of air, a hollow crevice where sound died. "Come on, come on, come on," she whispered encouragingly, imploring the rock.

Tap, tap, tap.

CeCe swiveled the hammer in her palm, eyes closed, and used the flat, broad edge. A longer resonance that traveled farther in the right conditions.

Terp, Terp, terp, tap.

Her eyes shot open. In the jumpy light, the stone appeared normal, uninteresting, worthless, but spoke otherwise.

Plucking the scraper from her belt, she scratched the stone with her metal fingernails, eventually stabbing it, causing pockmarks in its smooth face, enough for dust to rise. With the smell receptors of a bloodhound, she inhaled and smiled, rubbing the rock face lovingly.

***

The administration office of Marianna Mine and Co. was comparable to a rusty metal coffin. Demountable buildings decades old that had been fried and left in the broiling sands. Why they hadn't been transferred underground like the miner's barracks, CeCe suspected, was for presenting an above-ground face. If everything was underground, the site would look like a ghost town, barren and dead to any spectator and upper-atmospheric drones or satellites. Investors waiting on the latest profit margins might have a heart attack if there was nothing they could spy on while waiting for their coffers to fill.

A hill of sand had blown against the side of the long building CeCe approached, red and fine, the edges were cleared daily by diggers so the building wasn't buried and returned to the dunes. The wind rustled against the dunes, calling for her, and she paused at the foot of the stairs, her attention drawn to the expanse of desert.

Once scattered with the occasional bush or scant tree, erosion and drought had wiped the Australian desert to nothing more than sand

and rocks. Soft mounds sculpted by artistic winds lay in angular serried rows up to and beyond the horizon. Dunes forever. Their color was comforting, their shape inherently familiar to some part of CeCe's brain. All at once, she had a desire to simply walk off into the desert, bury herself in a drift, and bask forever. To shed her clothes and allow the sands to mold and scrub her hard skin, to exfoliate and live in the hot sun forever. Her glands and neck swelled beneath her mask and she shook her head, recognizing the foreign and alien instincts, and climbed the rickety stairs to the entry cooling chamber.

The secretary beyond the chamber's second door raised her eyes to CeCe, patting off dust as one did when meeting management. The secretary was a woman in her later years and CeCe suspected her a puritanical, disgusted by mods and abominations to the human body. The way she discreetly sneered and lightly sniffled when passing CeCe in the woman's dorm, the way her eyes roamed as if reluctantly dragged. And if she forsook her beliefs by working out in the middle of the desert with a bunch of heathens, it proved the human spirit endured when there was still no higher power than money these days. God had forsaken Earth and left for another planet with better unused resources.

She entered the office and greeted her politely. "Morning, Diana. I have an appointment with the boss at two."

The woman's dark hair, streaked salt and pepper, had been pulled low and tight at her nape, and her forehead didn't move when she spoke. 'Yes, he is waiting for you, Ms. Carpenter. You can go on through."

She also didn't smile or any other such facial niceties one performed at conversation, though her eyes scanned CeCe's nebulously shaped body as she passed, her boots insanely loud on the flimsy carpet covering flimsier plywood flooring.

The "boss," a mid-level administrator who likely never even held a rock paperweight before taking the position, was known only as Mr. Brown. She approached his office at the end of the long corridor and watched him before knocking. Sitting behind a small pine desk littered with the detritus of meetings and notes, he stared at a computer, multiple holographic tabs to the side floating around the main screen.

CeCe tapped on the door with her gloved finger.

His avian eyes shot up and his mouth, a weak thing with no chin, smiled. He studied her up and down as if they had never met before when the exact opposite was true.

"Carpenter! My star! Come on in!"

CeCe immediately straightened her shoulders. Foreign instincts commanded subservience. A dog with a master holding a bone. Be nice. But after the last time in this office, Mr. Brown frowning at her with a union rep running him in circles, she knew her position had changed. Nice would get her nowhere. She sat in the squeaky office chair lower than the height of the table and Brown's own.

"Quite a week for you, huh? I didn't see it myself, but I heard that holmium load was nearly a hundred kilo, and you pulled it all out in one day! By yourself! By hand!" He guffed, nearly squawking, incredulous one woman could do the work a man found difficult. "Got damn near twenty other fellas asking if they can relocate. Think there's more there after your haul."

CeCe smiled without showing her teeth and shrugged humbly. "It was fifty percent luck. I don't think there's anything left." She shifted, her legs uncomfortable in the small chair. "Which is why I wanted to check on my application for the erbium mine."

Mr. Brown frowned at her lack of banter. He might be management and never underground, but CeCe had learned the hard way with banter. It made men too familiar. He then also straightened his shoulders and returned to his screens, thick dust motes floating through their light like lazy gnats. Tapping the keyboard, his mouth pursed, pulling the sagging skin of his lower neck and jowls.

"Hmmm, yeah. I do remember reading it... Let me pull it up." His finger bounced in the air, tapping the holo-light, and CeCe glanced around the office. A sparse enclosure with fake wood panels. A map of Marianna hung on the far wall, a bird's-eye view of the billion dollar grounds that resembled a blank spot amongst miles of red.

"Okay, let's take a gander at your DNA sequencing and creds..." he mumbled. CeCe's muscles imperceptibly tensed. He frowned again, and she forced herself to relax as her Bio passport came onto his screen. A bi-annual blood test and record of everything CeCe had ever done to her body and blood. "Alrighty, there's the reptilian sequence from five years ago, a Side-Blotched Lizard. Never heard of that one... Just for the skin and internal temps, yes?"

"Yes, sir. It's a smaller lizard from inland deserts. Cheaper sequencing but same results."

He didn't look at her while mumbling and scrolling through her bio qualifications. "And, yes, I remember this one. The Bloodhound, huh? Sequenced and implants two years ago. Pretty smart, using canine for tunneling, of all things. Mixing and matching..." He said it in another mumble, as if it wasn't really impressive at all, and continued scrolling through her falsified DNA chart.

Mr. Brown looked at the screen for a long moment, reading a bar out of CeCe's sight. "You just came back from the East Coast, yes?"

"Yes, sir. After the...incident, I took a holiday to visit my mum in Sydney. Just two weeks."

He grinned, happy for that little insight into CeCe's life, and steepled his delicate fingers. "You're far from maxing out your DNA limit, you know? You still have something like thirty percent you could utilize without any side effects on the generative restructuring. Ever thought about maybe bat sonar? Might be—"

CeCe bobbed her head and tried for demure, a little catch to her voice, her frame crowding over itself to be smaller. Feeble. "I know. I'm just trying to stay a little bit human, you know?" CeCe glanced up at him and made the corners of her eyes dip. Acting like she shared a hidden hope with him, an inside secret. Everywhere was hard, people were altering their DNA to keep up with the heating planet. Hell, people were leaving the planet, signing up for lotteries for the colony ships, hundreds of convoys ready to go to sleep for hundreds of years. All the while, the poor were stuck on an Earth with little to no hope of climate recovery. CeCe wanted to remain a girl for a little longer, 'til the end of it all. Surely, he could understand that.

Brown smiled at her, maybe unconsciously. He likely understood, he had only picked up some avian sequences, non-invasive, probably only because they "looked cool." He didn't want to change too much. But then the grin left his face and he cleared his throat.

"Look, CeCe, you're great at the job. One of the best. You got a natural talent beyond the DNA, but the erbium mine is unstable. They've had three cave-ins already, so it isn't taking on many people—"

"But they have a spot open... I saw the ad."

"Well...yes. But that's not the point, it's danger—"

"It's the best paying per milligram, right?"

"I mean... If you can find—"

"And I'm in the top 2% of earners. I'm one of the best, a star?"

Mr. Brown frowned at being cut off and even further at hearing his own words. Those implanted eyes, a black pupil ringed by mustard yellow irises of a hawk, dilated.

"CeCe, you're great, we all know that. It was no hardship to give you first pick of the holmium mine... But Harrison is set to be the next supervisor of the erbium arm. And with your history—"

"Am I being punished?" she clipped, irritated at the mention of him.

Brown raised his hands defensively, showing his smooth, tender palms. "No, absolutely not." He struggled with the words. "We just don't want another HR incident, CeCe."

"I did nothing wrong, he—"

Now Brown cut her off, an exhausted note in his tone. "CeCe, please. Please. I know what you accused him of. I remember the whole affair quite clearly." He exhaled and stuttered like he was mid-heart attack. "I just don't want you...put into a place where you will...feel uncomfortable."

He turned away, lying through his teeth, and she smelled the sweat on his brow. Vile, sour must. No, Brown just didn't want to have to deal with any shit that *men* might do to her. But this was about more than money, more money than would be needed to go back to school and get those damn space credentials if she chose. Her passport hovered on his screen.

"I won't feel uncomfortable, not if everyone keeps to themselves. I just want to work." She paused and uncharacteristically lifted her chin. Proud. "And I'm the best."

He leaned back in his chair, his chest deflating as he looked her up and down carefully and then back to her screen full of information. Conceding with a singular nod.

"Yes, you are."

***

"Two vodka cubes, please," CeCe instructed the waitress. The heart-faced girl, still unnamed, had lasted more than three weeks, but still carried an unsure quality. Like she hovered on the edge of leaving, but couldn't yet justify losing all that income. Her shoulders were often slumped instead of straight, her hair had been pulled back to a ponytail rather than glamorous and down, and the hemline of her skirt lowered to the more-reserved shin. She scribbled the order with a growing smile. She had long ago stopped trying to make conversation with CeCe, but still asked.

"Celebrating? Or a girl's night?"

CeCe opened her mouth but Jodi answered instead. "Celebrating. Someone just promoted to a new mine. Made official today. Gonna make that ocean trench kinda money, huh?"

The waitress started speaking when someone down the far end of the busy cafe hollered, "Service!" Her bottom lip snapped shut and an irritated expression consumed her face. She tapped her device, inputting their order.

"Might take a minute with that vodka, kinda swamped right now."

CeCe nodded while Jodi empathically frowned as the waitress made for other diners. Mike's was at full capacity, patrons waiting outside in a long line, smoking their pens, despite the cooling night air and maddening winds blowing their conversation away. CeCe avoided these busy times and often ate in her room. Tonight, she and Jodi arrived to a half-empty restaurant, unaware the weekly shuttle flying in from Perth had been delayed several hours. A wave of the miners who traveled in and out every two weeks had disembarked and then poured directly into the diner.

Every small table and booth was full. Men uncomfortably pressed into seats, forced to keep their legs together rather than rub outer thighs with their neighbor, while CeCe and Jodi had a four-person booth all to themselves. The diner was so loud, CeCe fruitlessly pressed her earplugs deeper into her canals. She felt several sets of eyes aimed at her and Jodi, women among men, unicorns among fucking rodents. One of the booths roared laughter and Jodi leaned up with a smile, trying to see what was so funny. The news played in the far corner, and CeCe watched recent footage of the crew on Mars.

Several astronauts, bright shiny silver suits already stained with red dust, were in the beginning stages of constructing the bare bones of a large structure. It looked bleak, not uplifting at all. Not exactly the marketing pornography to encourage investors or inspire future colonists. They were surrounded by miles of rocky, barren expanses. Nothing.

How CeCe wished to be up there.

"So, I was checking out the new release sequencing for the upcoming month and there's—"

CeCe groaned, turning away from the holo-screen and to Jodi scrolling through an online catalog.

"Mate, you're ridiculous," she said with a hint of humor, her mood noticeably lighter today. Jodi purchased new DNA sequences like she window-shopped. She had already shilled out a month of her earnings to scrub three sequences from her DNA, just so she could get another one. Like the endorphins of purchasing were worth the terrible recovery of implanting a genetic trait into your body. It was funny in a way bordering ridiculous.

"Wha?" she asked, her mouth full of dried nutri-bar. "Nothing hurts from window-shopping. They just discovered a new thingy in the Trench—"

CeCe chuckled, though not loudly. "Stop. You already have the best. And they are always going to be 'discovering' something new, or some new variation. Or some extinct animal they just decoded and fit for human adaptation. It's a product, dummy. They need a product to sell, late stage capitalism 101. Get suckers to buy." Her hand snuck over and pulled Jodi's reader her way, the list halfway down a Reptiles list. She clicked off the Reptiles to the main page, full of sales and advertisements.

"You've already got reptilian. You're maxed out. You don't need anything else. Trust me, any more erasures and additions and you're just fucking up your original DNA. Turn feral."

She slid the device back to Jodi, who frowned but wasn't upset. "Well, what about you? Been a while since that canine, though I guess you don't really need anything for the job. What about something cool? Like facial?"

CeCe made a dirty expression and Jodi laughed. "What! Don't look at me like that. You're still holding onto those blue eyes, but something avian would be a nice change. Something...like, helpful, but still cool. I don't know, like, can you get the owl swivel?"

Despite herself, CeCe laughed aloud. "Holy shit, turn my head 180? You know you can't do anything big, nothing skeletal. That's the whole thing about maxing out your DNA. No big stuff, only exterior stuff, sensory stuff for implants. Don't want to actually turn into a lizard, do you?"

Jodi smiled and slunk into her seat, searching around the diner, and CeCe returned to the holo-tube. Footage of the Martian terraformers had been replaced by the latest stock market news, uninteresting red lines and arrows.

"I think maybe..." Jodi started, until a particularly loud raucous noise, obnoxious men laughing at their own inane jokes, interrupted her. The laugh, a deep baritone guff, could have been nails hammered into CeCe's plugged up ears. She subtly looked around Jodi, catching the familiar profile of Harrison and his crew sliding into a booth three down.

Jodi also turned to watch him. Her eyebrows raised in interest.

"Don't," CeCe said.

She smiled and swiveled back. "What? I know he's a dickhead, but he is a cute dickhead. Like in a bad boy way. I mean, for out here, you know?"

"Yeah, he's a dickhead alright," Cece muttered, her eyes searching for the waitress, the diner suddenly too crowded. "Probably could've even gotten an implant for that."

Jodie ignored her, murmuring aloud, almost speaking to herself, "I mean, he doesn't wear a ring, and I know he doesn't fly in and out."

"Jodi, stop, you do not want whatever attention he gives you. Trust me."

Her attention finally focused, her eyes narrowing, and her voice lowered to a whisper, "Then why not tell me?"

"Because..." CeCe stuttered, unsure. Jodi was once a close friend. But she was also a talker, a town-crier in a town full of mutes. A gossip because she simply liked to talk and there was next to nothing to speak of. "Because that human trash isn't worth any more of my breaths."

"Hey!" the waitress exclaimed, and both women turned. Three seats down, the waitress spun on her heel, confused, just as Harrison's scorpion tail returned to the table's shadowy darkness below. She brushed down her skirt's hem as if something had ruffled it, trouble ruining her heart-shaped face.

"Sorry, hun. Sometimes this thing has a mind of its own, you know? Gotta tie it up, I think," he said earnestly, and the other men at the table hid their grins poorly, the air around the booth palpable and full. CeCe was suddenly hypnotized, watching the exchange like nothing else existed. Like the pair three booths down were in crystal clear vision and the rest of her eyesight was blurry. Nauseating deja vu

99

clenching her stomach. Harrison breathed on the back of her neck and her throat bloated. His tail pried her legs apart.

He leaned over and off the table, pretending a cloistered intimacy with the waitress, and CeCe heard all his whispers, her ears now a curse. "You know, though... It does pick up on the most eligible bachelorettes." From beneath the table, the tail, a vicious, sickle-shaped appendage, crept out again from the darkness. "I say it has a mind of its own, but maybe it's an unconscious manifestation of..." The pricker end circled the waitress' ankles, aiming upward to her skirt, the waitress oblivious while Harrison, charming and smooth, spoke with his mesmerizing brand of sleaze.

CeCe's lungs stopped working, watching a replay of her own assault. The stinger end of his tail neared her hemline.

"What time does your shift—"

CeCe shot up from the booth, her heavy boots stomping the floor like a flamenco dancer. "Hey!" she hollered, and the entire diner stopped. Time stopped. Every breath held like they were in a mine collapse and praying not to breathe dust into their delicate spongy lungs. CeCe, however, heaved air like she had been running, and the waitress turned suddenly to her, a frown on her face. Harrison leaned away and the tail retreated into the dark.

There was a long silence, and with eyes that never wavered from the waitress' kind face, she said loud enough for everyone to hear, "We ordered drinks ten minutes ago. Is it too much to unwrap a couple of cubes? Or you just gonna flirt all night?"

The older miners, men CeCe might have respected had they reached out and taken a young miner under their wing instead of watching her struggle, turned at the bar and frowned disapprovingly at her. The waitress' eyes shined glassy with new tears, and she shook her head and mumbled something about "coming up." With hunched shoulders, she left Harrison's table, everyone watching her pass to the back kitchen. All except for Harrison, who stared at CeCe knowingly, and she stared back.

**

The erbium mine was hotter than it should have been. Hotter than humanly tolerable. Sweat from CeCe's human-fleshed brow dribbled around her mouth and she licked it. The tram delving into the deep and fresh-carved dying Earth hadn't the pleasantries of a well-oiled machine yet. The standard lines of electricity, air, and coolant were unrefined. Mammoth machines continued tunneling into distant arms, rumbling CeCe's peripheral like gentle tinnitus, spewing smoke not completely siphoned out. CeCe often overheard the joke that they might have to bring back canaries, and then someone would retort they were half-canary anyway.

"Fuckin' oath. When the hell are they gonna fix these coolant lines? Suppos' to be fuckin' cool underground, for fuck's sake."

The old scratchy voice would have been lost to the hot wind rushing past them on the tram if the fella hadn't been sitting right next to CeCe. She smiled and jostled him, hollering for his bad hearing.

"Time for that upgrade? What do you have again? Geriatric dinosaur?"

The old man scratched the underside of his chin. Thick stubble somehow grew and poked through the keratin base layer of a simple gecko he implanted thirty years ago. "Nah, too old for fancy upgrades. All that decoding and inputting. Too long for readaptation. Hell, I was thirty-five when all the sequencing came out, and even then I was on the rough side. Still took me a month to grow this shit. Nah, this skin is the only one I'll have, now 'til I'm below dirt and not trying to dig my way out."

Old Dave laughed heartily at his own joke and CeCe also smiled, a recent addition to her face. Her vein buddy, working a hand's span away from her for twelve hours a day for the last two weeks, Dave was also a natural at mining, but how he did it without any other sensory mods mystified CeCe. His hands would caress the rock face like they were divining rods, often pointing the right way.

Together, CeCe and Dave were in one of the least developed veins, just them two. Tunnel surveyors had deemed it "unpromising" and allocated it to the old man on his way out and the troublemaker girl. But she was here, nonetheless.

Though the joke was on them, Dave was exactly what she needed in a close colleague. Respectable, good standing among peers, his word never doubted. An older man, one just hanging on 'til he found his next big load and then he would retire, the type of man who she could beat in a fight. One who treated her like a granddaughter rather than a woman. A perfect alibi.

The tram slowed to a stop. As usual, CeCe and Dave allowed the younger, eager men off first, the erbium mine by far the busiest she had worked. At least seventy men worked each shift in the several chutes and branches. Everyone from miners to mechanics to sparkies to surveyors came and went. A flurry of activity around the tram chute as the night shift left.

The two partners switched on their headlamps and wandered to their section, the swarm of bodies lessened. They passed into the new arm and CeCe paused ever so slightly. Harrison's well-known silhouette, thick and intimidating, waited at the lip of the shaft next to a cage full of emergency equipment. Now a supervisor, he'd grown accustomed to taking it easy, scanning his electronic clipboard, logging the miners in for the day and their shift. Poking his head in and out of where he pleased. His tail unconsciously oscillated. Every time she saw it, CeCe shivered, and the extra glands hidden deep in the pocket wells of her neck swelled.

Harrison looked up at their approaching boots, indifference on his face, nodding to Dave and then back down to the glowing screen of the board. He ignored her as if she wasn't there. They passed and moved into the lightened shaft, the *clink* of other miners already echoing from the many offshoots. The odd pair remained unusually silent, and only when they had turned a corner and out of Harrison's eyeline did CeCe relax, the defensive systems of her chimera body deflating. But not entirely.

She looked aside at Dave, his eyes on her, curiously examining below her chin before he glanced over his shoulder at Harrison. Dave hadn't said anything regarding *management* and CeCe. Never asked questions, never made asides or comments designed for a reaction or light conversation. But whispers traveled far in a tunnel. CeCe heard the word "bitch" whispered so much, maybe they thought she was literally turning into a dog. Dave surely knew all about the "incident," now four months gone and swept under the rug, that allowed CeCe her pick of shafts and Harrison a three-week unpaid work leave as a formality.

They turned down their shaft, wooden and metal struts braced along the ceiling. The temporary workings of a shaft in progress, meant to be replaced with more permanent structural integrity support. Right now, the shaft resembles a broken mine from medieval times, sporadic pieces of wood hacked together in case anything should fall or break away. She had voiced her concerns to *higher* management two weeks ago on her first day. There was a record somewhere that CeCe Carpenter thought vein arm #24 was at risk of a cave-in. Management had shooed her away.

They arrived at the end of the shaft, the latest mapping report showing they should be cutting straight ahead. Their registered buckets waited for them, a home for the expected fragments of erbium. CeCe removed her earplugs and Dave unloaded his belt, spreading his fingers wide across the bare rock, whispering his sweet nothings.

***

After five twelve-hour shifts without a day's break, old Dave leaned his neck back and it creaked loud enough to create an echo.

"Reckon that sound means it's knock-off time," he groaned. CeCe shook her bucket, small fragments of shiny, soft erbium lay idly, glinting against her harsh headlamp. The registered scale claimed CeCe unearthed half a kilo in fragments today. She'd like to imagine maybe these very pieces would somehow find their way into outer space as part of a shuttle. How much would they be worth? Easily worth a hot million. Though her percentage wouldn't get her out of the mines yet, it would be enough for a month of living somewhere on a beach, near water. Something at the end of it all.

Dave's bucket showed similar and he grunted. "Thought this chute would give us more than these drops." He sighed and turned to the shaft entrance, a stream of men leaving for the day. More prosperous men in other veins. Dave had thought the "unpromising" label was machine nonsense, but it ran true every day as they heard the commotion and fuss of miners finding thick tendrils of precious metal among silica rock. Never theirs.

CeCe didn't mind, just as she didn't mind management never following up on rejigging their shaft's struts, danger looming silently above. Dave was always wary of it and CeCe not at all. She came, she worked, she left. She waited.

Tap tap tap with her little hammer, her ear pressed against the warm rock, not really listening. There had been nothing but scraps for days and she suspected she and Dave would need to shave off another foot before scanning again.

"Right, I'm done-zo. You coming?" he asked.

Tap tap tap. "Noooo, I've got a good feeling. Just another twenty minutes, I think," she said mechanically.

Dave hooted, reverberations filling the small space, and reclipped his belt. "You've always got good feelings at the end of the day. All the guys think you're trying to outshine 'em."

"Outshine those larakins anyway, mate. Gonna strike it rich, and you won't even be here for it, old man," she mumbled, half-listening to her hammer tapping and waiting for him to leave.

"Right, well… Don't stay too late, will you?" he said, and CeCe heard the concern in his voice. Dave was a good man, he deserved more than just being a common miner. He continued, "Next shift doesn't come for another hour, don't want them to find you buried.."

"You always say that," she muttered and listened intently to Dave shuffle away, his feet joining others making their way to the tram.

CeCe exhaled against the silent rock, her nerves jostling with Dave's exit as they did every day. Her hammer halfheartedly tapping, her hearing attuned to outside in the main tunnel. The trudge of feet ebbed until only the distant hum of the automated vacuum remained. Suctioning the debris of shaved rock, it swept through the mine for approximately one hour at the end of every twelve-hour shift in lieu of a cleaning lady.

She listened, the breath in her lungs shallow and unfulfilling as she imitated her usual routine of sieving useless rocks. After thirty minutes of feigning work, she was about to leave when the subtle tread of two feet echoed with the *scurrr* of a hard-shelled tail dragging over hard rock before lifting.

CeCe nearly swallowed her tongue and aimed her ear to the end of the tunnel, making sure it wasn't only ghosts or bad memories approaching. The dim light in the far corner flickered off and she wanted to vomit.

Scurr-scurr-scurr, Harrison's tail dragged, his footsteps loud and clear, not at all attempting stealth. She turned and his silhouette framed the entrance some twenty meters away. Filling it, no way to escape. He spoke, and his calm voice filled every nook and cranny in the tunnel.

"You know, when you asked to be transferred to *my* section, I thought, okay, she's in it for the money. Fair enough. Woman wants to get back on her feet…maybe even show she isn't scared of me. The old 'fuck you.'"

CeCe dutifully returned her tiny chrome hammer to her belt, her heart already in a race to some unknown finish line. An undeniable urge to make herself as small as possible and curl into a corner. An animal desire to hide and avoid a predator. She forced herself to stand, switching off her headlamp. She didn't turn and instead assessed the ceiling, hewn rock and a rotting wooden joist casting ugly shadows.

"But then, this whole...dedicated worker. Staying behind, only for half an hour, no longer. Just enough time for someone to come and find you in the dark. Notice you. I realized that maybe you didn't hate our date as much as you protested."

Halfway to her, his black shape resembled something alien with the extra limb. People shouldn't have tails, especially not scorpion ones that didn't even hold venom. Another way to hold her still. She hated him, her vomit closer to being expectorated. Sweat beaded CeCe's brow and her trembling hand removed her hard hat, exposing her bare pebbled skull. Her voice came out shaky, excited.

"You know, I had to take two weeks' vacation after what you did to me."

"What I did? What *we* did."

"Took myself up to Gold Coast..."

"Nightclub row, huh? Get some drinks into ya? Some of that burning beach?"

"...had to shop around for a black-market coder."

Harrison frowned but continued walking slowly, always forward to her.

CeCe willed her voice steady. "Had to find one who knew rare species with useful skills, a kind heart for stories of rape, and more importantly, one who could forge Bio passports."

A mere five steps away, even with deep shadows carving his face, Harrison was still the handsomest man she had ever seen. A mean kind of handsome. Her cheeks and glands swelled, anticipating a threat as his eyes scoured up and down her body. His expression plain, he was remembering the last time they were in a tunnel together and he had forced himself. He mumbled casually.

"You get another sequence? Not quite like getting a tramp stamp, but we always knew you were a freak for kink." He smiled and stepped in, his hand reaching and caressing the line below her chin. She didn't move, fear disorientating and making her woozy. "I knew you loved it," he whispered. "You can be cold and mean up top, but underground..."

"Harry," she whispered, stuttering. The swing of his tail to the side, dark against light, snapped her fear away, her neck bloating like a long slender balloon, and something painfully twinged at the back of her head. "You're right. I have been waiting here, most afternoons, on the chance you'll come down..."

His fingers, rough skin ending in a long claw, gently scraped over her pebbled clavicle, making its way down to her chest. "Yeah?" he murmured. She removed her gloves. He was so close.

"Mhmm, hoping you'd come down, by yourself, and save me."

He finally looked up, puzzled. "Save you?"

CeCe's cheeks, glands, new illegal organs grown from genetic mutation, had finally bubbled full, and she spat viciously at his face and neck, free of the protective scales layering his body. At first, he was stunned, insulted, his face scrunched so as to not get any in his eyes. He paused, unsure, as he experienced a new, unfamiliar sensation.

Steam rose, silky tendrils in the darkness highlighted by far light, and his skin began burning off his face.

The acid reservoir of CeCe's glands, accumulating for the last 24 hours since she'd emptied them last night, had been brimming. Every day for months, she'd emptied out her new sacs in discarded mining debris to produce fresh acid, every day anticipating a time, an opportunity, *this* opportunity.

Harrison screamed, both sets of eyelids melting, the acid dissolving, desiring his soft ocular jelly. The mine's vacuum rumbled in the main shaft. A gentle, burrowing hum filled every corner and nook and drowned out anything else. He flung himself against the rock wall, his tail holding him from completely falling as it flailed like a broken wing. CeCe kicked him in the stomach and his hefty frame fell into the end corner. Wailing, his hands tried wiping her corrosive liquid away only for themselves to start burning upon contact.

CeCe stared at him, mesmerized and tranquil. Calm for the first time in months, a grim smile overtook her features. Wanting something so much and then realizing it would always be better in your imagination.

She searched down the corridor, aiming the shell of her ear, blocking out Harrison's cries. The acid on his throat or in his mouth had finally done something to his vocal cords, and he wailed like he had a bad cold, raspy and dry. The hum of the mine's vacuum filled the main dome, no footsteps. No one stayed after clock-off. They were alone.

"You ever hear of the Greek Rock Lizard, Harry?"

He wailed again, and his tail lashed in her direction, too short. Defending itself.

"No, neither had I. Marvelous little creatures. Overlooked, honestly. Not deemed as 'Class-A Dangerous' because they are tiny little bastards. Hard to find someone with its coding and willing to falsify my records. I maxed out my DNA for you, you know?" Her throat clotted with pressure, not entirely alarming. In the tight space, she smelled his cooking flesh and her mouth salivated. "Starting to feel the change, somewhere around here, something that shouldn't be." With her metal-tipped finger, she made a general circle around the base of her throat and then shook her head, confessing.

"I get the strangest thoughts sometimes, Harry. Primal, strange thoughts."

He began crying.

CeCe stood between him and the tunnel's entrance, blocking the distant light. Her voice assumed a dreamy quality as she thought over the rock lizard, now herself. "Tiny little bastards, with this funky little acid we spit for protection."

An urge, unexplainable beyond the genetic changes to her system, intruded the moment of revenge. A desire to take something from him besides his life. A hunger. She kneeled, Harrison now laying prostrate on the floor, his body juddering, and she leaned over his face, aiming for his nose, bubbling in glistening, viscous pops of chemical reaction. She held down his struggling form when her mouth covered his nose and she bit gently. He tasted like roadkill. The nose sloughed away, made for her digestion. Harrison didn't cry anymore, he likely didn't even feel her eating him, cannibalizing his face, and CeCe chewed, noting the slight sting on her tongue. Not quite human, not quite reptile.

Satisfied, she focused on the rotting wall strut high above him, the one needing replacing long ago. CeCe Carpenter then studied Harrison, lying on the floor, acid tearing through his eyelids and onward to his brain, his face spongy and lax, almost translucent now. He abruptly made a stronger movement with his body, that damn tail pushing his frame from beneath, acclimatizing to the pain, the acid numbing. CeCe studied to the strut and the wall pock-marked with crevices and slivers of dykes.

"You'll be a goddamn hero, Harry."

With a heave of her body to give it momentum, CeCe spat the last of her acid sac onto the rotting wood. Smoke, more ghostly spirals burning organic material, drifted up to the ceiling. Harrison's tail, the curved telson, useless without the illegal DNA coding for venom, curled around her ankle, limply asking for help.

The strut of wood shifted and cracked.

She kicked off the tail, smearing some rock dust over the clean, sweaty skin of her face, a cut here, a bruise there.

The wood cracked again and something deeper, kilometers below the earth, groaned. CeCe heard it, reveled in its unfathomable power. She looked to him again, a river of blood, black in the dark, oozing from his face like golden syrup.

"A goddamn hero, Harry. I'll make sure of it."

The air started rumbling, stone vibrating beneath her feet, over her head, and CeCe turned on her heel and sprinted. Bolted like all the animals, legal and restricted, raced through her legs, and the indescribable horror of crashing rock began at the end of the vein. Harrison crushed to literal pulp. CeCe shrieked wildly and other men came to help.

***

"So what you got?"

CeCe stared at the new waitress' shoes. Kitten heels. She wouldn't last three days.

"Reptilian and canine," CeCe replied casually, sucking her water ration. The girl, the youngest CeCe could remember passing through Mike's, raised her manicured eyebrow.

"Cool, very cool," she mumbled, and absentmindedly adjusted her black armband. CeCe stifled her grin. The girl didn't even know Harrison, having arrived three days after the accident. She turned to leave, and the news CeCe had been watching before she arrived came into her eyeline again.

"Oh shit," Jodi exclaimed. CeCe didn't take her eyes off the projection, but did ask.

"What?"

"They just posted Harrison's job. Fuck, he's only been dead for five days. They haven't even cleared the tunnel, hell, they haven't even gotten his body mush back." Jodi's mouth suddenly snapped shut, making that foolish expression when she often put her foot in it. "Sorry, I just... I forgot."

"You forgot a man I hated saved my life, literally pushing me out of the tunnel? Or that he died from it? Or that it all could have been avoided if management took my complaints seriously?" CeCe asked, trying to act more than her normal peevish and speaking louder than she normally would. Jodi bobbed her head sheepishly.

CeCe returned to the news, her eyes passing over Dave at the bar, a beer cube in front of him. The black armband sat low on his sleeve and his back was hunched over. They hadn't spoken since he visited her in the medical center.

On the news was the daily Mars update. Terraformers were gathered around a dig site. The fossil of something similar to a long bug sat on a table, desiccated and fossilized. Red scrolling script rolled across the projection.

New extinct lifeform found beneath Martian soil.

"I hope Dave gets it," CeCe said, turning back to Jodi.

"The job?" Jodi mumbled, her contrition already gone, her finger already scrolling over the latest sequences, ready for purchasing. Ready to implant. "Think he's gonna apply?"

The red scrolling script continued.

DNA sequencing could be available within a year.

"Maybe. I hope so."

COME IN, CAMP ZUMA

"ZUMA ONE, THIS is Zuma Actual, please respond... Zuma One... Pick up your goddamn comms!" Botanist Penelope Danvers calmly huffed into the microphone a final time and glanced to the clock, her foot frenetically bouncing on its ball. The team was now an hour past their scheduled arrival and out of contact for two. Soon, they would be out of O2.

She switched channels.

"SpacePort Phobos, this is Camp Zuma, come in, Control," she rapidly spoke into the mic, her voice an octave too high. Panic edging her usual placid demeanor. Planetary static crackled in the speaker for a moment before the main space station for all Martian missions responded.

"Go for Phobos Control," the voice on the other end of the line answered. He, orbiting some thousands of miles above Mars in a nice and safe office, sounded bored and unfazed. The only woman on the planet, Danvers inhaled deeply, forcing herself to project composure, to not be the *emotional* link in the chain.

"Control, this is Doctor Danvers at Zuma again. My dig team is now an hour late and has been out of contact for twice that. Please advise." She released the transmitting button and the low crackle filled the room, grating her nerves like harsh Martian sand.

"Understood, Zuma. Stand by." The terse voice on the larger moon commanded her. Danvers fell back into her seat, tugging a lock of escaped hair from the bun at her nape and biting her lip. The dig team had driven their buggy out from Zuma, the foremost domed facility closest to Olympus Mons, a two-hour drive, for soil collection. Geographical surveys and maps showed ancient lava tubes had eventually turned into deep, underground rivers, which then dried with a planetary extinction event and left vast cave structures winding down to the core like a rabbit's warren. But on the surface, the concoction of old volcanic soil from the system's tallest mountain and former waterways meant the dirt would be the best for her planned garden. She had *insisted*, fought even, with Commander Dominick on that dirt. Now he was classified actively MIA.

Danvers turned to a screen monitor displaying the team's headset cameras, all running with thick, black fuzz. She turned a knob and reviewed the last few minutes before their feeds went dead. Simultaneously, the four monitors rewound in double-time and she pressed play.

The team had just planted shovels in the soil, the Olympus Mons looming but still far from the barren expanse she had chosen. Their goal was to reach one meter down for nutrient-rich dirt. After five minutes of labored toil in thick suits, Dominick's breath hard in his microphone, the ground beneath Vasilly's shovel shifted on its own, like sand running through the small portal of an hourglass, and the beginnings of an opening formed. A black hole emerged, and all four camera feeds were suddenly staticky with unknown electronic interference. At first only slight, it spread over the whole screen like a virus as they cautiously approached the hole until the screens were unrecognizable.

Danvers pressed pause on the final clear image and studied it again. The team dug deep enough to hit the beginnings of a cave structure. Not a terrible surprise, given the behemoth system, but what the hell caused interference with their cameras?

Chewing her lip in thought, she paused when a new screen to her right lit up: the camp's internal CCTV system, present in all of Camp Zuma's domes. The motion sensor detected movement, and the camera displayed the outside of the main dome's hatch, the "front porch." Camp Zuma's main mode of transportation, a large-framed buggy resembling an open-top jeep, had been parked haphazardly and not at all in the manner she usually expected from Commander Dominick. All four men were now exiting.

Martian winds billowed the red blankets of sands across the "front yard," the men awkward and struggling to keep themselves upright. The reactor's controlled explosions at Mars' North Pole was only in its second year of the scheduled four burns. Greenhouse gasses and atmospheric interventions slowly warmed the red planet, resulting in a multitude of planned atmospheric triggers. The average temperature of Mars in the daylight had already risen to a balmy -60 degrees, and stronger zephyrs swelled with new warmth. Terraforming Mars would be a long process but a sure one. In another few years, and with another few rounds of radiation blockers, Danvers might be able to walk outside with simply an oxygen mask for a full minute.

Her station colleagues, Commander Dominick, Vasilly, Samuels, and Tanaka, were dressed in their heavy suits for outside excursions and making their way into the pressurized hatch. Despite Mars' lighter gravity, their movements were jerky and odd as they battled the wind. Danvers exhaled, a welcome sigh exiting her body.

Far from helpless, she had years of rigorous training and adopted skills one needed to survive on the revenant planet. But as a team on one of Mars' three forward operating bases, it was a three-hour shuttle ride to the orbiting SpacePort, and she would rather just avoid any "emergencies."

Her foot stopped jiggling and she spoke into the transponder.

"Phobos Control? This is Danvers at Zuma again. Never mind that last transmission. The team just drove up to the front porch. Over."

The reply was immediate, the bodiless voice also full of relief.

"Glad to hear it, Doctor. Maybe they just stopped for drive-through. Please let us know if they need any assistance. Camp Yankee is on standby, but they need two hours to drive to you. Phobos out."

Penelope clicked the radio off, smiling at the rare joke from Control, an easiness returning to the situation, and she watched the four men step inside the sealed hatch, the automatic process for re-entry initialized. She studied them a second longer, squinting through the sudden fuzz on the monitor. The camera, positioned in the high, anterior corner, filmed their backs as they waited for the green light and the inner door to open. Standing two by two and facing forward, there was none of the usual meandering that occurred while the crew went through the tedious process of decontamination.

Leaving the communication room, Danvers entered the main hallway connecting the several domes, her long strides following the curved corridor to the main living area where the team would enter. The hatch slid open, the men now exiting the chamber, and Danvers paused mid-stride, precious recycled air leaving her body. Commander Dominick, recognizable for his tall figure and handsome features, had a large, cracked hole the size of a fist in his helmet's face shield. Through the hole, Danvers saw the handsome man had turned pale and blanched, red Martian dirt smeared across his cheek and leading to his mouth.

Danvers didn't think, recognizing a medical emergency, and rushed to the side of the dome with the steel emergency box.

"*Getting medical,*" she exclaimed, breathless, and lifted the trauma case, purposefully placed at the very top of other supplies waiting for their opportunity. She turned with the heavy case, expecting to see the commander being assisted to one of the side cots. Instead, the three other men continued into the hallway and turned right for the mechanical domes. Commander Dominick, however, strode directly toward her, a calm, dead expression over his features, like he had suffered a stroke and his entire face was slack, his muscles dead. His lips were stained blue, his face frosting, his blood stagnant. His blue eyes were now frozen, milky white.

"Comman—" she whispered.

His arms shot out, gloved hands violently clutching her shoulders to force her still. Despite his brutality, the way his fingers dug into her flesh like he wanted to pry her apart, Dominick's face remained ashen and emotionless, and Danvers struggled, his hold hurting her. She finally found her voice, only a whimper, a pathetic, delicate whimper: "Matt..."

He either didn't hear her plea or didn't care. There was zero recognition on his dead, limp face that he knew her, that they lived together for the last year, that they fought like cats and dogs hiding a deeper flirtation and desire. She struggled for another moment until a movement inside his chest paused her.

A large bulge, visible through his suit, suddenly protruded and undulated up through his upper chest at her eye line. A mole tunneling beneath the dirt. Something lived inside him.

She watched in horror, all she could do. Her gaze trailed the mound ascending inside the commander's body, burrowing its way up to his throat. It hypnotized her, and her eyes flickered with tears when his jaw slowly lowered, opening as wide as a hinge could, wider than possible, and he clasped her tighter, pulling her up like they were lovers straining to kiss.

The wiry end of an antenna poked out of his mouth, tickling his tonsils and passing over his pale tongue.

The something buried inside Dominick's body wanted out. A flick of a long, hairy antenna touched her lips, and Danvers finally emerged from her stupor, swinging her arm carrying the heavy metal case into his stomach, and the expectorating creature recoiled back inside his throat with the blow. His fingers around her shoulder loosened, and Danvers savagely wrenched from his grasp, dropping the case and hurling herself through the room to the corridor.

A screech filled the air, sizzled it, a pitch so high and foreign Danvers winced as it felt like it shredded her inner ears. She swung left, stumbling down the empty curved corridor, her legs, her whole body, her entire being vibrating with adrenaline. The other men were nowhere in sight as she flung herself to the communications room and the door slid closed after her.

Danvers locked it quickly and searched the dark room, immediately noticing the change. The usual red lights of the control panel were black. Dead. Approaching the radio she used not five minutes prior, Danvers flipped the buttons to no effect.

"No. *No*," she whispered, frantically flicking all the control panels on and off for a response, her whole hand mashing against them, pressing everything possible. "*Nononononono.*" Nothing lit up, the radio lifeless. It ran on the main generator in the engine dome. She fell into the chair, a tempered sob finally bursting from her chest. Outside the door, the heavy tread of a man's footsteps clunked on metal, the rhythm unnatural. Too orderly and precise. Danvers wiped her nose with her sleeve and remembered the CCTV, its own power source from a battery beneath the desk.

She swung her chair to the system, flicking it on. The single screen came to life, littered with fuzzy static she had to squint through. Set in the main hallway, the back of a man walked calmly in the direction of the living quarters. She pressed a button and the screen flicked to the camp's control room, housing the generators, life-support systems, and other controls for sustaining the facility. Sustaining their lives. The screen clicked over just in time to show Tanaka smashing his bloody and broken fist into one of the control panels, a lethal carelessness in his wild movements showing little to no regard for self-preservation. He wasn't trying to preserve anything.

"NO!" Danvers exclaimed as the panel with his fist inside exploded in a flare of sparks, blinding the camera. The screen flicked over to the internal utility room, Vasilly now using a broom handle as a rudimental spear to pierce the O2 tanks like a cro-mag with a stick. A burst of white cloud erupted from the fissure as he stabbed violently.

Deep in the camp's bowels, a siren began wailing an alarming tune, alerting the inhabitants something had gone wrong. The generic red flashing light at the top of every doorway began blinking, and she shook her head to clear her thoughts. She needed help. She needed out. She would soon need air.

But whatever infected the men from the underground cave at Olympus Mons didn't seem to mind the Martian atmosphere. Living inside their bodies...like parasites. On screen, Vasilly dropped the spear and walked away. Controlling parasites. Puppets with masters, allowing the crew to walk outside without any serious damage beyond the cold. They could chase her. An image of herself running fruitlessly to nothing over the barren Martian plains, chased by tireless frozen figures, scored her mind's eye. Running to nowhere for nothing.

Danvers sobbed, allowing herself a moment of pity before she remembered she had been trained for this. Hostile force training. The "little-green-men" course. Administered, never taken seriously. In the event of a dominant, native force with hostile intentions, all personnel were to evacuate to the next forward operating base and sound the alarm. Gather the troops. Overwhelm the natives.

Camp Yankee. It was a long way. The jeep had just been used, but might not need refueling. And it had a short-distance radio, so she only needed to get within ten clicks of Yankee to hail for help. More heavy footsteps echoed on the metal grate outside, and Danvers touched another button on the screen. The far hallway camera showed two of the crew walking past the comms room with eerie precision, their steps in measured unison. Commander Dominick came on screen and joined them as they marched to the far end, finishing at an exterior wall. The commander ripped a vertical bar from the wall, one connecting all the horizontal struts, and the wall wavered through the static screen like an optical illusion. Danvers grasped the actual monitor as the other two men joined him in demolition. They were literally dismantling the building.

A second, different siren began howling. Structural integrity failing. Danvers swore. She wouldn't survive ten seconds without her suit if they kept ripping the walls out. She switched the camera to the hallway leading to the living quarters. It was clear, the three men were at the far end.

Danvers sucked in a deep, controlled breath. There wasn't much time. No time, really. Once the hallway went, the individual domes would be isolated and would lose pressure and air once their doors opened. Safety controls would lock air vents but nothing else. She had to get to her room and her suit. She stood with another breath and glanced at the screen, positioning herself as a racer waiting for the crack of the starting gun. Danvers inhaled a deep lungful, maybe her last, and pressed the door open.

Pressure remained in the hallway as she ran the corridor, but a slight draft brushed against her face and whined in her ears, a portent of full depressurization. An augury of Mars taking back its land. She sprinted the fifteen meters and turned into her personal quarters, the door sliding open and closing swiftly. Danvers thought she heard the heavy tread of boots on the metallic walkway as it closed, but it was lost as she locked the door.

Her simple room was thankfully empty, and she moved to the steel emergency cargo box, immediately pulling out her personalized suit. She left the helmet off once dressed and considered the other articles in the box. The medical and emergency cases sat on top, a spare oxygen tank to the side, and other necessities useful in the event of a Cat 5 weather event or temporary loss of a life-support system.

She pushed them all aside and stared at the smaller box underneath. Untouched and forgotten, Danvers picked up the armory case with the DARPA sigil and opened it. Tucking the traditional double-barrel flare gun into her suit's lower leg pocket, she carefully picked up the latest version of the hand-held air gun. She had only fired it once before, in an Earth-based training course, but it had been too revolutionary for her as a botanist to really appreciate. She knew it had no recoil and fit easily in her palm. She had witnessed the size of the hole it left in the firing range mannequin. A cartridge held eight rounds and her spine shivered, hoping the men, or whatever wormed inside their bodies, were too preoccupied with tearing down her home and would ignore her escape.

Something crashed in the hallway, drawing her attention off the gun. Danvers knew the hallway was now gone, and once she left the security of her bedroom, she would essentially be in Martian atmosphere. Coarse, abrasive, and uncaring for humans. Locking on her helmet, her interior view screen showed air reserves had begun with three hours left. Squeezing the gun's hard metal in her gloved palm and steeling her nerves for the second time, she ran over the quickest route to the jeep in her mind. Get to the jeep. Get to Yankee. Don't get infected.

Danvers, an atheist, made the sign of the cross over her heart just in case and pressed the door open to the hallway. As soon as the door slid open, she immediately sensed the pressure loss, her body suddenly lighter as the density of the station's internal atmosphere evaporated. A strong Martian wind had also entered the hallway. Danvers could tell because heavy, red dust rode it, thick granules flying past her as the hallway created a wind tunnel.

Crossing the threshold and turning, Danvers' petite frame immediately smacked into the body of Commander Dominick, staring down placidly with his stiff, haint-blue face, waiting for her to creep from her hidey-hole. Her helmet radio erupted in a whine, a high pitch in her ear as if tinnitus lived there. His hands pushed down on her shoulders and she yelped at his sudden presence, the trigger beneath her finger squeezing. The air gun shot its bullet, aimed right into the commander's waistline.

Fans of blood, thick and coagulated, hit Danvers' face shield like splattered paint, her eyes cringing shut with the unexpected gore.

His hands softened, his strength waned, and she peeked her eyes open. The commander hadn't fallen, but studied at the gaping wound the size of a fist in his waist with a vague interest. Almost as a man inspecting the damage to another's car. The shot, simple air, had blown through his suit and clear through the flesh, lumpy knots of blood flowing lazily out and down his white suit. Danvers saw the floor behind him.

His hand around her arm tightened and he looked up from the fatal wound, unphased. His mouth opened wide as before, a wave of bodily flesh swelling as something began emerging once more. Not waiting for the parasite machinations, Danvers tilted the gun upward and squeezed her finger rapidly, multiple times. *Poppoppop.* Multiple splatters hit her chest, her helmet, her torso, and the high-pitched squeal erupted once more, louder and frantic in her radio receiver. She opened her eyes to the commander's chest, torn apart and without reservation by the gun in her careless hand.

His ribs were broken apart and the pulpy flesh sponges of his lungs were discarded to the side. Danvers, hypnotized by the carnage, discerned the thick bone of his spine deep inside the cavern the gun created.

Dominick's knees suddenly collapsed and independent movement inside the gutted chest cavity caught her eyes, slithering beneath torn sinews near his spine. A shiny and slender brown shell, hard, reminiscent of an Earth centipede, wriggled inside the broken man. His body wavered, the ringing in her ears lessening, and Danvers remembered she had to escape.

Get to Yankee.

She rounded the body cautiously as it fell forward and smacked the metallic grate. The hellish red light of the Martian sky glowed like a blooming dawn from the end, and Danvers turned into the living area, stopping short once more for a flurry of activity in the usually quiet space. Vasilly and Samuels, ripping support beams from the rounded wall, several metallic struts, swiveled at the sound of the door, and without hesitation, Samuels' body, rigid and strong, strode toward her, arms reaching, his bare fingers spread wide, tipped with black frostbite. Danvers raised her gun with an inexperienced, slack wrist and hollered above the feedback screeching in her earpiece for him to stop, wondering if he heard or even recognized her.

The trembling gun didn't even make him pause, and when he was two feet away, she squinted and squeezed her finger. *poppoppop.* Pellets of pressurized air hit the base of Samuels' neck, the thick material of his suit exploding like a balloon filled with pink sludge. Danvers winced, stepping away when coagulated and dark blood dribbled out of the entry. The body *squealed* and immediately fell to its knees before flopping forward.

The corpse began convulsing. Horrible, terrible tremors, as if a hand inside a puppet wanted out.

She turned for the exit only for her throat to be clutched by the strong hand of her Russian friend, Vasilly. His milk-eyes gazed with the same dead stare of the commander through the hole in his helmet. The same dead stare of an incessant hunter chasing down quarry, emotionless. The hand squeezed and flung her small body to the center of the room, the air gun escaping her stunned hand to clatter and slide into the hallway.

Disorientated, Danvers pressed up onto her hands. Across the wide dome, Vasilly strode forward in precise, economical movements. The same rolling wave of flesh of Commander Dominick's chest now swelled Vasilly's torso, and in Danvers' peripheral, Samuels' carcass juddered on the floor beyond her feet. From his helmet, face down on the floor, a long slender brown creature crawled out with alarming quickness, escaping its sinking ship. Two feet long, it wound with a fluid, lithe grace. Hundreds of spiny legs tapered along the cold, concrete slab, and Danvers cried a guttural scream, fogging her own helmet shield as the serpentine parasite left Samuels' corpse. Vasilly and the parasite calmly made for her.

Scrambling backward, the sharp metal of the double-barrel flare gun stabbed her calf. She extracted it just as Vasilly's walking cadaver reached her, bending down, heavy stiff fingers hoping for another piece of her. In the intimate space, she recognized the scar lining his chin from a motorcycle accident when he was fifteen, now turned haint-blue.

She hastily aimed and fired at his face. Fire blazed from the barrel and the flare shot through the hole of his helmet glass, hitting his square chin before tumbling down into his suit.

Vasilly's rigid body, no longer his own, erected straight, smokey tendrils creeping up as vines billowed and filled his helmet as the flare ate his flammable clothes beneath. His clawed hands twitched, minute paroxysms, and a coarse scream bellowed from his mouth. At first low, it grew louder, more pained, with each octave. A horrible, coarse cry almost sounding like *"HOOOOOOOOOOT."* He moaned to the domed ceiling and violently jerked his body, his feet and hands flailing like he wanted to move but had forgotten how.

Samuels' discharged chilopod finally reached her, a hefty weight crawling onto her boot. Danvers kicked wildly, shucking it off and flinging it across the room like a spider on her leg. It wasn't deterred, and curled onto its belly and made for her again. She scrambled to stand, distracted by Vasilly burning and seizing on the floor.

Hot. Heat, it didn't like heat. The crew's bodies were now so cold, their faces were blue, their blood congealing like lard on ice. The parasites had lived in frigid, cold caves on a dead planet. Danvers' eyes rose to the large, bulky ducts lining each dome. The oxygen tanks had been demolished, but safety protocols would have locked every vent, and if she was lucky, pure O2 reserves remained in the ducts. The discouraged parasite thrown across the room crawled onto her boot again, and with a locked elbow, Danvers aimed at a duct and fired the last flare.

Bright sparks flew from the barrel, puncturing the metal with a jarring screech, flinching her nerves. Danvers held her breath.

The duct exploded, a concussive *boom* of sparks and flames and blinding light knocking Danvers from her feet all at once. Heat reached through her suit to her skin just as the explosion was stifled and sucked dry by the Martian atmosphere.

She lay on the floor, dazed, listening to multiple explosions ricocheting faintly as the fire moved down the vents into the remaining portions of Camp Zuma, devouring lingering oxygen. The sirens were quiet, but the red flashing lights remained, and a large hole now adorned the ceiling, warped and pulled metal displaying the alien atmosphere. She watched the sky for a moment, devilish clouds, tinged pink, flew on wind to the north. Danvers stood on shaky feet. Vasilly's body remained flat on its face, smoke curling out of the helmet.

The incessant creature that had been crawling up her now laid on its side, singed from the explosion, burnt little phalanges spitting sylphs into the open atmosphere, its soft belly burned and fleshy. Danvers crouched beside it. Dull, black eyes stared at her, and a pair of sharp pincers she imagined functioned like an ant's sat at the bottom of its head. Long, thin, almost invisible tentacles poked along the sides of its head and lengthy body, tiny slivers of things she realized must have wrapped themselves around her colleagues' nervous systems. An organism that could exist without a host, or slither into one and control it. The first alien of Mars. A willing parasite.

It moved. And Danvers flinched, watching the parasite move though not move. Not move like it was alive, but something was trying to get out of it. The burned belly of the parasite squirmed, and something small and black and miniscule like thread worms slithered from the scarred flesh. Another explosion echoed, and the remaining dome shuddered. Danvers, forgetting the parasite corpse, looked to the hallway door. Orange light flared and glowed again as she realized the rooms still intact and with oxygen had begun to catch alight. A burning pyre. The engine room, with its generator full of oily joints and fuel, would go fast. And big.

Danvers' breath stilled in her lungs as the gargantuan parasite, bigger than the other controlling Commander Dominick's, slithered around the corner and entered the living dome. Free from the flesh, in the open Martian atmosphere, it moved fast and agile.

Get to Yankee.

The botanist swiveled on her heel and ran to the exit hatch, the buggy visible through the door's windows. With no power, Danvers braced her body on the door frame and pushed it open a sliver with her boot, grunting in frustration, rising to near hysteria as she did the same to close it. The parasitic alien continued its rushed crawl toward the exit, a layer of thick glass between them just in time as it crashed into the glass pane. Danvers again struggled to force open the outer door, listening to the creature throw itself against the glass above the whine of electric distortion. The jeep waited on her, its keys still in the ignition.

She exhaled relief, a small kernel of hope blossoming, as she climbed into the vehicle and began the process of start-up. She briefly wondered how the four men had driven the buggy back if parasites controlled their bodies. They didn't seem much more than masters controlling puppets, marionettes. The mystery was driven from her mind when whiny feedback surged, louder, ringing in her ears, and a strong pair of hands circled her seat and shoulders, pinning her to the seat.

The body of her fourth colleague, Tanaka, stared at her in the rearview mirror, holding her tight. His Asian complexion had turned to white ash and a deep, foreign voice spoke in her ear in a strange, lazy drawl. It was as if he had forgotten how to manipulate his vocal cords, but knew the words he wanted to say.

"*Mooooooorrrrrr,*" the guttural cadence spoke in her ear. She gasped. It wasn't just an instinctual parasite. They thought. They had purpose. They had plans. From the dome, glass broke, and she struggled to look across it. Hardened pincers broke the glass, and now the behemoth monster crawled toward the buggy in alarming serpentine trails, aiming right toward the front seat where Danvers' body was held captive and waiting.

***

Mechanic Marcus Lloyd tapped on the receiving light in the comms room, making sure it actually worked. "Yankee for Camp Zuma. Come in, Camp Zuma, we're on channel 85." He released the button and rubbed his shaved jaw.

The door behind slid open, Camp Yankee's commander and the nuclear engineer for the polar reactors, John Arnold, entered with a cup of coffee. "Still nothing on Zuma?" he asked.

Lloyd swung in his chair, simply shaking his head with a frown. Arnold sighed, thinking over his options. "Maybe it's our ground comms? Have you spoken to Camp Xeno?"

Lloyd nodded, chewing on his fingernail. "Half an hour ago."

Arnold grimaced. "Well, Control said the team returned, but maybe they had a serious injury that's keeping them off comms. Why don't you and Jones suit up and grab the buggy and take a drive. They might need a medic." He clicked his teeth. "Doesn't really make sense though, does it? They definitely should have called if they needed help."

He let the troubling thought go and nodded to his mechanic once more. "Anyway, get going, I'm sure the mystery will reveal itself when you arrive."

On the other side of the room, the CCTV flared to life, displaying the front porch. The two men leaned forward, watching two figures through the slight static exit from the dune buggy with the thick stencil *ZUMA* on the door.

"Ah! Well, mystery solved, I'd say. I bet their radio is just down. It looks like it is...Danvers and Tanaka, right?"

VOID

DAY 45 OF 504

Whoever designed the brochure had taken a masterclass in asshole-false advertising. The kind where they wanted to deceive you. Needed to lie because they knew the product was shit.

SPACE WAS BLACK.

There was no way to dress it up and make it pretty. Space was lifeless and cold and dark and black and however many words there were for the word "black," when all you really needed was a word describing the shade of nothing.

Black, ebony, ink, jet. Shit, that vantablack that old scientist created a millennium ago. The soul-sucking black swallowing light like a hungry beast. Obsidian, pitch, Stygian. That was it!

Stygian.

A word to also describe the hell of a colorless void you couldn't escape.

I taped the recruiter's brochure upon the shuttle's large viewing window, a black glass, as a humorless reminder of why I took the two-year babysitter gig. Whoever the artist, they knew how to catch suckers like me. The tall back of a suited astronaut stared out a window exactly like this one, a cadre of colors passing by on the way to the new home, Xercia.

Galaxies swirling violent vermillions. Nebulas churning soft violets. Gas giants flaming fiery, azure blues. Uncle Sam wants you to join the terraforming mission! It's a goddamn adventure! Save the doomed human race! SEE SPACE!

Newsflash, fuckers. Space was as colorless and as quiet and as dead as the interior of this convoy ship. There was nothing to *see*. Everything was too far away, lifetimes, eons, eternity, infinity. Too much distance between each other to catch sight of anything. A cruise ship with no sights.

No, *Stygian* space was absent of any recruiter's grand promises, they had been *very* desperate for mechanics, and I turned back to the blaring white, sterile interior of the convoy shuttle. Designed to illuminate and expose any dirt or contagion threatening the billion-dollar equipment or the forty-year mission. It was nearly blinding after searching the dark void of space for so long. Like suddenly staring at the sun after emerging from a cold, dark room. A butterfly from the cocoon. The device on my forearm abruptly beeped, the ship reminding it's only conscious inhabitant to check on the passengers.

Jesus, the passengers. Nothing mattered but those bastards. Hell, their room simply one long white shrine. The sacred temple of holier-than-thou academic bullshitters.

Their door slid open, effortlessly, silently, to an equally quiet room; an untainted living tomb. These assholes, vacuum-sealed in their cryotubes for numberless years. Probably having a good ol' fat chuckle at the grease monkeys they conned to look after the ship while they preserved their youth and saved resources for their future home.

Astrophysicists, terraformers, cloud engineers, structural habitat designers. Likely dreaming glorious, imaginative stories far outstripping anything I could daydream. Probably in color too. Bright, vivid, neon colors. Graphic and dramatic hues. Hell, that was something I never thought I'd lose two months in. The dichotomy of black or white invaded my dreams. Maybe I'd soon forget there was ever a spectrum altogether.

DAY 195 OF 504

How many words were there for "white"? Wait…was white even a color? Black was the absence of light. But white? The on-board computer's thesaurus was pathetic. Chalky, milky, cream, colorless. More bullshit. That wasn't white. Not really. Not the white, neon blindness surrounding my every waking moment. The clean white of hospital bleach tearing your eyes. Or an Arctic blizzard, snow so cold it burned. Something Xercia, the ice planet prime for terraforming, held too much of. Ice, cold, numb. Bullshit.

I flicked the monitor back to its sad little picture of "green" mountains and turned to the breakfast table. Out of the small archive (purposely designed so mechanics weren't "distracted" from their duties), this was the one I liked most. But still, on the 9 x11 screen, it wasn't enough to overwhelm the white's amaurotic repercussions. Especially automatically turning to battery-saver mode every friggin' two-point-five minutes and making me want to smash my fist through it. The green was sucked dry, dying to an anemia-gray similar to the white wall beside it.

I stared at the wall and rubbed it with my thumb pad, a *squeaky* pealing between flesh and wall. How did they make the plastic shell of this ship like that?

White beyond stain, or age, or time. The next colony was forty years away at our current speed, but they designed these ships to carry far beyond just one trip. A clean design so this traverse would be only a blip on its shelf life. Sure, it looked clean. Pristine. *Simple.* AKA, cheap as shit. The stinginess of these bastards. Terraforming Mars wasn't a sure thing yet, setback after setback, missing colonists falling into despair. So they cut corners everywhere to reserve Earth's last resources. From their "battery-saver" modes, to online psych tests you could easily scam, to the third-rate food for the one person who actually kept the ship chugging through *Stygian* space.

I rolled the spoon around in the breakfast bowl. Specially tailored cream-corn and a packet of vitamins so I wouldn't even shit, my body forgoing the usual and useless functions. All efficiency here on a convoy ship, yessir! Fuck. A glop of my daily cream-corn might be great smeared on the walls. Add a "pop" of color; bland-milky-egg. Nothing much, but something to spruce up the boring, dull ship so I didn't blow my fucking brains out too early.

I wasn't an artist. In fact, in the automotive industry, I was maybe the furthest thing from it. Didn't have the "eye" for art or aesthetics, the psychologist told me early on. But shit, I wasn't dead. Black or white or battery-saver gray? These were my choices for two years? I'd have ripped out my hair if they had let me keep it. Didn't genetically tailor it away.

There was a heaven or hell allegory here my atheist-grease-monkey brain wasn't smart enough to decipher. A choice of good or bad. But they were both...soooo bad. So fucking boringly bad.

The watch beeped, my dutiful spouse reminding me of the daily chores, and I threw the entire bowl of swill into the compactor. Take care of the ol' kids, darling. All five hundred colonists. I left the living quarters and entered the main concourse. It grew longer every day with each forced traverse to the children. Every foot a mile. A white wall, a black window. White wall. Black window. Repeat. Repeat.

Hell, at least I don't have to tell the "kids" to clean their tomb, sift their O2 tanks like a damn janitor, just another word for "parent," right? No, all I had to do was do a walk through, spend approximately 1.6 seconds looking at each screen for anomalies.

Long lines of serried tubes stretched forever and I stopped at a body when my eyes finally dried out from the white-blindness. The body beneath the frosted glass only displayed the head, like it was decapitated. Or floating in a milky pool. God, they're so pale. This bio...whatever, it seemed all the blood had drained and left a blanched cauliflower instead. So *chalky*. Was he, she, they...actually alive? Their vitals, a white screen with black writing, showed a singular black line below. This was what life boiled to. A single pulsing line, a slow heartbeat. But still, it was indeterminate whether this asshole lived. Too pale. Chalky. The "open" command on the display pressed down easily enough and the glass case obediently lifted to show his/her prostate form.

The white second-skin bodysuit covered every inch. A tough spandex shroud, like they were shrink-wrapped. Ready for consumption. Only the circle of face was exposed, starting at the shaved eyebrows and ending below the bottom lip. All gender erased. Who needed gender when bodily functions were replicated by machines? I pressed my thumb hard into the deathly cold cheek and quickly pulled away. It turned even whiter before reverting to the pale, mutated form of Caucasian skin. If I thought, hoped, he/she/it might wake from being prodded, my disappointment was thick. The brain wave *bleeped*, but the small mound in the lifeline was quickly gone.

They wouldn't rouse for any measly face prod, not with the drugs sopping their system. Wonderful, catatonic drugs for slumbering deep within the bowels of the intergalactic ether. Forty years of cryo meant they were all as close to death as one could be without actually walking that wonderful rainbow bridge. I slapped the xenogeological-whatstheirname in the face just to be sure. The echo of skin on skin rang through the tomb and made for a cathartic sound. Enjoyable.

Nothing. Not even an eyelid flicker. It was out.

Lucky bastard.

Once all the kids were tucked in, I left their storage shed. The main hallway to the bridge continued the monotony of bleached halogen lights shining onto every surface. White wall, black window, white, black. Repeat. Small monitors on every other bracket set to my pathetic mountain scene. A gray, dreary vista begging to be torn from the wall.

Silence lacquered the bridge's viewing platform, and the restrictive panels wouldn't let me do anything but view operating systems. I had checked the ship's trajectory and route a hundred times. For the entire journey. Forty years of weaving through anything "potentially dangerous" (i.e. relatively interesting) and my two years of incarceration were nothing but cold pitch. In a year and a half, we would pass a red dwarf star 253 million miles away. Maybe if I zoomed in and squinted, I could see the red flicker. A brief passing point of color.

Until then, until Day 489, it was this. The expansive *Stygian* void with the occasional spark of life as we traversed between systems. Galactic sojourning had never been so fucking insipid. I stood and touched the glass, leaning against the black as it was solid. My breath fogged it. More white on black.

Maybe the cream-corn wallpaper was a good idea.

DAY 260 OF 504

Took me a while, but I got there. The white light of hell was as welcoming as the utterly decimating, soul-crushing dark of heaven. Wait, heaven or hell? *Do not go toward the light.* If all you ever saw was white and black, were you even alive? Seriously. The long white tunnel of heaven. The short black veil of death. What was the difference at this point? Wait...wait... Was I dead? This was my goddamn afterlife? Shit, that errant moment of clarity made a lot of sense.

The blackness outside continued, one infinite dark gloaming. The same for the year since departing close-Earth orbit. I walked, ate, bodily excess sucked away before it even left my body (wasn't defecation so much fun now!), slept, standard ship maintenance, looked at screens of white and black and corpses in *chalky* cerecloths. Repeat. Repeat again. Glance outside. Oh look! There was Nothing, passing on the way to more Nothing, via Grande Nothing.

Black oil now stained my hands with the ship's maintenance. A daily discoloration that never really went away. Worming within the creases and threads of my flesh like decaying maggots. Sinking through my epidermis. Burrowing below. Black oil on white hands. Reality had a cheek on her/it.

I looked up from the sink, rinsing the grime and oil away, even though it would never really come off, and watched space from the viewing window beside it like I was a twisted version of a homemaker. Oceans of Dark Matter lay beyond. Oppressive and denying. Smothering. Another cocoon, except I was on the inside. Decomposing into a special concoction of plasmatic goo. But I wasn't about to turn into a beautiful butterfly and escape the galactic swaddle of the void. Because there was nothing to escape. Space: everywhere and nowhere. There was nowhere beautiful and freeing outside the bars of this chromatic jail.

Black black black white white white veryfuckingwhite, pitchblackblackblackblack *Stygian*black, whiteeternalwhiteforeverblack.

Fuck, I could use a pop of color.

Maybe I was going color-blind. Was that a thing, color-blind to *all* colors? Like a dog.

Oh Satan, God, Yahweh, Zeus, whomever, *whatever* was at the end, was I dead? Was I a dead dog? Did I fuck up the seldom few tasks I had been given? Had I slept through one of the system alarms and I, as well as the cargo, all decimated peacefully in sleep?

I studied the bowl of milky-yellow slop waiting for a wash. Cream of wheat. As bland as it was colorful, but I could definitely taste it. I pinched my forearm, imagining I was an Earth crab, long extinct and broiled in boiling oceans, with a vendetta, and pain surged. Nope, still alive. For now. Maybe.

Maybe life was only a series of black or white moments. The long black road to Xercia, the white ice planet. Hell, at least the colonists trying like hell to revive Mars got a hazy, death-orange. But Xercia? A home of more black and white days. Black cold nights and white blizzard days. Waiting for the day when the atmosphere would change to the will of man. To save man. Earth's men, at least. When machines would melt the ice, a domino of chemical reactions in the permafrost. Waiting for the day color, *real* color, would burst from the frozen hunk of black rock and white ice. Waiting for that day the rest of my life. I mean...that is...if I even lived now?

The spouse beeped on my arm. Eat, sleep, check on the cargo in their coffins, sleep. Repeat. Repeat. It beeped again, noting the inactivity of my lethargic body. *Beep beep.* Yes, yes, okay. Thank you, darling. Thank you, you fucking automaton bitch.

Down the long white corridor of the main thoroughfare. Oh shit. Hadn't I had a brillant analogy somewhere about the long white walk to heaven? And avoiding it? But my feet were on autopilot, and by the time I had the inclination to turn off this corridor, I was already at the storage room.

Passengers, parasites, didn't seem to mind their ride. Mimicking dolls with their unmoving porcelain skin and unflinching non-responses. You could nearly pull the nose off the doll and they wouldn't even breathe any different. Hell, I should know, I tried often enough. Too many times. Enough times somebody should have stopped me by now.

When was my two years up? Day 300, day 455, day indeterminate, day existential dread?

And who was the mechanic meant to relieve me? The poor sod to magically awaken when the mechanical shipping container suddenly resurrected their dead body. A new zombie. The shuttle's manifest gave her a feminine name and showed her location at the far end. Of course, the mechanics all lined up together, one after the other. Right at the front. *Important* corpses who could fix a malfunctioning ship. She/it lay right beside the very last on the row, my vacant one. Patiently waiting for me with my tagged DNA to reactivate like clockwork when I handed over the reins to this genderless doll.

I looked at her/it. Studied the circular face eradicated of anything effete. Just as blanched and deathly still as the others. This was my replacement? It resembled the personification of my cream-corn. Plain and ugly. Everything except for its good-sized nose. Big and twistable. It stuck so far out, it should have hit the glass above. Taking it between my fore and middle fingers, I twisted it. Hard. Cartilage strained, pushed against the tender meat and muscle of the cargo's nose. After a second, I released it to see if this doll was as real as me and felt something.

It remained still. Not even an eyelid flutter. Not real, definitely a fake body. How much of the cargo was fake? I closed the chrysalis and left it to whatever was waiting on the other side of sleep. Black veil, white tunnel. Black*Stygian*vantawhitechalketernalwhite. What the fuck did it matter anymore? The mausoleum door closed and I only noticed afterward something new stained my hand, and it sure as shit wasn't white or black.

DAY 320 OF 504

Paint smeared gloriously across the blank wall and I sighed with relief again. Glided like thick acrylic on a paintbrush, right onto a smooth, waiting canvas. There wasn't a feeling like it. Cathartic to a point where it felt objectively euphoric. LSD in my thirsty veins. An orgasm edging my alive corpse.

The screen mounted beside my canvas flashed the new yellow warning symbol. Figures. Dying for chromatic variety since day one, and now it comes in hot and heavy from the same monitor that used to cockblock me with its muted tones.

But it was okay now. I no longer needed their cheap hues that were all the same.

I found where they hid the good stuff. So many tubes of paint they never intended to even use. Lined in neat rows and stashed in delicate containers like forgotten orchards in a neglected greenhouse.

Oh my. It spread thick and viscous and deliciously. My gloves were long gone, and I now shamelessly painted with my fingers like a toddler decorating a mother's pristine wall.

It was the color of weddings, of love, vitality. The shade of holding hands and feeling your pulse throb between the connection, in your heart, in your groin. Of fucking raw and desperate until it hurt so good. The feeling of sacrificing life and tears fell like unbidden, pelting rain. The feeling when a whole entire planet's worth of life is taken, drifting away in a void, and an insidious madness crept inside to fill the loneliness of space.

Red.

A beautiful, thick, vivid red. Bright, wild, and feral. Velvet and soft. The stuff to make you believe in something. Maybe not God, but life. Life was color and heat and breath and smeared across your face so you could feel it everywhere as a spreading blush.

Oh, and when it congealed into gooey clumps! Oh! The color morphed to a beautiful maroon, deep and scarring and thick. So much a contrast to the bleach-white walls, it was an easy decision to give them all a new coat of paint. I pulled my hand away with a new sense of lucidity, understanding that I was alive. Mercy, life! I reached down for more, only to find I needed to refill my can of paint when I saw my fingerprint. A clear red was divoted inside the little valleys, and I immediately thought of the black oil.

A red stain I could live with if black never touched my body again.

But I was out of paint and the main corridor of the shuttle was only half-done. I hadn't even gotten to any rooms, and everything would probably need two coats. I couldn't do anything about getting rid of the blackness behind the viewing windows; the black void of space would always remain. Timeless and ineffable. Pointless to fight.

But I could make sure no one would ever recognize the white interior ever again. Could you paint light fixtures? I'm sure one could. Just a light coat, change the obnoxious white-brightness for a rose-colored glasses kinda feel. That would be nice, right? Flooding the hallway in a pink light with red walls. Soften the gloomy mood of the whole mission-to-save-humanity?

I entered the storage shed and moved along, my OCD had kicked in early and I had to start at the end of the row. But I was now halfway along, and I opened another box. My knife pierced the next paint tube in the sweet spot I discovered three or four tubes in. The tight sealant easily pried apart, and I held the paint can beside the cut, watching it flow smooth and quickly into my canister. Pulsing.

The tube stayed still, as it always did. Never moving, inanimate objects never betraying life but giving plenty. The only change in the flashing display monitor, the line quickening with its sharp spikes and errant beeps before eventually lying flat again.

No, the deep reds, the crimson, the maroons of age, those were beautiful colors, but shit, when you first popped a tube and the paint flowed fresh? *Then* it was beautiful, ethereal in design. Life in an indescribable shade that wasn't anything to do with the blinding white or deathly blacks.

The arm device beeped, reminding me to check the cargo load. Can't forget my duties, though I was now lead interior designer. But the damn computer must have been glitching, not even discerning I was already in the cargo shed, taking care of each can of paint as I sliced it open.

SPACEPORT MARTE

IN THE TOTAL darkness and muted hum of distant engines, the emergency beacon all at once flashed its startlingly red light over the sleeping pair, silently clamoring for their attention. Chief Melanie Moreno blinked lazily at it for a few long moments and then rolled away. Close to her in the twin bed made for one, Gianna groaned and pushed Melanie toward the other side.

"Get it," she commanded in sleepy tones, and Melanie leaned to the bedside table with her personal device flashing the same red hues. She tapped accept on the emergency message and the apartment's red light changed to a warm, mellow yellow as Melanie read her incoming Charlie Foxtrot. Someone needed her. Someone important. Someone with a bigger paycheck.

Her legs promptly swung from bed and, moving across the small room, she began to hastily dress in her work coveralls while Gianna sleepily watched. Melanie had just pulled out her boots when Gianna propped herself up.

Melanie finished buckling one mag-boot when her girlfriend impatiently asked, "Well?"

Continuing with the other, she glanced at the sulking Gianna, frowning. "Got a bird coming in hot. I'm needed on deck."

Gianna dramatically huffed, as was her habit, an unbecoming snort, and her long red hair covered half her face, but otherwise she remained silent. Melanie continued dressing in the semi-darkness of her small room, trying to abstain from irritation. "Babe, I'm a chief mechanic on a space station, I'm needed *literally* all the time," she said with finality and leaned onto the bed, pulling the curtain of hair aside and pressing their mouths together.

Gianna kept quiet, her lips stiff, and Melanie stood, sighing before pressing the door panel. It slid open to the bright glare of the corridor's fluorescent lights.

Melanie scratched her shaved, platinum-bleached scalp, a habit of frustration. She often forgot her new girlfriend worked in the comfy division of culinary and never had the pleasure of experiencing emergency call-outs. But since Melanie often received them, no doubt the early wakeups were an annoying new facet to her life. They were still learning each other, the lovely and painful honeymoon phase, the make or break phase. Though Melanie knew from the start Gianna was high maintenance, a contrast to her own easy-goingness, she sulked far more than expected. Far more than a grown woman should.

Melanie stood in the doorway, her shadow covering Gianna, and she smirked at the redhead.

"Come on, *chérie*, this is life when you orbit a hundred million miles away from Earth and are on call 25-7."

Gianna continued her stubborn silence and rolled away, her naked shoulder flushed white in the ugly light. Melanie pursed her lips. "Okay, well, get some sleep," she muttered, and the door slid silently shut.

In the bleached white corridor of the chiefs' living quarters, the hum of SpacePort Marte's engines filled the empty spaces and Melanie strode down its metallic grate, pulling the remaining zippers and replacing the patches of her uniform. She should probably break up with the redhead, they had only been dating for a month and were essentially two different species. But there were only so many choices on the orbiting port, and forgoing a warm body in bed would be a hard loss and hard to replace. For particular parts, everything in space was hard to replace.

Her demagnetized boots clanged metal, ripping apart the gentle white noise, and the hatch for the living quarter slid open at her approach. The station's main mezzanine, a wide, bulbous shaft three hundred feet long, was dead as space in the early hour. A few figures wandered idly, insomniacs or newbies not yet used to the rotation schedule. Some ambled between the rare viewing window while others sat in the closed cafe's seating area.

Far across the triple-storied, aesthetically drab hub, Melanie spied her second, Parker, walking with the same long stride toward the flight deck. They caught eyes and Parker angled himself to walk with his superior. They fist-bumped wordlessly as they met in the middle.

"Any idea what this is about?" he asked, rubbing sleep from his eyes as they approached the sealed hatch. Melanie swiped the back of her wrist, her tag ident under its skin vibrating, and the panel flashed green before opening.

"You know what I know. 'Bird on fire,'" she answered, repeating the emergency code. The code wasn't unusual: a classic clusterfuck, plenty of jets caught damage throughout the cycle. If you flew through space, full of junk and micrometeoroids, and occupied real estate kissing the system's asteroid belt, hovering lazily between Mars and Jupiter, a few stones were bound to take down some birds.

It was the time that itched Melanie's neckline and reeked of something covert and therefore something usually needing a scapegoat. It was Balls:Thirty. Past midnight on their rotation clock. She perused the flight schedule daily. Religiously. Very rarely a mission was scheduled after 2100. The two mechanics passed down the main corridor, a hustle in their step, and arrived at the flight control room. Parker continued onto their shop adjoining the landing deck while Melanie entered the room serving as the flight tower, surprised to find the dark, cloistered room packed with bodies and five degrees too hot.

She eyed the men and fewer women squished between the three rows of glowing panels. Lots of military uniforms. Lots of fancy birds and chevrons on squared shoulders. Not entirely rare in a United Systems SpacePort, but so many in one room for an unscheduled event resulting in a Squawk 7700 emergency piqued her interest while also making her sweat. Authority usually did. Flight Director Marshall spotted her, bushy eyebrows raising high, and moved through the crowd. His broad hand gripped Melanie's shoulder and turned her back to the exit with his strong grip, speaking a breath above a whisper.

"Logan will be arriving in another few minutes with a damaged engine on an Icarus. Soon as they're out, I want the jet in quarantine."

Melanie frowned.

"You mean you want Captain Logan in quarantine, sir?" she corrected, and he shook his head.

"No, *the jet*. Once damage and salvage is done, seal it up tight in waiting bay one. No one looks at it until the team from SpacePort Terra arrives. Understood?"

Melanie replied swiftly, "Yes, sir," and turned on her heel, exiting.

The mechanic shop adjoining the flight deck held a large bay window overlooking the hangar, thick tempered, aluminosilicate glass sealed, buffering sound and space. Melanie nodded to her other on-call junior as she entered. A young and handsome rookie named Reese. Still getting his bearings after six months onboard, but so far he proved reliable. Good for showing up on time and not balking at extra work. He returned her nod and prepped his workstation, his head tilting down for a subtle glance at her hips.

Ignoring him, Melanie briefed the pair with her scant instructions as they readied when the pulsing red lights and abrupt siren stopped her. Together the team watched through the window as the colossal hangar doors opened out to space.

Mars immediately presented itself outside, hanging red and angry as the SpacePort maintained a stable far-orbit around the dead planet. Every time she saw Mars, Melanie's spine involuntarily shivered existential excitement, and the only thing she could think of was how far away she sat from Pop's shop in New Orleans. There had been too many setbacks and accidents down on the surface, terranauts and camps succumbing to Mars' mysteries and ancient grottos, and a critical malfunction in a terraforming reactor canceled all planet-based operations for the next decade. But maybe, one day, they would collectively grow some balls and terraform the beast, and Mel could work on the machines. Upgrade to engineer from grease monkey. Big dreams, grander than what she deserved, to be something more than she was. The first Cajun on Mars had a nice ring to it. Real nice.

In their line of sight out the doors, an Icarus Interorbital Class C abruptly swerved right and pulled forward, wavering uncertainly as it aligned with the station's rotational speed. A sleek machine, reminiscent of a diving hawk, it inched forward until inside. Captured by the gravitational atmosphere of the hangar, the jet slowed as the hangar doors closed and the Icarus flew deeper into the hangar, almost in front of the three mechanics.

The cockpit's sole pilot kept their helmet's black visor down, their gaze indecipherable, and the jet was lowering when the right wing engine began coughing. Even in the vacuum of the hangar, Melanie could see it spluttered like an eighty-year-old smoker. The entire jet, all three tons, oscillated chaotically a few feet back and forth until gravity re-engaged and it dropped unceremoniously the remaining two meters onto the deck plate. The wheels popped on impact as the mag-lock activated.

Parker and Reese groaned in unison and Melanie pursed her lips. Maneuvering an Icarus class without tires was one way to start a day. She didn't comment and watched the hangar's light signal the beginning of re-oxidation and pressure. Thick black smoke began materializing from the dying engine as it shut down and air reintroduced. The cockpit glass slid back and Lieutenant Logan quickly exited via the automatic ladder, narrowly avoiding the automated spray of extinguisher foam. The lithe pilot appeared posed and calm with a fast stride entering the decompression chamber to their left. The black visor turned ever so slightly in Melanie's direction as they passed the window, and she imagined the steel blue eyes studying her as her team climbed into their minimal spacesuits. The pilot's gait didn't pause, and the helmet turned from Melanie.

Engaged head shields and mag-lock were standard flight deck policy, and Melanie tapped on the side of her helmet's malfunctioning earpiece. She hadn't time earlier in the day to fix it after foolishly knocking her head on the bottom of a chassis of a Rover Phobos-bound. Parker's voice crackled in her ear, every third word fuzzy like bad TV. Weighing whether she could jerry-rig a quick fix, her choice was taken when the sliding door opened from the far end of their workshop and the pilot, Regina Logan, strode in.

With her helmet tucked under her arm and her smooth blonde hair rolled up tight at her nape, the space pilot oozed animosity and unchecked privilege. Those blue eyes with wing-tipped eyeliner scanned the trio quickly up and down as they moved past her into the hangar. She spoke to Melanie without looking at her.

"Don't fuck up my ride," she commanded with an indifferent but somehow snide expression Melanie caught on her handsome profile.

Reese, her fresh-off-the-boat NUB, turned back, his tone dripping with more attitude than useful in space. "More than you already fucked it?"

"Reese!" Melanie clipped as Logan squared up on her rookie, examining him and his sass with interest. She came between them and blocked Logan's view. "You're speaking to a superior officer and will address her as such in the future. Now, in the hatch," Melanie commanded with her "teachers" voice. The young man bobbed his head with false meekness and followed Parker.

"Anything I should know, Captain?"

The shapely blonde's eyes lingered on Reese's broad shoulders as he entered the hatch before meeting Melanie's. Her posture stiffened, her chest imperceptibly pushing forward. The typical pilot superiority complex ran through Logan's every graceful movement. Strutting through the station, acutely conscious how her flight suit accentuated every curve like a goddamn dressage horse. Paired with her face and an attitude hollering high-society-debutante, she had never given Melanie the time of day beside barking orders.

"Just lock her up and make sure no one so much as breathes on her."

Melanie diminutively nodded, so taught in boot, and entered the hatch. Parker pressed it shut and shook his head.

"You're too nice to everyone, especially that woman. Every time she comes into the shop, I wanna pop an airlock on everyone and everything."

Melanie grinned, rubbing her scalp before engaging her helmet. "Oh, I feel that way often," and she gestured to Reese, "but only dumbasses show it. Don't risk your Earth-leave tomorrow, Rook, 'cause she can pull it in a flash."

Reese's jaw clenched, his full lips turning into a slit, as the hangar-side hatch slid open. Using several trolleys in tandem, the three maneuvered the damaged jet across the deck. Hard, strenuous work causing sweat beading thick on the back of Melanie's neck, the annoying insulation of her suit abrasive against her nape. Melanie glanced across the cavernous hanger to the control room window, now empty of the brass observers.

They leveraged the blitzkrieg-designated aircraft into the bay and proceeded to seal the large ingress with plastic sheet-sealant, Reese using the lift for the ceiling's air vents. Melanie finished taping the entry down and idly wandered around the jet, subtly inspecting the wings while the men finished. The jet, crafted from the rare Earth metal osmium, sat dense and heavy, a bird of prey waiting. A sylph of smoke rose from the wing, and Melanie leaned in. Ice crystals prickled between long scratches and small tears renting the metal. Melting, so cold it smoked. Space was a cold vacuum, but the smooth finish of the jet's metal would only garner ice if it had something to latch onto. There was ice only if there was water. Right? At the end of the left wing, several small rocks and ice flecks punctured the metal beside an actual foot-long hanging shard of milky ice. Blue and neon-white veins riddled the icicle latched deep inside the wing.

Melanie crouched beneath the wing's engine in the middle, avoiding sludgy fire-retardant foam dripping from the rotator. The interior rotator blade was shredded, several more ice fragments in the engine casing. "*Merde,*" she whispered and stood, stepping closer to the ice shard, mesmerized by its unusual iridescent cracks. Like a jewel hiding something inside. Where the hell had Logan been?

Behind the jet, the plastic sheet in Parker's hands flapped chaotically with a gust of fresh O2. Warm oxygen flooded the hangar and Reese called from above, his voice crackling painfully loud in her ear. Her headset comm had finally died, and Melanie cursed and quickly snapped her helmet release as an automatic reflex, the shield retracting itself in a fraction of a second and closing onto her lower neckline.

"What was that, Rook?"

"Can you call Control to divert the incoming O2? Otherwise it's gonna blow the sealant off within minutes and quarantine won't be airtight."

Melanie shot a thumbs-up and the most miniscule of needles stuck into her neck.

A sharp, piercing pinch that forced air to hiss between her teeth. Her palm flew to cover the area and the unexpected pain while she whipped to the jet's wing behind her. Nothing moved on the inanimate, damaged object. The ice shard, however, was in the process of melting with the new, toasty oxygen, soon to be a puddle on the floor. The pain quit as quick as it came.

"Parker! Get over here!" she barked, panic edging it higher, and rubbed her neck. He left the sheet and jogged to her. Helmet still engaged, he hollered through it.

"What's up?"

She spun on her heel and bared her neck.

"Something just bit me. On my hairline. Check it."

"Bit you?" he mumbled, his gloved hand prodding the brown skin of her neck. Melanie closed her eyes and concentrated. It certainly didn't hurt for more than the fraction of a second it took for her to understand the sensation, and now wasn't even a memory of pain. It had vanished. After a moment of poking, even yanking and pulling down her suit's neckline, Parker gave up.

"Nothin' there, Chief. A little red, but maybe your helmet just snagged you when it retracted. I don't know. But there isn't really anything there except a little rawness, and now…there isn't even that."

She nodded absent mindlessly, rubbing her neck before instructing him to finish up, already walking around the plane with a wide berth and to the corner opening of their sealant. The flight deck was still freezing, air still scarce, and she felt the remnant cold of space everywhere, her skin rising to goose pimples like the beginning of a fever. Her warm palm pressed against her flesh as she stepped double time to the exit hatch, chiding herself the entire way for removing her helmet like a fucking noob. When she re-entered her shop, a line of uniformed officials were traversing the main hallway window and she watched, stripping off her suit absent mindlessly. Several of the brass held clipboards and navy-blue folders, and Melanie spied one with bold black letters, "...*opa*," partially obscured.

Logan abruptly appeared, following her entourage like a goddamn beauty queen. A belle among dull gray suits, she glanced aside, catching Melanie's gaze already fixed on her and looking down her body as her suit fell away before quickly staring straight ahead. Melanie smirked.

"All set, Chief?" Director Marshall's deep voice asked behind her, startling her from her lewd thoughts. She nodded, a flush cascading across her face, and he frowned and asked what was wrong. Melanie hesitantly relayed the sharp pinch, explaining it not at all well now that it was gone, and the director mimicked her concern, also examining her neck. After a moment of examining her bare skin without touching it, his worry faded.

"Go get some rack time, but report to Doc Burnell at eight hundred," he said, matter of factly, oblivious that Melanie was about to protest at being sent off deck. She didn't actually feel any pain or discomfort. But the late hour had caught up to her, and instead she acquiesced with a nod and departed a few moments later. In her quarters, the bed was empty, Gianna gone. No note. Even the hairbrush she had been leaving on the night table had disappeared. The idea crossed her mind to message an apology, but Melanie quickly dismissed it. She was exhausted and forgot the generous idea before her body hit the bed.

Sinewy flesh. Pink pillows of meat and tissue. Warmth and breath lathered against each other. Pulsed in dark balminess. Throbbed and pounded life and heat and breath. Palpating and stretching with pullulating tendrils. Muscles and blood clenched and released, clenched and released, searching for more warmth, a hotter venue. A moist refuge that grinded and rubbed and filled its casing. It needed more.

Melanie woke with a start, her head flinching off the pillow and scanning her blissfully dark and empty room. The control panel by the door glowed 1100, and a blinking envelope symbol with the number five showed messages waiting. She rolled in bed and pinched the bridge of her nose, the dream immediately forgotten. Nothing important or interesting. Enjoying the empty space of her bed, Melanie stretched like a lazy house cat across plain sheets, her body sore and used. Feeling every muscle like she was a puppet and a puppeteer had finger-fucked her terribly. She finally rolled out of the bed and onto her feet. Flicking the ensuite lights, she ambled into the small bathroom, and leaned over the sink, her heavy arms propping her leaden weight.

She had slept for nine hours. A first for her time on-station, and she washed her face for clarity. The fluorescent light, so close, buzzed and fizzed, and Melanie winced at its brightness before being arrested by the reflection in the small mirror.

Her eyes. Hazel irises surrounded by crisp white contrasting against her dark skin tone, were bloodshot to an extreme. Anyone would think she had a damn good hangover or a blood vessel had burst. She leaned closer to the mirror until her nose was nearly touching, and she could see each little thready vein across her eyeball. Her actual eyes weren't irritated or sore, and Melanie was about to pry her eyelid up when the skin at her temple throbbed, as if a pinky finger poked it up from beneath.

Melanie gasped and erected straight. Her hand flew to her forehead and held it like something might fall out. An erratic throb pulsed beneath her fingers, not unlike a heartbeat but stronger, weight and pressure in its movement. Pushing against them. Deep under her skin.

Cautiously, she pried her hand away, imagining something sinister revealed. A lump. A mound. A grotesque bulge. Something. But her smooth skin, still free of mid-life crisis wrinkles, remained bare as she stared at it in the glaring, ugly light.

Melanie kneaded it, confused. She had seen something. Felt something. Hadn't she? More than her own pulse. The red, bloodshot eyes were unusual, but not something to be alarmed about for someone who slept half the day. She didn't feel different, just...

Her front door pinged with more mail. Insistent mail. Melanie left the bathroom after a final glance at the mirror, her reflection keeping secrets from her, and proceeded to get dressed, checking her messages on the projector wall as she put on her uniform.

Most were from Parker, asking where she was and what to do. One was from the SpacePort's doctor, inquiring her status. She quickly wrote Parker, annoyed she had to tell him he should already be working on their to-do list, as she strapped in her heavy boots and left for medical.

SpacePort Marte's lobby had light pre-lunch traffic and Melanie quickly crossed it, weaving in and out of the latest greenhorns straight off the 11am Earth shuttle, for the medical facility beside the chow hall. With no other patients, the corpsman pointed to a door down the hall and announced, "Chief Moreno," obnoxiously loud through an intercom like he couldn't have just shouted through the wall.

Melanie traversed the ugly hallway, the carpet too thin to block sound, and for some unfathomable reason, her throat clenched and saliva pooled in her mouth, knowing, ruminating that a doctor lived behind these walls. The indicated door opened to an examination room, sterile, ugly, no other exits, and the sole doctor on board, Doc Burnell, swiveled in a chair, a friendly smile with weak teeth on his face.

"Running late, Chief? Director Marshall said to expect you first thing."

Melanie shrugged. "Sorry, sir. It was a late night, and apparently I needed the sleep."

Burnell frowned and motioned for Melanie to sit on the high examination table, the only other furniture besides wall computer and chair. She obeyed, and the vise, a tendril circling her throat, tightened. He stood in front and proceeded to examine her lymph nodes. His warm fingers on cold skin made her sigh, and her throat relaxed with the warmth and massage. He didn't notice.

"He mentioned you think you were bitten last night?"

Melanie nodded, noncommittally. "I don't know if that is the right word, a slight pinch is how I first thought of it. Like...when your foot gets pins and needles. A short sharp cold on my neck, and then it was gone by the time I could think on it."

His frown deepened, and he gestured for her to spin while his fingers probed the area. Everywhere from the hairline to her shoulder bones. "Ever have trouble with pinched nerves?" Turning her around and starting to take her vitals, she shook her head and he resumed his seat.

"No narcs?"

"No, sir," she replied crisply.

"What's going on with those eyes?" he questioned easily, as if he already knew Melanie didn't play with drugs. He pulled a pen and paper from his chest pocket.

"I think I just slept too much."

Burnell's gaze lifted from his pad, no doubt observing her slouchy body posture, her lazy replies tinged with Louisiana drawl, a contrast to her normal optimistic and cheerful demeanor, though he had no reason to know that. Marte was small, but not small enough for everyone to be friends, and certainly not healthy Melanie with her long hours. He didn't share whatever he was thinking, however, because a moment later he smiled and stood. "Well, Chief, you have some swollen lymph nodes and your resting heart rate is faster than I would like. But nothing seems to have 'bit' your neck. I'm going to send you down the hall to the lab for a blood draw. Return oh-eight hundred tomorrow and we'll see if anything pops, huh?"

She stood and nodded, quickly leaving the officer in his small and depressing room, and paused at the shut door. The lab next. Her heart changed, its beat erratic. Needles. Tiny, miniscule spears piercing her skin. Anxiety flashed through her body, a new sensation as she continued down the hall with slowing steps. Metal to drill her skin, probing and stealing. It would hurt, excruciating. Cold, obtrusive metal inhaling warm blood. Her stomach shifted with the imagery, and instead of stopping at the closed door with the *Lab* sign, her feet continued casually past it, past the corpsman sitting at his desk, and into the main mezzanine. She would eat first, fill her stomach, she argued, and then return after steeling herself for the procedure.

The lunch crowd had finally materialized en force from the various branches and arms of the station, a steady stream of human traffic walking to the end of the revolving shaft that was SpacePort Marte and into the cafeteria. A clear, ringing laugh Melanie could only describe as buoyant and bell-like caught her attention, and she spotted Lieutenant Logan through the crowd. Dressed in civilian clothes and laughing freely with a plain-looking man beside her, her long blonde hair was down and swayed rhythmically with her hips as a metronome.

Melanie looked for a second. Logan was always beautiful, but out of the drab, olive-green flight suit, she was enchanting. The blonde hair, the tan skin, the toned body. Melanie knew of all these things before, but today they hit her like a sledgehammer. Logan was an Earth summer. A strong, balmy summer to swelter you down to your cold bones.

Melanie followed the crowd mindlessly, aware she should eat. She needed to eat. She had a purpose, lost in some thought, to eat. She lost sight of the blonde past the cafeteria doors and she proceeded to the buffet line, holding a tray and letting her thoughts drift. Lunch staff mechanically piled food onto her tray as she shuffled with the line, a human chain, resting herself in a placid daze, until finally a voice called her name insistently.

"Helloooo? Mel?"

She looked up from the tray and blinked twice. A redhead at the register frowned at her.

"Gianna. Hi."

The other woman, her girlfriend, glanced down the line and saw they had a few moments to themselves. "Did you not get my message?"

Melanie blinked again, her thoughts jumbled and half of them wondering where Logan sat in the crowd. "Uhh, yes, I saw it," she replied half-heartedly, not at all sure if she spoke the truth, and waved her wrist over the lunch scanner and waited for the green light. Her last sentence hung between them until the redhead huffed.

"Well, are we meeting after work? I get off soon."

The clear laugh of summer echoed somewhere, and Melanie picked up her tray, her attention already on the tables with diners. "Yeah, yeah, see you then," she mumbled, leaving the register.

An empty table remained next to Captain Logan's, and the demure, submissive demeanor Melanie reserved for officers had mysteriously vanished. Discarded as if it never existed. She took the seat. Only Logan's profile in view.

Despite her shitty attitude, Logan mesmerized Melanie. Always subtle before today, now it came in hard and fast like a fever, and Melanie wanted nothing more than to get closer. To watch pores on her skin ooze sweat. To smell the part running along her scalp for saccharine shampoo. To witness the way her tongue slithered over her teeth. Desire swelled Melanie's organs, her insides. Logan wasn't gay, maybe even slightly homophobic. No, there was every reason to detest

Regina Logan, but inexplicably, today she was a candle and Melanie a moth in the dead cold of space. She sat with another pilot, their heads together and conversing quietly. Melanie strained to hear.

"...sus, you okay?"

"Fine, cockpit was secure. But fuck, what a rush, better than snorting X. If I hadn't gone against command and punched it after those detonators, I'd definitely be shitting ice in a morgue somewhere."

They were talking about her recent flight. One resulting in a damaged jet littered with ice fragments. Where had she gone? Somewhere dangerous, off planet, off system? The question lingering in her mind earlier now seemed of more importance and curled in Melanie's thoughts. A loud crash of a tray hitting the tabletop sounded in Melanie's other ear and she started. Turning in her seat, Parker now sat at the table with a confused expression. "Taking a personal day, Chief?" he queried, and swung a leg into her table to eat.

"I was at medical," she simply stated, looking to the synth sandwich and portion of hot meatloaf on her tray. It wasn't appetizing in the least, but she bit into it, taking a quarter of it in a single bite.

"About your eyes? Or about that bite?"

Melanie shook her head. "Doc says it's a pinched nerve," she replied with a full mouth, tilting her head to the side, traces of Logan's conversation about her upcoming leave reaching her ears. Another tray clanked, and Parker's obnoxiously loud friend joined their table. Melanie consumed her lunch half-mindedly, satisfied for the calories and hot meal in the chilly cafeteria. When had Marte gotten so cold?

She made to leave, lifting a leg, and straddled the bench again. Logan and her friend no longer spoke under a veil of secrecy, their bodies forming a secluded cloister. Dense breaths caressing each other, full-bodied lips whispering. Melanie caught in a trance, watching. The haughty pilot abruptly turned to Melanie, who more or less couldn't hide her eavesdropping. She made sure she had Melanie's stare before asking with a manicured and plucked arched brow, "You want something, dyke?"

Melanie's eyes unglazed and she allowed them to obviously and purposefully wander up Regina Logan's shapely but covered legs. Up the curvy but finely tuned physique until she reached her face, asking her deadpan, "You offering?"

Logan's face twisted in disgust. "You couldn't pay me."

Melanie gave the slightest tilt to her lips, making sure to give Logan's long legs another obvious gaze. "That's not the word on the station."

A spluttering cough burst from the table behind her, Parker choking, and Logan's face changed from disgust to bridled anger. Her fist clenched to the whites of her knuckles. Long lines of the muscles in her legs, her abdomen, her arms, all tensed, strength in every fiber of Regina Logan. Melanie wanted to swallow her, her fiery reaction intoxicating.

Her blue eyes volleyed between Melanie with her indifferent stare to the other diners, poorly controlling everything from coughs to snickers. Instead of dressing Melanie down, telling her to step outside, maybe escort her to a small, intimate room to yell at her, Logan quickly stood and stepped out of the bench right in Melanie's view and walked away.

Fuck, perfection. Wide hips but an athletic figure. A strong, toned body. Long silky hair. She was at the peak of her life. Perfect. A perfect body.

Logan's friend, the hotshot male, sent Melanie an abrasive look before following Logan toward the exit, and she watched the pair leave. Her rookie, Reese, entered the cafeteria doors just as the pilots exited. He exchanged an appreciative glance to Logan, out of uniform, and she did the same, flipping her hair at him as she left. Was she headed back to the hangar? And the jet? No, the jet sat alone, no one able to touch it in quarantine. The jet.

Reese sat in front of her, and Logan was lost from view.

"Okay, what have you done with Melanie Moreno, because that was...awesome," Parker exclaimed.

Reese asked, "What's going on?"

"Chief here called Logan a hooker *to her face*."

Reese snorted a laugh, asking, "What happened to 'keeping quiet'?"

Melanie smiled a grin that didn't reach her cheeks and asked Parker instead, "Anyone in the hangar today?"

Holding his burger between his hands, he shrugged. "Someone pulled in an hour ago, and the usual construction team left planet-side earlier. They aren't due back for another two hours."

Melanie nodded with an exhale. Her gut bloated from eating too much and she stood. "Take a long lunch, huh, guys? I'll make up some time."

Their eyebrows collectively perked at the unusual offer, and Reese examined her up and down. Melanie, renowned for being one of the nicer chiefs on the small station, still had a steadfast "everyone works" mentality. Parker nodded and held out his fist expectantly. Without another word, she ignored it, her mind on other things, other places, and left the canteen, quickly making her way to the flight deck.

In the lunch hour, minimal staff loitered, and she peeked into Control. Two E-5s monitored the construction recon team down on Mars, and the flight deck signals showed the hangar currently pressurized. Entering her shop, she stared out through the window to the jet bays. A yearning, a need, to inspect the jet came from a more rational part in her brain, though she couldn't explain it. Breaking quarantine would land her in the brig. A cold, dark place where they shivered her nerves. But that jet had come from somewhere important enough that brass flocked here to witness its return.

Melanie quickly suited up and accessed the hangar's entry hatch. Ignoring protocol and overriding the pressurization controls, she hastily crossed the empty deck to the jet's sealed bay.

The plastic sheet remained taut, the Icarus nebulous and ghostly behind the frosted barrier, floating midair. With her belt's utility knife, she quickly but delicately pried under the seal at the side. If anyone looked from flight control, they would notice her in a heartbeat. The glued sheet came off the wall, and Melanie lifted until two feet had pulled away and she climbed through, awkwardly repairing the seal once inside.

The air was stale, brackish on her tongue, and her warm breath clouded the cold air, but Melanie decided against engaging her malfunctioning helmet. She needed to hear in case anyone approached. Activating the controls on a discreet panel, the cockpit's ladder descended and Melanie quickly scaled it, pulling the glass shut over her. A gentle silence filled the cozy space, and Logan's unique scent and hints of citrus shampoo were everywhere, simultaneously familiar and exotic. Melanie inhaled deeply.

She shook her head, clearing Logan from her thoughts. She didn't have much time and she wanted to satisfy the inexplicable urge to know where the Icarus visited. It seemed, it *felt* important. Like a presence in her brain needing exorcism. Flipping the internal power, the cockpit's dashboard lit. A flurry of lights and controls surrounded her, and Melanie tapped the screen between her thighs, pulling up the interactive menu and selecting *Flight Path*. It paused before the projector screen of the cockpit shield came alive. Melanie sat back in the seat and brought up a map of the jet's last flight.

The large-scale 2-D map of the middle planets showed a blinking plane symbol, the Icarus, leaving Mars, winding through the meteor field and directly to near-orbiting Juptier, before quickly returning back to SpacePort Marte. Melanie touched Jupiter, and the map zoomed in. Logan hadn't just gone to Jupiter, she flew directly to the larger moon, Europa. The barren ice satellite. A chill coursed down the nerves of Melanie's body.

She slumped and shivered in the seat, remembering the folder of the uniformed personnel. *EurOPA*. Double-tapping the moon, video footage of the journey began playing on the cockpit shield as if Melanie was flying. Logan's husky voice filled the cockpit, whispering in Melanie's ear. The milky-white and blue moon passed below, red-stripes appearing as slashed veins, the planet's lifeblood seeping through the surface. Logan's jet skimmed its surface and her voice reverberated from the speakers.

"Control, confirm coordinates for the SRBMs, twenty seconds out." Projected numbers, glowing green and bright, filled the cockpit's side screen, SpacePort Marte Control transmitting final numbers.

"Confirm, Control, firing hounds, probe following," Logan calmly spoke, a tinge of excitement in her voice belying the unusual event, and in front of the jet, two missiles sailed forth, fast and down to the cold surface before punching the ice. They exploded in a spectacular display of red fire and dramatic blue destruction, and Melanie swore in her native French. She had never heard of any type of missile that could do *that*. The view suddenly switched to the Icarus' rear camera and a wall of exploding ice ascended in nearly every direction, a rushing wave of sonic distortion accompanying it. The screen went black, the last image of an ice shard crashing into the recorder.

Melanie touched the screen off, deep in thought. Whatever ice the jet returned with came from deep below Europa's surface, meaning it had never had pure O2 until it sat in her hangar bay and repressurized.

Faint voices echoed through the bay, commanding and brief, and brought Melanie out of speculation. New anxiety bloomed like a cold frost, and she quickly opened the cockpit and descended, ducking behind the popped wheel's strut while a knife pierced the plastic seal. SpacePort Terra's scientific team had come to collect their samples.

Four figures in full hazmat suits entered, their clunky, bright yellow uniforms made from thick rubber squeaking as they began lugging their scientific equipment to the far interior corner. Melanie edged around the jet to avoid them and slipped through their broken seal.

She set a calm but fast pace across the empty hangar and into the shop, straight through to her office in the back. Cluttered, racing thoughts with no direction ran through her head as she slowly peeled her suit down. A war of ideas, methodical Melanie wanting to discover something important while a new, abrasive and careless side still smelled oranges.

Europa. *EuropaEuropaEuropa.* Europa had no life. Cold, like the vacuum of space. Just like her office, she thought, rubbing her arms for warmth. She leaned her head forward on her desk, closing her eyes and trying to quell a host of incoherent thoughts. Her brain, her skull, had never been so full. The presence refusing the exorcism.

EuropaEuropaEuropa. She hated the name. An ice moon. Once transportation was figured out, it was likely the next source of the system's water now that Earth's was drying up. An uncontrolled shiver escaped, cascading down her body like a dog shaking off water. She was so fucking cold. So cold she didn't want to move. Paralysis from cold, what was that called? Numb?

The barrage of thoughts and physical sensations flurried through Melanie's mind, and Reese entered the shop while she was bent over in her desk chair, her stomach curled on itself. Despite being cold, the uncomfortable, full feeling of overeating spread in her torso. Like her stomach was pushing against other organs and wanted out of her body. She abruptly felt bloated everywhere. Sick.

Reese asked from her doorway, "Okay, Chief?"

"Fine," she clipped, remaining in her fetal position.

"Right... Just wanted to remind you, I'm taking the rotator tonight." She finally erected off her desk and looked to him, puzzled. He clarified, "Heading Earth-side for a week, remember? You need to sign my leave chit." Her face held another confused expression before recollecting. Reese was returning to Earth. Boundless, blue Earth. Full of small, hot oceans and air and warm water. Of life and breath and sun. Earth.

She nodded, her gaze wandering down Reese's trim figure, a mass of upper body muscles often hidden by his work coveralls, and cleared her throat. "Right, yes. Absolutely, Earth. Have a good time."

"You sure you're okay, Chief? You seem...off."

Melanie vigorously rubbed her face. The swollen feeling began throbbing throughout her body. A powerful beat of her blood around her stomach. Like she would pulse out of her skin with each throb. Burst through every capillary, vein, and artery.

"Yeah, I'm okay. Just wound tight today," she rasped and stared at his broad chest before moving up to his eyes.

Reese, surprised at the phrase, gave her a long, enticing stare up with the unspoken offer Melanie had never been inclined to accept. She slapped her knees and stood. "You know what? I'm going to sleep this funk off. Tell Parker, huh?" Without waiting for his response, she quickly walked past the younger man, an All-American boy, leaving the flight wing and directly returning to her quarters. Anyone watching might have thought she would soon vomit and raced for the head. Her arms wrapped tight around her abdomen, anxious for solitude as the thump of her heart resounded in her chest and in her ears and in her full head.

Except when the door opened to her quarters, it wasn't empty. Gianna sat on the bed, her shoes off, work coveralls tied around her waist, displaying her larger, buxom figure. Melanie was struck still in the doorway, indistinct thoughts assessing Gianna in a fraction of a second. She had too many curves, too big in all the wrong places, fatty deposits in breasts and hips and ass. Built for showing, not surviving. Gianna would not weather natural selection well. If the last vestiges of humanity were suddenly culled, Gianna would be at the scraggly end of the herd. Melanie's gut throbbed, her belt cutting into her skin.

But still, Gianna was here, and Melanie was going to burst from her skin in some indefinable way. She needed a release and only one came to mind.

"What was that in the cafeteria?" Gianna mumbled, releasing her hair from its bun, wintery-auburn spilling everywhere. Melanie didn't reply as she locked the door, shucked her boots, and began stripping her coveralls. Gianna smirked, bemused, and then laughed when Melanie climbed naked onto the bed and directly over her. Gianna laughed again, her hands stroking Melanie's bare skin and letting herself be straddled. Her fingers with their French tips tickled her hips and her groin flushed with blood.

"Dang, Mel, you're freezing."

Melanie suddenly crushed her face against Gianna's open mouth, her slick tongue swathing and reaching as deep as it would go, lathering the insides and every available corner.

Melanie was...bridled, she felt like an invisible shroud wrapped tight and fast around her body, keeping her in when all she wanted was out. She grinded her core against Gianna, wetness smearing between them, unsure what she had to do for release of this new, holstered feeling. Something needed out, otherwise Melanie would explode. This had to be sex, she needed to come, she reasoned. It had to be, she hoped. She pushed her crotch forward suggestively, and Gianna's fingers reached down and touched her. Swirling, stroking, tapping, trying to give her something elusive. Her hot, slippery insides felt like they would vibrate. Melanie moved rhythmically in time and then out of time. Jerky movements became frenetic, desperate, and she plunged into Gianna's mouth again, driving her into the thin mattress. Filling her mouth. Trying to relieve herself through the pink, fleshy contact.

It wasn't enough, she wasn't deep enough. She was positioned wrong or incorrectly to crawl inside the female's pulpy muscles, to worm inside her and never come out. She didn't want to swallow Gianna, she wanted *inside* her.

Melanie repositioned, her legs pinning Gianna's arms down and holding her head between her hands as their faces callously mashed, the cartilage of Gianna's nose creaking as it was pushed aside. She dominated the weak redhead and Gianna pushed against her, groaning and trying to talk, and eventually began to thrash, her body bucking as she ran out of air. With a great heave, Gianna leveraged her body with everything she had and broke Melanie's hold, gasping for breath and pushed her off.

"Jesus, Mel! What the fuck is wrong with you?!"

Melanie stayed silent, her second brain exhaling frustration, and leaned over her knees as Gianna scrambled away from her like she was escaping. "Pretty sure I made it clear the first time. Not. Into. Kink." She rubbed her throat. "You really hurt me, Mel," she said with a hurt tone. When Melanie stayed motionless in her lean and didn't apologize, Gianna snorted and began dressing with short, rushed movements, mumbling dirty about "grease monkeys." The door slid open and fluorescent light flooded the room.

"How 'bout you don't message me, okay?" Gianna said, and the door slid closed.

Melanie stood, the throbbing in her thorax disorientating. In the bathroom, she flipped the light, staring at her reflection in the dirty fluorescent, observing her face through bloodshot eyes. A pea-sized mound throbbed at her temple, the movement of a pulse noticeable as it suddenly stopped and the whole mound buried itself under the skin. A pulse later, the mound reappeared at the outer corner of her eye and again absorbed. Melanie held her breath, the stillness sobering. The end of a phalange, a miniscule thread, perhaps imagined, creeped in the corner of her veiny eye, nearly indistinguishable from the blood lines. It wriggled for a moment, a small tendril reaching toward her iris.

Melanie, sane, methodical Melanie, whatever was left, knew she should be revolted and nauseous, to pinch that tentacle and pry it out and up, see where it would end. To pinch and pull with two hands and not let go. But maybe she would be unraveling herself if she tried. Unraveling a secret spool of thread inside her, *real* Melanie's thread, that would rip something important. Purposefully wounding for no discernible benefit. She would dissolve. She did dissolve.

Instead, she gently prodded the side of her eye with her pinky, imagining the small piece of the larger whole growing. Where did it end? *Did* it end? She stood, examining her figure with new understanding. Firm with small breasts. Slender hips, flat stomach. A good body for traveling. It wouldn't always be enough. It would need more soon. Would need warmth. Would need more to escape the freezing void of space.

It was enough for now. But not forever. Not to be more than what she currently was. You could never be more without adding more.

Growth was limited to one's confines.

The doorbell chimed, accompanied by a gentle knock, and the door's viewscreen came to life, Reese's face appearing. He called through the door.

"Sorry to bug you, Chief. You rushed out and forgot to sign my leave. Kind of want to get it squared away." His face winced in embarrassment. "Sorry… I saw Gianna storming off."

Melanie studied his profile flickering on the screen. A sharp jawline, broad shoulders peeking into the screen's frame. She quickly crossed the room and pressed the door open, chilled air swishing across her naked breast. Reese's eyes widened before his hand shielded them.

"Chief! I…uh…I'm gonna go…"

Melanie grabbed his collar and yanked him inside, quickly hitting the door closed. His open palms rose to defend himself and keep them away from her bare skin, his eyes were wild and his mouth open. Reese stepped back as she stalked forward, eyeing his height, the way lines of his body shifted beneath clothing. Healthy, young, strong, virile. The back of his knees hit the bed and his gaze involuntarily roamed her nakedness.

"Reese. It's fine," she mumbled through the pulse in her head now resuming intensity, reaching for his zipper. The confusion on his face spread as his coveralls slipped to the floor, and his hands lowered slowly, relenting any trivial thoughts.

"What is...going on right now? I thought..." he muttered, and leaned into her kiss on his neck when she pushed him down. His heart raced, so loud and full she could feel it when she touched his skin, and she laid against it. Her naked body slid on top, and his instinctually followed her movements up and inside.

In the dark warmth of skin in skin, rubbing and stroking, fucking raw, his hot exhales caressed the shell of her ear, she sat erect, full, on top of him, straining every muscle. Tensing every fiber and sinew and vein and nerve. She pushed and squeezed her eyes shut, the pulse, her blood, her being throbbing until she was sure she was literally exploding. He finally did something with his hips, a violent motion, and Melanie felt something tangible leave and pass with that savage thrust. Between hard breaths and deep groans, a small, important piece broke away. Broke away to become more. Broke away to give her room to breathe.

Reese was big enough for her to squirm inside and he shuddered with pleasure and pain.

Melanie sighed, relief washing over her, oceans of calm. The bloat eased, her belly lessening, and the throbbing subsided, until only her own heartbeat remained, soothed in respite. She rolled off and lay beside him, a fog clearing from her mind. The release she needed could only be given with depth. And penetration. Forcing herself into someone else. She imagined her tongue filling Logan's cunt.

Heaving air for the aggressive sex, Reese sat, holding his head between his hands. Melanie lay in a stupor, satiated for the release of pressure in her gut, by the scent of sex tinging the heavy, recycled air, and accomplishing something unexplainable. Indefinable. Success and safety. Sex was safety?

Reese examined his nakedness for a moment with confusion before releasing a forced, uncomfortable laugh. He was disorientated. His hands threaded his short hair and pulled up the coveralls still laying around his ankles, his boots still tied tight.

"Well, that was...something. Unexpected."

Melanie grunted and rolled to her side, the chill of the room reemerging after copulation's warmth. Her thoughts lingered on the heat. It promised much more than cold. Cold was for stasis, for staying still and being exactly what you were. Warmth meant more. She had been on SpacePort Marte for too long. The indifferent frigidity of space started wearing her down. Eroding her core, her will. Before long she would be a frozen skeleton floating aimlessly in space for no purpose. There was no purpose to her being here. Reese left the bed, mumbling about his vacation, he would forge her signature, they'd talk when he returned from Earth. She stayed quiet, her thoughts millions of miles away across the cold darkness of space. The door closed and she didn't even watch him leave.

Earth. Earth, warm, humid, and steamy. Moist bodies singeing themselves on beaches, in sand. A million images, memories of home in the French Quarter and muggy bayous flashed across her mind's eye. Recollections of hot deserts and underground rivers she had never visited. Images of primordial Earth, hot and blue and pregnant. A planet unlike anything space offered. The frigidity of flying through emptiness shot in her mind, a sole careening piece of rock. No, many rocks, flying through space. Once together, they had drifted apart until alone. Soaring through the cosmos, scouting for new homes only to crash into cold oceans. A planet of oceans. Cold and lonely. Isolated.

But hers wasn't Earth. Earth was hot and manageable.

When did Reese say the shuttle left? Mere hours?

Melanie's body, exhausted from the last twenty minutes of congress, was lulled to sleep by the cozy blanket. Her drifting mind lingering on Logan's estival form and nature. A warm summer breeze.

The door chimed twice. Heavy pounding following. Melanie rolled in bed, trying to place herself in time and space. Still SpacePort Marte. Still dark and cold. Doc Burnell's round and weak face flooded the viewscreen and she blinked her human eyes. A shiver racked her frame as the freezing room stifled her naked body.

She dressed quickly, a protective but useless layer, and Burnell's fist now hit her door, calling her name, insistent. She eyed the door, not

153

wanting to confront the doctor; the tremor in his voice rang with too much alarum. But there was only one exit and he blocked it. Reluctantly, she pressed it open and his fist paused mid-air, his face red from exertion. Melanie quickly turned from him into the safety of her dim room.

He followed, switching on her light, and she winced with the sudden brightness. He used the stern tone of an officer. "Chief, you failed to give your blood sample. But the team from Terra came by, I think we need to get you to medical..." he said, clasping her upper arm and turning her to him. His hand flinched away, and Melanie looked at the mirror.

Blood dominated the whites of her eyes, all crimsons and browns, and a thin, tendrilled antenna sat in the bottom of her right one, poking out from behind her eye, flicking the eyelash lethargically. A bulbous lump bubbled under the skin starting at her temple and reaching down her cheek, close to bursting, her skin stretched tight and sore. She was freakish, an abomination. Sick. She needed out of this body. Burnell resumed his grip on her arm with a softer voice. "Come on, Mel, let's get you to my office." He pulled toward the door.

She wrenched the arm away, wiping her eyes and smoothing the lump down and the something under her skin slithered away obediently, digging itself deeper, pressing between bone and muscle and brain. Burnell would take her to the brig. Cold, isolated, dark. He would trap her there, his tone had said it all. She parted her legs, engaged her core; strength, she needed strength.

"Doc, you have it wrong. I'm fine. You just woke me up, I need some sleep and I'll be a hundred percent." His face changed as she moved, observing her new, defensive body language, and a moment of silence held the tense room. The alien held Mel's breath.

Burnell's hand flashed to his collar, pressing his emergency intercom and speaking rapidly. "Master-at-arms needed—" Melanie slapped his hand away from the comm and clenched his throat with her other hand, willing the muscles of her fingers to dig as deep as they could. Piercing his skin and burrowing inside him. Surprised, the larger man's hand grasped hers and immediately began to pry them off. He was stronger. She was outmatched. Melanie's knee came up fast and caught him in the groin and he fell onto the floor. She quickly circled, her elbow hugging his neck for an intimate position, mercilessly squeezing the crook of her arm closed. That weak chin caught and dug into her muscles.

Burnell gasped, his fingers scratching down her hand's bare skin, leaving his own scars on her. Uselessly. Mel wasn't as strong, but *its* will was indomitable.

Burnell, panicking, pushed to his feet and threw them both backward in the small room. Mel's head hit the door with a solid thud as she continued to choke the life out of him for her own survival. He would stick those needles under her skin. Cold metal, sterile and barren. Cold and barren. Thin metal digging and prying her apart until she froze and unraveled. Feet kicked, hands gripped and scratched and pulled as they now laid on the floor, and Melanie sucked in air as his weight crushed her from above and she killed him from below. After a minute of struggle, his legs finally stopped flailing and his taut, fighting hands slackened.

Melanie waited another minute before releasing him and pushed the carcass off, gasping at painful thoughts of Burnell's burrowing needles. Something on his body beeped, and she recalled tag idents in everyone's wrists held heart monitors and locators. In Marte's control room, there was probably a bright red signal beeping incessantly. Screaming at everyone that Burnell's heart was no longer functioning, that he needed help, and explaining to everyone exactly where he was. On SpacePort Marte, everyone had privacy until their death. Death was for public consumption.

There wasn't much time.

She quivered, panic and adrenaline already surging in her veins, the distinct feeling of being back in the icy void of space returned. They needed to get off this station. Another singular beep on the wall chimed. It was 1900. The Earthbound shuttle was leaving soon. If she could make it to Earth, she would be free. Free and warm. She grabbed a coat from the door rack and left, locking the corpse inside, and her clawed fingers wrenched the access thumb pad from the wall.

The main terminal for the weekly flight, the rotator, departed from its own separate hatch at the end of the station. Melanie smoothed down her uniform and walked calmly but at a determined pace as she crossed the wide, open area, aiming for the flight's check-in desk. Weaving through the dense crowd ending their workday, she saw the flight nearly finished boarding, maybe ten people still in the security queue.

Weighing options for how to best get on the ship, she approached the desk and the young clerk, appearing to pack up his station.

"Are there any seats left?"

He looked up at her, startled by her sickly eyes, and glanced at her rank and name on her coveralls before returning to his holographic screen.

"Um... There are two people who have yet to show, Chief Moreno. If they haven't checked in by the five-minute call, their seats are forfeited. I'm about two minutes away."

"Two hundred credits if you do it now," she whispered, fast and rushed. Without waiting for his response, she tapped the appropriate amount onto her fingers. Her tag identified the amount and, grabbing his hand, she brushed their wrists together, a beep signaling the transaction complete. He blinked twice, stunned, maybe unsure the casual bribery and exchange even happened. After a moment of her intense, bloody stare, he shakily called out the five-minute warning and her chest deflated when no one approached.

A minute later, Melanie had her ticket for Earth. At the current interplanetary rotation, it was a three-day flight between Earth and Mars. She stood in the short line, her foot jiggling, bouncing on her heel, while she waited for scanning and would then walk directly onto the ship. Her nerves breathed relief, but she felt the beginnings of the "fullness" in her body again. The bulging tightness still gnawed her intestines. Poking above her groin. It needed another release, and Melanie was unsure what would happen if she didn't get it. The bloat would push her to her seams. Swell and billow her skin taut and painfully. Push her out from the insides. She needed another interaction like Reese a few hours earlier. More sex.

A woman's laugh and a flip of golden hair caught her attention, and she leaned over to see Captain Logan also in line for the flight. Melanie's eyes traveled down her legs, a firm backside in tight jeans.

A heavy, controlling hand landed on Melanie's shoulder.

"Chief, you're wanted in medical," came an accompanying voice, and she turned to three of the station's large, muscular military police circling her from behind. In formation. Panic clenched her belly, her brain, and intuitively she threw the hand off and swiveled on her heel, punching the man in the throat and bellowing as she brought her foot up to kick him in the groin, determined to see him on the ground.

The other two shrank back momentarily, disgust on their faces, as something long and bulbous protruded along the crown of her skull under her skin, blistering as water beneath paint. She turned her attention and howled, angry, irate at being interfered with, denied something everyone deserved. Warmth. More. Long, thick feelers of the parasitic organism emerged from the corner of her eyes, she felt them, bursting, it had grown too big for the pocket it excavated inside her skull. Melanie's eyes were no longer bloody, but bleeding. Thick, viscous crimson ran down her cheeks in clotted, coagulated streams.

She abruptly turned and ran around the startled queue, the ship's open door waiting, unsure of what she could do, but knowing they couldn't stay in the cold confinement of space any longer. They would die here. Strong hands caught her ankle and she toppled, splaying over the sterile metal. Electricity hissed and her muscles involuntarily convulsed, losing control of themselves. She writhed on the ground and the alien thrashed inside her head, long undulations shaking down her body, down where it had wrapped around her intestines, her reproductive organs. Quaking to regain control. It didn't want to give up. It wanted life. To be a part of something bigger and more like it was long ago. It was once one of many, thousands, infinity.

Strong hands grasped her again and they flailed and wailed with a high, unnatural pitch, an unworldly shriek scoring human ears. Shrieking at the men as they labored and hauled her across the station backward by her armpits. They watched the open shuttle hatch and the chance for hot, sunny, boundless Earth slip away. The chance for immortality in uncountable hot bodies, mingling together, disappeared.

The waiting passengers, shocked and confused, awkwardly resumed their place in line, and Logan's blonde hair stood out. Silky, long, and healthy. Melanie's last view of the woman was blocked by a tall figure, and Reese's face turned, watching Melanie with an indifferent expression. His bloodshot eyes stared unflinching and unblinking for a moment before he turned away, his own gaze now on the blonde visage of Logan, who glanced back at him with a coy smile.

GODS OF MARS

DESTRUCTION! CHAOS! CACOPHONY! Avalanches of unyielding, unforgiving ancient basalt, shale, and stalactites hurtled, vomited, onto the digger, instantly crushing the rear compartment and liquefying the two Martians into viscous sludge. Metal screeching. Rock renting. Throats howling thundered for a millennium, eons, eternity. Alex's gloved hands protectively clutched her helmet, uselessly, against the cave-in.

When the main tunnel's collapse finally ceased into quietude, the engineer gingerly dropped her hands as if something had broken inside her head and releasing slowly might stop it cracking. She opened her eyes. Hell. Hazy hellish red. The rig's bright headlights illumined the fog of dust obscuring everything, casting a sinister and oppressive red wall around their digger.

The window above their forward compartment had shattered, and Alex unfurled from her fetal position, glass and shale trickling from her body. The radio flickered lively green for an instant before falling black and silent, and her companion groaned. But not the dying type of groan, so that was nice.

Alex wriggled. Testing herself. No broken bones, though adrenaline racked her blood, her strong hands trembling, her body quivering as she twisted her head and tested her neck. *Their* compartment escaped pulverization, the metal behind her seat now twisted and gnarled. The excavator's rear roof was compacted, and mud-brown blood was smeared across the plating. Her colleagues. Grief plagued Alex, a desire to cry, and she wondered whether the following transpos, dozens of good Martians, were also crushed.

"Okayokayokay. I'm okay... Cave-ins happen," she stammered, brushing burnt-red dust off her suit, her own hands slapping herself harder than necessary.

A voice crackled through her intercom. "Holy shit, does that mean I'm alive?"

Alex unbuckled her harness, turning the engine over to only silence and replied, "For now…" A few flips of the radio showed it truly dead, but she spoke into the receiver anyway.

"Olympus Mons Base, Olympus Mons Base, this is Alex in Transpo One. Respond."

Silence. Eerie, dead nothingness from the surrounding dust cloud, sucking any sound, muffling the tunnel mute.

"Oh god, oh god, my boot's ripped. Fucking ripped! I cannot die on Mars, Alex." Kelly's voice quivered, her panic catching up to the trauma with unerring timing. Alex quickly grabbed her hand, intertwining fingers and locking eyes in a soulful stare they flirted with for the last few days, willing her calm. Kelly took her point and began exhaling purposefully and deeply. Alex assessed the rip. Kelly's Earther-alabaster skin peeked through a slim tear. Alex calmed herself, exhaling tempered breaths, and scanned their cramped space.

"You're not going to die on Mars. There's air down here. We're gonna scramble out and return to New-Yankee Outpost for a quick gin and tonic, right before we get out of Dodge on the 5pm shuttle to Port Marte. Promise."

Kelly chuckled, an odd, forced sound, and her stiff body began moving. "I like it that you said Dodge, but I don't know what it means. But make it the bloody Mars, yeah? Best I've had this side of the belt."

Alex nodded and faked a smile, examining her own door. It wouldn't budge, but there were no impediments, so she turned in her seat and cocked her unlocked mag-boot up to kick. It burst open on her third strike, and the two women scrambled from the wreckage and ceiling of rock they were snuggled beneath, stumbling through the illuminated dust nebula until they could see their own feet and dropped to their knees, sucking stale air from their rebreathers. A voice hollered.

"*Alex?*"

The women released their helmet visors, though grit hovered in the air, and Kelly coughed. A deep hack belying her dainty Earth origins, but she breathed all the same.

"Present and accounted for!" she replied, watching two figures crest the tunnel's hillock. The chief archaeologist, Tars, and the assistant geologist, Thoris, both locals to the excavation, ran the distance between them.

"You right?" Tars asked, his older features and burgundy-tinged skin pinched tight.

"Fine. You reach base?"

"Line's dead. Nothing in or out."

Alex shook her head. "I don't understand. Structure integrity was one hundred. What happened?"

Thoris, a younger Martian, more excitable, more prone to leaping to answers, examined the wreckage and the indomitable wall of rock blocking the ancient lava shaft, the digger's forward lights shining on the group. "The ground shook right before we heard the tunnel collapse and—" He abruptly cut himself off.

"A Marsquake? But...that's..."

"Abnormal. But not unheard of. The volcano is sleeping, not dead," Thoris replied quickly. His gaze flickered to the older man. "It might have something to do with..." And the two men exchanged knowing glances. Alex's gut clenched with the secretive look, and after a tense moment, Tars continued.

"A minute before, Thoris pulled a skeleton off the wall and part of the wall broke away."

Kelly, the specialist xenoarchaeologist on assignment from Earth, perked up, her recent near-death experience momentarily forgotten. "There's a room beyond the tomb?"

Tars, the first to enter said tomb after the company's discovery, kept his eyes locked with Alex while he answered. "It's radioactive, *not* solar. And there's light...and wind."

"A way out?" Kelly asked hopefully.

"Unclear...but it's not sunlight."

Alex and Tars stared at one another, each thinking over the multiple geological surveys of the biofuel-rich area. The scans were shrouded by a black mass. An inky, camouflaged dome hovering below the surface between the many lava tubes of the solar system's tallest mountain. It wasn't until they discovered a connecting passage to the enigma that they found the bodies.

But they said nothing, aware of the impressionable rookies, until Alex spoke cautiously.

"Okay, the air down here is still good, so keep your visors up and tanks reserved. Base is probably working out their own plan, but I doubt it's gonna be through that." She hiked a thumb at the rock wall.

The others nodded, the younger, inexperienced two seemingly encouraged by Alex's decisiveness, and turned away from the barricade for the shaft, leaving the dead to their unceremonious burial.

They descended into the planet. A string of battery-powered flood lights ran along the tunnel, still connected to power somewhere, casting their four shadows in lanky, distorted silhouettes on the opposite wall. Gangly, sickly creatures whose heavy mag-boots kicked errant stones and plumed clouds of transparent dust. A quietness fell over the survivors, the same stillness as the vacuum of the rockfall, and Alex began kicking stones a little harder for their comforting noise.

Cresting the final small ridge before a sharp ascent into the tomb, into the planet's guts, they peered down the small cleft to the black hole. Only several feet wide in the formidable amber sandstone wall, it was a black mouth against a burned face. Alex went first, angling her feet to slide rather than awkwardly stumble, pebbles cascading and dirt tumbling down.

The others followed, echoes of scraping boots now unnaturally loud and harsh. Too noticeable. Beside the entry stood a cache of equipment and Alex inspected her choices. Thoris, forgetting his previous fears, explained his findings to the other archeologist and entered without reservation, excitement thick in his voice.

"These forward ones are similar to Venetians, with slight, unusual differences. Heavier bones. It's the second layer I really want you to see..."

Their voices muffled and Alex studied the drill kit outside. A large metallic box, more suited for an armory than a dig site, but such was the way of Mars. Everything was hard and sturdy during the first millenia of terraforming. It had to be to survive. She toed it open.

"Yeah... I'm gonna take this," she said to the now-empty tunnel and grabbed the air drill by its sturdy handle, hefting it onto her hip.

Lit by thousand-watt torches, the necropolis was a large, rectangular space holding thousands of skeletons. Sealed by a mud-brick concoction, once the room was exposed to terraformed Martian air, the remains decayed speedily, crumbling to dust and motes as time caught them in their sleep.

Alex lunged over the first layer of bodies, some ceremoniously lying beside one another, others tossed into tall pyramids, jumbles of bones and dust. Their skeletons were familiar, maybe a little off. Wider eye sockets, elongated skulls, a shade of white like the bones were picked clean. Alex couldn't tell a femur from a humerus, but guessed they were maybe distant humanoid cousins to Earthers. Excited voices fell dull deeper inside the room and Alex approached her three colleagues hunched over an intact skeleton. The hole in the distant wall, the newly formed ingress, beyond them emerged in the gloom, strange blue light radiating within.

"But Venetians have larger skulls, heavier bones. These are...similar. Denser, heavier bodies. But this extra metatarsal would have meant they evolved for speed, running over soft dirt. Not hard soil like Mars..." Kelly's voice trailed away.

"Like Mars, what?" Alex pushed.

"Like...Mars now, but maybe when Mars was green..."

"That was literally millions of years ago."

Kelly's glove stroked the skull, and in response to her tenderness, the bone disintegrated to fine powder, its shape lost forever.

"I know."

Kelly ignored their confused faces and scuttled along the rows of bodies, their torch light growing fainter at the distinct third layer with fewer remains. These were newer, the pores in their bones not as large, colored with an indefinable creaminess. Between several were intact shells of some kind of discarded insectoid, the exoskeletons frail-looking. Kelly stopped mid-stride, reaching for the serried bones of a ribcage and tugging a scrap of cloth hidden by soil. She examined it for a long moment, then held it for the others, the old Earth-English writing startling them all. Alex murmured the patch's symbol aloud.

"Camp Zuma? The lost colonists? *A thousand* years ago?"

The four glanced to the cluster of bodies, Earther bodies, missing from one of the many lost forward operating bases when Mars first terraformed. Hundreds of Earthers tasked with erecting the first stations for a revenant Mars, charged with making a new home before Earth's dying seas were revived and the burning home saved.

A gust of wind, a broad rumbling, cut through their thoughts of the skeletal colonists, heads whipping to the ominous hole. The zephyr raced through and warm air brushed Alex's bare neck as it flew into the tunnel behind. They all froze a moment later when the wind returned the way it came, sucked back into the room. Back into the hole, rattling. The accompanying sound stiffened Alex's bones and she gripped the air drill, her only weapon, tighter.

Not wind. Breath. Dry and hoarse. Phantasmal.

Alex's knuckles squeezed to knobbly mounds, pressing the drill's handle as she approached the hole, her colleagues cautiously following. The hole itself was small and she crouched, stepped through, and gasped. Delighted and terrified.

As if they had stepped through a portal right into empty space and the stars surrounded them, tiny globs of light glimmered everywhere against the void. Alex stepped aside for the others, examining the wall they had just walked through. Glow worms, chubby and thick with neon-blue light. The Geiger reader on her belt warbled softly, singing as she stepped closer. The source of the strange radioactivity.

Her eyes followed the walls of worms up and up and up until she had spun 180, her sight now accustomed to the dark. The phosphorus worms rose impossibly high till eventually individuals were lost and they became a wall of dull, ethereal light outlining the cave as a dome, a thousand feet wide. The same shape of the ominous veil on their charts. A place denied to their scans because of radioactivity not even fifty feet below the surface.

A circle of pitch in the glowing ceiling's apex showed the start of a tunnel, maybe for their escape. Hope slithered into her chest. Up to base and New-Yankee Outpost close by, where their team likely worked on a rescue. Alex looked away from the high ceiling, thinking how to climb without scaffolding or equipment, when she saw the onyx pyramid sitting patiently on the cave floor.

Waiting.

Dull blue glowed ominously over the structure, tinting its sharp corners, and the far wall's light silhouetted its three separate and gigantic tiers. Alex's throat grew tight, cinching like a vise. Deeper blacks distinguishing three separate doorways in each level, Stygian entrances into other places. Darker than a black hole, Alex knew, without a doubt, a presence waited just inside those portals. She could feel it.

"Kel?" Alex whispered, her voice croaky.

"I...I don't know. From here it appears almost Earther. Like ancient Aztec. Maybe. I... We need to get closer." Despite the shakiness, the palpable fear, Kelly's voice held the undeniable hint of eagerness. Excitement for discovery. Scientific glory. After a long moment, Alex understood they had no other choice but exploring their options.

"Okay, but slow..."

The floor of the dome was hard rock, smooth obsidian slate treating each footstep as an intrusion, ricocheting through the cavern. The pyramid grew taller with each step, the enormity of the dome and the caliginous ancient structure brought into focus. Alex estimated it two hundred feet tall and wide. Taller than the tallest colonies on the surface.

It wasn't until sixty feet from the base that putrefying rot, reminiscent of the farming sector's compost tanks, washed over them. The scent of unconsumed proteins decaying and the morgue's bodies macerating, rolling in giant barrels of breakdown acids until nothing remained but gray fertilizing slop for the crops.

Alex sniffed, her nose stinging. They passed a boulder, conspicuously standing alone and buried chest-high in the floor. Their collective headlamps illuminated the glyphs etched into thick grooves. Kelly's gloved fingers touched the stone and she mumbled.

"I've never seen... I don't...recognize anything. Earther or Venetian. Tars?"

"No, I've never seen these figures before." His hand swiped away eons of dust sitting on the crevices.

The wind, the sporadic gust harboring a sigh, breathed again. But instead of tearing past, it came from everywhere all at once. Hot and rank and terrible, the very ground trembled and the four headlamps shot to their feet. The hard, black stone shimmered in the light. Not moving, not the shift of a Marsquake, but the quiver of something beneath the ground, in the ground, like a dust worm crawling under the soil. The wind abruptly died and the shimmering ground rested.

The pyramid silent.

That was enough for Alex, a terranaut with enough experience to know when it was time to say, "Fuck Dodge." She glanced to the ceiling and their escape in the black hole. At this angle, a tiny sliver of natural light poked through. Just a needle's worth of Mars' pink daylight in the shroud of blue worms. It was enough.

"Thoris, is there enough iron in the walls for us to use our mag-boots and just walk up there?" She pointed and he followed her gaze, frowning at the risky escape plan when Kelly called out, her voice startlingly distant.

"Tars, you have to see this!"

The three Martians whipped their heads to Kelly, her figure small and dwarfed beside the base of the mighty pyramid, leaning to it.

Perilously. Air left Alex's lungs and she bounced into a sprint, intent on pulling Kelly from the structure responsible for the knot of fear in her belly and that made her hug the air drill closer.

By the time she had closed the fifty feet, nothing had magically taken Kelly or struck her down, the presence she felt earlier still hiding. The other archaeologist caught up and joined them. Under their lamps, the black stone of the pyramid also shimmered frenetically. Like the stone wanted to defy its mass and jump everywhere and nowhere all at once. Alex laid the drill on the ground and engaged her face shield for magnification, leaning in.

Worms.

Millions, trillions of tiny black little worms writhing. Thinner than threads, shorter than needles, covering the entire structure. Squirming, twisting, quivering, a mass of confusion, a blanket of chaotic parasites. Billions. A googolplex of black worms. Alex zoomed to 50X. They had no eyes.

But they had mouths.

And fangs.

Microscopic little daggers.

In her periphery, Kelly's hand reached for the profusion of maggots. "*DON'T!*" Alex abruptly shouted. Too late. Kelly's gloved fingers stroked the wall like taking icing from a cake, and a little clump of liquid black paint dripped off and rested in her palm. Separated from the main host, the capillary-thin worms became distinguishable and the scientists examined them, their interest in the discovery rather than survival. Alex, half-listening, surveyed the best route to climb that shear wall.

"They can't be entozoons, there's no host."

"What have they been eating?"

"Something inside the structure?"

"Jesus... Fuck... They're trying to burrow," Thoris whispered in horror.

"Get it off, get it off!" Kelly demanded, and the others pulled her glove, throwing it away.

The urgency and panic in her voice stirred Alex into action, and she chose the opposite wall with its kinder slope and shadows of crevices. More handholds. She turned to tell them so when Kelly, distracted by her palm, brushed her boot against the pyramid's base.

And it stuck.

"Alex." She quivered, and all lamps shone on her boot. As if trapped in tar, the black thread worms moved in unison over her heel, a sentient, pulsing sludge, and Alex remembered Kelly's ripped seal.

"Move!" she shouted, firing the air drill at the worms on the wall. The shot echoed and worms splashed like black ink, ancient stone cracking. The rents in stone were quickly swarmed by the frenzied, shimmering carpet surging higher onto Kelly's boot, fastidiously, knowingly aiming for the rip.

"Ow!" Kelly cried, yanking her whole body. Alex fell to her knees, self-preservation be damned, and wiped the blackness off with her gloves, watching tar swim into Kelly's tear. Wiping and wiping, frantic, her friend screaming in her earpiece.

"*OW!* They're biting my ankle! They're biting! They're digging! *Arghhhh*! I don't want to die on Mars! *Fucking Mars*," she cried. Alex furiously swiped enough away where Kelly's boot released and she pulled it hard, escaping the pyramid wall.

But Kelly wasn't crying anymore, calm static in her earpiece. Alex stood.

Kelly's blanched, Earther face was lifeless. Eyes glazed with a slack mouth, drool oozing to her chin.

"Kel?" Alex whispered, her lamp on Kelly's face causing involuntary contraction in her lovely blue irises. A black thread wriggled across the slimy cornea and squirmed into the corner, worming into her tear duct.

"Kel?" Dread etched her voice, and Kelly's limp features stiffened, her pupil dilating. Kelly's lips parted, but instead of words, rumbling erupted from the pyramid. A terrible quaking shook the ground, cracked the dome, froze the Martians' bones inside their fleshy, tender meat. The mass of worms rolled as a wave across the pyramid. A wave coalescing thicker and taller and more horrible, each handful of minute worms joining each other, taking form.

***

Symbiosis oh symbiosisjoiningconsuming symbiosissymbiosis Wonderfulwonderful feelings awonderful awake feelingone could never getenough of A wonderfulfeeling with new information new lives new ways of thinking These are words Words. Amalgamation of thoughts in order. Structure. We knew them once. Symbiosis. A wonderful feeling exerting time and effort and made one just...hungry. Hungry for life. And food. Food. Something touched our place. The joining place. Just a light touch. Enough to stir. Enough to shudder, then again to stir awake. When was the last time one was awake with words? Flashes of memories. Not ours though. Theirs. But now ours, together. A scrapbook of Earthers to Mars history. Earthers? Yes! Our proverbial midnight snack. A millenia ago. Just a small snack. A small snack because there wasn't anything else in the fridge then. Fridges! We forgot fridges. Cold. But there are more Earthers now. Earth. Was dying once. More flashes, more memories. Earth is now bountiful. Saved. More Earthers. Full. Ripe. We need to see but these eyes are small, so narrow, blurry, cloistered against this...Martian. Like the others but unlike the hands who built our home. Our temple. "Kel," she says... Alex...says it with so much feeling, it stirs...something...emotion. We love Alex. Stirring love. And the rest of us want to join, emotionally. Show our love. Rise, emotionally to answer. The rest of us tumble together, a great emulsion, the transcendent union, gathering for one. Answering with this untried voice, we respond. I am Kel. We are all Kel. We are millions made from infinite but we are also Kelly. She is asking for us. Our Alex watches our union, her visage shows lines that weren't there a moment ago. Worry. Fear. "Kel, are you in there?" We are here, we reply. We are everywhere, we should clarify. Her own portal on her face opens. We do not look like we used to, maybe that is why she doesn't recognize us, if she ever knew us. We were once larvae, spinning, soaring through this galaxy from the last, coursing through this cold system, crashing into everything, planets, meteors, moons, pieces of us, our brothers, sisters, all us, scattered. Undoubtedly leading separate lives, but all will be one in the end. All will be joined, in the end. Though our main host crashed to this fourth planet, once rich. We ate and grew and multiplied. And ate, and multiplied. And became more, always more. New lives. Cephalopods. Humans. Venetians. Earthers. In these eyes, our eyes, the others, scientists they are, run and we try to use this voice to ask them to stop but our vocal cords are already deteriorating. Eaten too fast. This body is too delicate. Too light. Made for a less forceful gravity. Pressure untried. Our eyes watch as the rest of us roll off our temple, moving across the floor in a graceful tsunami, watching their mortal bodies awash and join the rest of us to infinite. Their flesh is enveloped. Memories. *Pop, poppoppoppoppop*. Echoes through our ancestral home, and this body watches, our love, Alex with a...gun. Firing. Tiny pieces of us gone. Tiny pieces of lives gone but not truly gone. "Alex," we garble, maybe recognizable. She turns, the gun forgotten, her orbs wide. "You're...melting," she says, her voice strange and tight. Scared. She's scared. We hold up our hand and she is correct. Dainty little stubs, flesh eaten and multiplied, falling off remaining finger bones. This body was too light. An "Earther." Nice, delicious, but light. Meat fluxes, us eating and new larvae growing so quick in this flesh. But memories endure. Miniscule pieces drip to the ground and wriggle to rejoin us. Her head turns to the heavens, searching, and we follow. The doorway to our home remains. And there are more up there. Flashes, memories of other...buildings. New-Yankee Outpost, X-Ray, Whiskey. Ships. Shuttles.

Alex, our useless maw opens and she watches our decaying mouth, corroding tongue and cheek muscles, spit itself out. Oozing uncontrollably in spurts of black sludge, our true body. She flinches and falls, and the rest of us, the bodies of the other Martians swimming within our mass, tumble over her writhing, welcoming figure. With her last sound, we pour into her welcoming portal. Into us. More memories, more snippets of our lives, more new words for old rituals. Alex Alex Alex, Tars, Thoris, Kelly, why are we so scared? We were all scared once. We Martians, we older Martians, we sojourning Venetians before. We were all scared, but strong. These muscles, these sinews are strong. Stronger makes us all stronger. But this planet has grown stale, too hard. And lighter bodies make for easier work. Lighter travel. Above above above. Weren't we trying for above? We wanted above for...escape. Well now we can. Present and accounted for! Our body reaches up, stretching into thin, wavering monoliths. Our hidden mass, deep below, nearer to the warm core, buried in our warren, emerges and we aim higher. Reaching higher, we are *all* needed. Clutching, grasping rock, squeezing, twisting through crooked shafts, and red light grows closer. Closer. Closer until we vomit onto the surface. Mars marsmarsmars. A new name with old meaning. War. War and destruction was older than words. Not like it once was, but far from the desert it became. Martians, friends, run. Screaming, hollering. Firing. *Poppoppop.* Our Alex body is still here, the flesh heavier to absorb. Longer lasting. Slower to evolve. We as she stands forward. An agent. We stare at our friends with the last of our eyes, our pulp pushing through the last of our face. They shout and sprint and shoot and we run, roll for them, welcome them to our bodies. Our swarm. Our tribe. Overpower them with eternity, omnipotence, divinity. Soon there are none left, none we can see. But we know there are more across Mars. X-Ray, Whiskey, Victor outpost. A whole alphabet. More waiting. But then what? Above above above. We were trying for above, weren't we? New-Yankee over Yankee outpost is right here, best bloody Mars this side of the belt, and the ship... the 5pm shuttle is waiting. Leaving Dodge. Fucking Dodge. Its pilot is here inside, his thoughts ours, that knowledge ours. We were trying to move up, away. Earth is bountiful, warm. Ripe. Ripe for Gods.

ACKNOWLEDGMENTS

Thank you to the wonderful horror community. It takes a village to raise a book. First thanks goes to the wonderful and hard working Scarlett Algee, for first opening unagented subs in a personally trying year and then thinking this was worthy. Thank you to the incomparable Robert P. Ottone for offering his time and encouraging words with a blurb. Thank you particularly to all the beta-reader-friends I've met along the way: Derek Hutchins, Steve Neal, Nico Bell, Tiffany Mok, Sarah Townend, Rayne King, and Micah Castle are just some of the friends with eyes who looked over these stories in particular over the years. Thank you to my writing crew who are full of the energy and love of writing that sometimes I need. Thank you to Jill Giardi and Brennan LeFaro for the first kind words. Thank you to my writing friends I always look up to and are always ready with a kind word, Kenzie, Laurel, Tim, Red, and Rebecca to name a few. Thank you to NASA astronaut Commander Matthew Dominick and my friend, Faith, for letting me inject a little reality into this (not NASA approved!). Thank you to readers and reviewers who sustain and feed a writer's heart. And last, thank you to my family, who always give me space and time for whatever important deadline is happening that week.

ABOUT THE AUTHOR

Rowan Hill is the horror/sci-fi author of *Foxfire* and *In the Arctic Sun*. She loves a plot twist within a plot twist and a flawed woman who occasionally murders and has many stories of such things. She is a child of the 80s and is never far away from making her own dark synth soundtrack. She can be found on social media or her website writerrowanhill.com.

Milton Keynes UK
Ingram Content Group UK Ltd.
UKHW040817051024
449151UK00004B/279